KV-513-307

ROOMS IN THE CITY

a novel
by

Nicholas Hasluck

ARDEN

This is a work of fiction. Names, characters, places and incidents are the products of the author's imagination or are used fictitiously. Any resemblance to actual events, locales, or persons, living or dead, is entirely coincidental.

© Nicholas Hasluck 2014, 2020

First published 2014 by Arden
the international general books' imprint of
Australian Scholarly Publishing Pty Ltd
7 Lt Lothian St Nth, North Melbourne, Vic 3051
Tel: 03 9329 6963 / Fax: 03 9329 5452
enquiry@scholarly.info / www.scholarly.info

The moral right of the author has been asserted.

ISBN: 978-1-925984-55-2

Cover design and typesetting by Art Rowlands
Set in Sabon LT Std 11pt/16pt

For Sally Anne

THE FIRST ROOM

A T THAT TIME WE HAD VARIOUS ROOMS in the city that were
suited to the unusual nature of our work. Their location was
known only to some of those whom Toby Asplin liked to call his
inner circle, for within that circle were the few whom he really
trusted, confidants whose identity was never entirely clear to me,
nor to the rest of our outfit, and probably disclosed to 'C' alone
– our anonymous but ever-present superior in faraway Whitehall,
the counter-espionage controller to whom Asplin submitted his
coded and increasingly terse reports.

We used our rented rooms, situated mostly in the busier parts of
the city, in order to interview prospective agents and informers, or
to question those who crept back to us from time to time with their
supposedly important findings, hands out for the promised fee.
They kept us interested, these mercenaries, by crafting hints about
shipping lists or armaments or troop movements, foreshadowing
dire revelations in days to come before they slithered off again,

disappearing into the streets and alleyways below, eyes alert for the next transaction.

Too often, their so-called findings were laced with misinformation concocted by our German counterparts, the enemy operation that was supposed to be the subject not the censor of our inquiries. So it sometimes seemed to me that our rooms in the Athens of November 1915 were little more than vantage points poised on the edge of a chaotic no man's land, overlooking entanglements of unreality, afflicted by the truths and untruths of war. Our rooms were linked by that at least to the turmoil elsewhere. The Western Front had become a grim mosaic where the language of gains and losses seemed meaningless and where much of what was said about plans and offensives to lift the morale of those who served the Allied cause – in the trenches or behind the lines – had to be taken with a chunk of coarse salt.

I kept these fugitive thoughts to myself (like much else that worried me about our clandestine pursuits) being determined to do my bit dutifully and without complaint, as so many others have done in times past when they heard the call to arms. Nonetheless, sent to Athens to act as an interpreter, attached to the intelligence services housed in the pine-scented premises of the British School of Hellenic Studies, it troubled me after a few weeks to find that I had gradually, almost invisibly, been drawn into a more sinister role in Asplin's unit, for the simple reason, as he explained it, that I was obviously accustomed to keeping things to myself and I seemed to fit. It happens everywhere in wartime, he observed ungraciously. To make things happen one has to make do with whatever is at hand, from manpower to weapons.

The unreliability of our informers meant, of course, that the dingy rooms at our disposal – sparsely furnished lodgings with a bed, a wardrobe, and a table flanked by two rickety chairs – were mostly in a state of turnover. Whenever the location of one of our rooms was discovered by the Palace police or the agents of the enemy, the address in many cases having been divulged by a disaffected or insufficiently bribed former 'friend', the room in question was immediately replaced by some other habitation. This in turn, cramped, dimly-lit, equally down-at-heel, was rented out (pursuant to our usual practice) to a provincial worker or some other fictitious tenant – a loner who had made his way to the city in search of work.

The out-of-town loner's role was quite often played by our driver, Alexis Brusa, who had, at Asplin's insistence, managed to suppress his initial distaste for impersonation and was beginning to enjoy his posturings, cap pulled down to hide his bald head, a thick scarf tucked under his chin to serve as a costume. Animated by this meagre disguise, the truculent Brusa haggled with landladies and their indignant sons, raising a fist occasionally when the part demanded a show of strength, foreclosing any further argument by leaving his mark on the rental slip with a decisive grunt.

Rumour had it that before Alexis Brusa came to us from the slums of Mytilene he had once backed over a fellow driver to enforce repayment of a debt. It was probably this, or some other incident like it, that added flair to Brusa's theatrics, encouraging him to look beyond the steering wheel and improve his act, fending off histrionics on the other side with a hard, unblinking look until he had closed the deal at a figure less than the price chalked up on the board outside.

Brusa's formidable presence ensured that his counterfeit demands for living space were heeded and that his illusory loner – if only on a rental slip – enjoyed a brief but perilous existence, before the room was vacated, its purpose served.

* * *

Ruses and subterfuges were our stock-in-trade, for in Athens at that time rooms in the city were hard to come by, especially within the central district where most of those we had to keep an eye on scuttled to and fro. A neutral city, the place seemed overcrowded with itinerants – representatives of foreign powers, traders in munitions, entertainers with raucous voices, import agents with dubious bills of lading, double agents and their contacts equipped with matching cards and tokens to make themselves known to each other. The streets swarmed with all sorts of adventurers and opportunists as the German-led Central Powers vied with the British-French Entente to recruit Greece as an ally in the European struggle.

The process of recruitment tipped first in one direction, then the other, as King Constantine listened to emissaries from his brother-in-law in Berlin, Kaiser Wilhelm, before reverting to supporters of the popular leader, Venizelos, for counsel weighted the other way. Venizelos, known as the Lion of Crete, was fully committed to an Allied victory, according to Toby Asplin. But the fact was that the King disliked the Lion, feared his popularity, and had recently forced him to give up the office of Prime Minister. Throughout this period of unease, these vacillations of opinion, rooms and lodgings in the city were regularly on the market, true, but not always at a price within our tiny budget.

We had a room above a doctor's surgery in Odos Soutsou; a small second floor room opposite the German Legation (occupied for the most part by one of our chaps with a pair of binoculars); a spacious suite masquerading as the office of a Refugee Commission in Silenus Square; and so on – rooms that were affordable and with owners who weren't inclined to ask too many questions. Although the renting of the refugee suite, I seem to recall, was one of several deals that later became a source of worry to me. On that occasion, still new to the game, not thinking quickly enough towards the end of the negotiations, I had inscribed my own name – Robert Kaub – on the rental slip, another matter I now kept to myself.

One couldn't afford to make mistakes, not in a city seething with competing enmities and consequent eruptions of violence. Notwithstanding its neutrality, Athens was rapidly becoming more like a war-infested swamp lying beneath the soaring columns of the Parthenon. It was a world in which secrets were badly kept and doubts about the one beside you were commonplace, a characteristic of the turmoil mirrored in myths of bygone ages and now, with a similar potency, in the streets and squares around us.

The constant turnover, the variety of rooms we had to acquire and quickly abandon after some unexpected act of betrayal, didn't entirely surprise me, for I soon realised that anything could happen in this ancient and contradictory realm. Democratic ideals had been dreamed up here before being eroded in due course by human flaws. The Parthenon itself, cruising serenely above the city, had been blown up in its time, the best of its marble features stripped and shipped away. The widely-revered Socrates, a proponent of free and open discussion, had finished up being accused of corrupting youth and was forced into oblivion accordingly. His acolytes had dwelt upon the meaning of justice while simultaneously revealing the essence of pernicious art and dire plots. And we ourselves – Asplin's unit at the British School – were masquerading as Hellenic archaeologists. All of this was Athens.

But what did surprise me, astounded me in fact, on the fateful morning we found a would-be informer, Cy Lapides, in one of our rooms, a knife in his throat, was how it came about that the room in question was put at risk? Why was it selected for a meeting with this particular man? A sudden death by stabbing in our own domain reeked not only of betrayal but of further deaths and betrayals to come. An attack upon the precautions that until then had served us well.

So who was this Cy Lapides and why did he matter, I had to ask myself, staring at the corpse with Toby Asplin beside me, equally aghast? Who was this man from Smyrna? A con-man, according to an entry in our card index system, who was said to be 'grasping and more than usually unreliable!' What secret did he bring with him to the empty room and why did his assailant, who must have known (or been tipped off) about the time and place of the meeting, feel obliged to get rid of him?

* * *

The judgment about Cy Lapides on our card, a verdict entered in the system before his mute body was found – propped up against the bed in runnels of blood, the knife-handle beneath his chin glinting – might well have seemed reasonable when written down, but in the presence of the corpse it left us feeling disconcerted, abject, affected not only by doubts about our methods but also by the eloquence of death, the deceased's final entreaty in that dusty light, a limp hand supported by the iron bedstead, a gesture infused with a power of its own, reaching beyond the rhetoric of death to the living.

The questions kept coming. As if reminding us that we still had work to do in this world, including the anguish of looking back, going over things again, from our first encounter with the dead man to matters of concern along the way.

In that regard I recalled immediately that I had complained about fixing a meeting in our room when Asplin swept through the door of my quarters at the British School that very morning, a good half hour or so before the time set aside for our rendezvous with the man from Smyrna.

Perhaps I was conscious even then of a sense of foreboding about the risk attached to the newly-acquired room I had staked out less than a fortnight before, a dread that it might lead us not to the usual sycophantic face of a would-be informer, avid for drachma, overripe with promises and blandishments, but to another entirely different kind of opportunist – a schemer with still secret information on a grander and more dangerous scale.

This premonition proved to be accurate eventually, although I was not to know when the feeling of unease first gripped me that the crucial piece of proof would not be the man from Smyrna's proposal or curriculum vitae, presented to us calmly at the pre-arranged meeting place, but his blood-stained body slumped in an odd position against the bed, staring at us with a stricken gaze, as if recognizing in a moment of desperation, which can sometimes happen in the course of an interview, that he couldn't handle the last few questions, the final thrust, and wasn't ready for whatever might lie ahead.

'What do we know about this fellow?' I had asked Toby Asplin when he came to my quarters. I was determined to find out as much as I could before we dashed off to keep our appointment. 'What can you tell me about Cy Lapides? This so-called man from Smyrna?'

I was at my shaving-mirror as I spoke, knotting my tie. I could see Toby Asplin behind me on the strip of Persian rug by my dresser, spick and span in his linen suit, smoothing down his dark glossy hair, fiddling with his moustache. He was keen to get moving, to bundle me downstairs and into our four-seater Sunbeam that was probably waiting at the kerb below, engine running, Brusa at the wheel. But I wouldn't be rushed.

'Cy Lapides!' I had to keep my scorn in check. 'He was ready to meet us here at the British School. Now, instead, you've fixed a meeting in one of our rooms. I don't like it. He sidles up to you at the Panhellenion Café, so you tell me, claiming to be recently-arrived in Athens. Here from Smyrna. But nothing to prove it. And within a few hours he's inveigled his way into meeting us at a place we'd prefer to keep secret. A *new* room, in fact.

According to the index card, he's supposed to be some sort of import agent. Tiles and pottery and so forth. The usual nonsense about shipments coming in and going out. Code for information, perhaps. The rest is mostly a blank. I smell a pottery-sized rat.'

I pointed to the Lapides card to underline my point, there on the dresser, in front of my guest, inviting Asplin to check my summary. 'Nothing to show what he wants of us,' I added, 'apart from a few sly hints, according to your notes, about a forthcoming offensive in his corner of the Aegean. Hints we've heard before.'

The irascible Toby Asplin fastened not upon the card but upon its presence among my tie pins and knick knacks. 'Left lying about!' He had the card now and was flapping it at me, beating the air as if it had been uplifted not from its place of repose against the leather box containing my studs and starched collars, but from the depths of an Athens gutter – spattered with droplets of filth that could only be removed by drying it out right away. 'Who cares about the risk? None of my subordinates, apparently. Not even my trusted confidants. A vital card there for the taking as if it simply doesn't count.'

All of this was somewhat farcical to my way of thinking, as I harboured a suspicion that it was Asplin himself who had created a problem by setting up a meeting in one of our rooms with a man we knew next to nothing about.

It was this sort of impulsiveness, a propensity for sudden action – usually driven by an excess of zeal – that was rumoured to be troubling Asplin's superiors, even the omniscient C in Whitehall. That and Toby Asplin's scarcely veiled support for the former Greek Prime Minister Venizelos, at a time when the British Foreign Office and its military commanders seemed to be in a muddle as to what to do about the stalemate on the Gallipoli peninsula and how best to win over Greece.

'Rest easy,' I counselled Asplin in a soothing voice. 'I spoke to our archivist yesterday evening, and picked up the card after dinner in the Mess. It's been with me ever since. Held well and truly under wraps.' I tapped the collar box. 'Brought to light less than a few minutes ago to await your arrival. Ready for our chat with Cy Lapides.'

* * *

I had forgotten how excitable Toby Asplin could become. My placatory words about the man from Smyrna's card and its safekeeping in my collar box, far from having the soothing effect I had intended, brought forth an outburst.

'Under wraps, he says! Under wraps! A glib response if you'll forgive me for saying so.' In a characteristic gesture Asplin had buried both hands in the pockets of his pale linen trousers and begun to stride. 'Glib to the outer edge of waffle. You know as well as I do that our systems have to be bullet-proof. We have our critics. In Whitehall. In Naval Intelligence. On Lemnos.'

He rounded on me, finger upraised. 'This fellow Furnell, for instance. Arnold Brooke Furnell! A Lieutenant Commander, no less. All the way from GHQ in Alexandria, where the only thing they ever seem to think about is how to abort the Berlin to Baghdad railway, or whether some jihad aimed at Suez is on its way. So here he is an Athens, our esteemed visitor, sniffing the breeze. A review to improve coordination, or so he says. But what's it all add up to? What's it mean in practice? Picking us to pieces to suit their own agenda. A missing card could be the last straw.'

A lack of coordination between the various British agencies – before one even began to think of sharing information with our French and Serbian allies – had certainly complicated our work of late, but at times it almost seemed as though, in Toby Asplin's mind, we were threatened more by mysterious forces on our own side than by those working against us for the Turks and the Germans.

His latest fears were probably due to a sense of personal insecurity. An Oxford-educated barrister before the war, Asplin's enlistment had led to his secondment to Sir Ian Hamilton's staff on the island of Lemnos followed by exposure to the horrors of the Gallipoli landings, at Cape Helles and Anzac Cove. Wounded, shipped out to Athens to recuperate, Asplin's connections to the chief of the expeditionary force, and those beneath him at the command centre on Lemnos, meant that Toby Asplin, the former advocate, renowned for his forceful personality, was soon delegated to set up a counter-espionage team within the Eastern Mediterranean Special Intelligence Bureau – or simply, in its shortened form, within 'Intelligence' – even though his first-hand experience of combat had been surprisingly brief.

Outranked by the heads of the other agencies, and by most of those who passed through Athens, Asplin was well-aware (it annoyed him) that he was described behind his back by 'certain people' in the services as an amateur. Being a novice myself, I sympathised with his frustration. Things had gone well to begin with, but the harder we worked, the more we expanded, the more difficult it became to cover all the enemy initiatives, to monitor the hotchpotch that was Athens in those tortuous days. The boundaries between counter-espionage and propaganda ventures, for example, became increasingly problematic.

Indeed, less than a fortnight before the day fixed for our meeting with Cy Lapides one of the government broadsheets had published a long account of headless corpses being washed ashore on a beach near Old Phaleron, victims of the British secret police allegedly. Then, just as the controversy was dying down, dismissed as simply one of the many baseless rumours that swept through the city from time to time (all too often nurtured by Baron Von Kessell's coterie of German sympathisers), we learnt from one of our informants – much to our horror – that the story wasn't entirely fiction. Hessian sacks had been found by

12

local fishermen containing the beheaded carcasses of three pigs. The sacks and their contents had been disposed of, according to our confidant, quickly enough to avert an official inquiry, but regrettably, not before rumours of British wrongdoing had begun to spread.

We let our informer have his fee, but worse was to follow. It was only a few days later that Lieutenant Commander Arnold Furnell turned up at the British School, without forewarning. A swarthy, long-serving naval officer, straight-backed and sure of himself, there he was before us in blue serge and gold braid, with papers from GHQ in Alexandria to show that he had been instructed to review our operations, and the operations of our colleagues at Salonica.

Taciturn as a rule, or so I inferred from my exchanges with our unwanted visitor during his first day in Athens, Furnell was nonetheless inclined to blurt out jots of information about this or that to serve as small talk, although in some cases he should have known better. And so it was that at morning tea on his second day in Athens, when the talk by chance turned to ruses designed to confuse the enemy, Arnold Furnell happened to let slip, with a loud guffaw, that he himself had supervised the beheading of the controversial pigs.

The plan was to put the carcasses in sacks and let them drift ashore, he explained, then let it be known that this was an example of Turkish infamy. Unfortunately, according to Furnell's rendition of the story, his confederates on shore – a group that probably included our informer – must have double crossed their employer, and in pursuit of yet another (and presumably higher) fee, had sold the secret to a German sympathiser. Passed up the line, the carefully contrived scenario destined to become a rumour about headless bodies in hessian sacks, soon came to Baron Von Kessell who made the most of it, reshaping the story until it reflected badly on the British.

Stunned, devastated by what we had just been told, Toby Asplin tackled the storyteller furiously, castigating Furnell for the blood-soaked extremity of his actions, regaling him with the risk of the plan backfiring (as it had done) and, above all, denouncing him for his failure to liaise with the British intelligence teams ashore, an alleged lack of coordination being the very thing that he had been sent to Athens to investigate.

Lieutenant Commander Furnell, with the obstinate look of a seasoned naval officer who had been battered by worse seas than this, listened to Asplin's tirade quietly, sipping his tea, saying nothing. Until Asplin had finished. Whereupon Furnell raised a gnarled hand to repel any renewal of the onslaught, saying briefly but savagely. 'In wartime you do what has to be done. And sometimes, when the stakes are high, the quicker the better.'

That such a man had been sent to review our operations left Asplin fuming, but the orders were there. Cooperate! Brief him fully! The innuendo that a professional had been despatched to fix up an outfit that had fallen into disarray was inescapable. Asplin was stuck with it, but the thought had left him constantly on edge, especially in Furnell's presence.

I sensed that Asplin was on edge as I quizzed him in my quarters about Cy Lapides. My superior was worried about Furnell, no doubt, but also about our forthcoming meeting with the mystery man from Smyrna. But I had to persevere. Find out what had prompted Asplin to arrange a meeting at our recently-acquired room.

'Talk about keeping our processes impeccable is all very well.' I held out my hand to retrieve the card from Asplin, concealing it in the inner lining of my jacket, before moving on to gather up my notebook and pencil – tools to help assess the would-be agent from Smyrna who was probably on his way to our secluded room right now. 'But why couldn't he come here to the British School if he had to see us? Which would leave him free to fall back on the usual cover story? Selling artefacts from Smyrna or whatever.'

Asplin's expression became grave at this. He had found a perch for himself on the edge of my bed, seated in the triangular space created by my partly-drawn mosquito nets like a sultan-in-exile holding court in the doorway of a cheap pavilion. 'The fact is …' The former barrister glanced quickly this way and that as if he feared we might be overheard to our disadvantage, even in a room attached to our own headquarters. 'The fact is that a message from Lapides reached me after I arranged to meet him here. It shook me. I had to answer it.'

I took the hint and closed the door to the landing. 'A message?'

'Yes. Alexis Brusa brought it to me. It seems that, unbeknownst to me, our very important visitor, the esteemed Lieutenant Commander, prevailed upon our driver in my absence to provide a tour of the city, going first to the Acropolis, finishing up eventually at the Panhellenion Café. Which is where I met Lapides a few days ago. Lapides must have recognised our car, or perhaps he was well-briefed by whoever sent him here and knows a bit about us. Not just about our presence at the British School, for that's where we had previously arranged to meet, but about Brusa and other members of our team.'

Asplin shifted on his perch uncomfortably. 'In any event,' he continued, 'yesterday afternoon Lapides sent me a note. To say that a man he had seen previously in the vicinity of the British School had spotted him in the street. No words were spoken, for the man in question had simply smiled and made a threatening gesture. So Lapides in his note sought my permission … no, he begged my permission, to change our meeting place. He feared that the person he had seen was after him. And only by a change of plan could he avert the risk of death.'

'A gesture? What sort of gesture?'

15

'A knife gesture, he called it.' Asplin demonstrated by drawing a finger across his throat. 'Like that, presumably. It all sounded rather melodramatic to me, but as you know one can't afford to misinterpret the fears of these would-be informers. If they're not trailing one of our opposing agents, they're being followed through the back streets themselves. Best to play safe and fall in with whatever they propose, provided they take the usual precautions to evade pursuers. So I scribbled a reply to that effect, proposing a meeting in our room tomorrow morning. Which is now *this* morning.' Asplin glanced at his fob watch. 'In about twenty minutes' time.'

My colleague rose to his feet as if to round off the tale. 'Having scribbled my reply to Lapides, I decided to bring you in on it. Hence my note to you before dinner.'

'Which is why,' I chipped in, still piqued by Asplin's earlier diatribe, 'I felt obliged to fetch the card from our archivist after dinner. Does anyone else know about this morning's meeting?'

Asplin grimaced. 'Now there's a peculiar thing. Not being entirely sure about Brusa's reliability I decided to have a chat with our esteemed visitor.' The speaker made a chopping motion. 'The carcass man! Furnell. To find out whether he had noticed anything unusual at the Panhellenion Café or elsewhere in the course of their excursion. Naturally, and probably out of an undeserved sense of courtesy, I made no complaint about the commandeering of our car and driver, although I was tempted to do so. I carried on as if engaged in minor chit-chat, but I certainly wanted to hear what he might say.'

'And did he say anything of interest?'

'Well, that's the peculiar thing, and I don't know what to make of it. What he said amounted to this. While walking with Brusa in the street outside the Panhellenion, Furnell noticed a chap he knew to be a businessman from Smyrna. Surmising that this was the very man we had arranged to meet, for I had briefed him about that too,

Furnell went on to say that he signalled to the fellow. In the way he used to do when they had dealings together. To let the man know, or so Furnell claimed, that this brief encounter in the street was to be followed by a more significant meeting in the morning.'

'Did Furnell say what his signal consisted of.'

He didn't say, and I didn't press him. I was talking to him shortly after sending my notes to Lapides and yourself, by which time I had changed the meeting place. That seemed more than enough to remedy the man from Smyrna's apprehension. There will be time enough later, I concluded, after you and I have spoken to Lapides this morning, to go back to Furnell and ask him about the nature of his signal. I can't imagine him making a cut-throat gesture in broad daylight.'

'But nor could you imagine him putting pigs in hessian bags.'

'True. I'll have to press him hard about his so-called signal.'

'And about the nature of his previous dealings with this fellow.'

'Exactly. There's something very odd about the whole thing …
but still. One has to keep moving.'

Asplin buttoned up his jacket. *Keep moving.* Reassured by his usual mantra, our leader had obviously regained his aplomb and was keen to get going. So I opened the door to let him through to the landing.

'Yes,' I called after him as I locked the door, noticing that Asplin was on the stairs already. 'All things considered, it's about time we had a good long chat to the said Cy Lapides. To hear his side of the story. Test him.'

I put away my key and turned to face the row of marble statues lined up in the half-light along the landing wall, an array drawn from the archaeological school's vast collection, some with missing limbs, others with chipped torsos, or damaged profiles.

They stared back at me with sightless eyes, the impassive bystanders, these old reminders of mortality, a thought that prompted me to add a warning to my call in a way that seemed quite uncanny half an hour later, by which time we were dwelling upon the scene that awaited us – the corpse, the bleeding throat, the contorted features, the lifeless gaze.

'It probably doesn't matter where we meet.' I crossed the landing to join Asplin on the stairs. 'This is War. We may well learn more about the likely outcome of the next Allied offensive by meeting Lapides in our room, face to face. You can learn a lot by the look in a man's eye. It can tell you what the future holds.'

* * *

Where was Alexis Brusa? The Sunbeam four-seater we had expected to find outside the front gate, engine humming, hub-caps and wheel spokes gleaming, the black brow of its canvas hood ready for action, was nowhere to be seen. And no matter how often or how fiercely Asplin examined the streetscape for some vestige of Brusa's vehicle, shielding his eyes against the glare with an upraised hand, the car still failed to appear.

'Damn the man!' Asplin let his hand drop and began rubbing both hands together. 'Chilly!' he said. 'We'd better wait inside.'

So we retired to the front room of the little gatehouse with its peeling wallpaper and archaic bulletin board. It was better to be here, inside, than loitering in a cobbled tract adjacent to a tram stop and a trio of shivering palm trees. But the gatehouse room was chilly too, and it had a musty odour. The bench for visitors was occupied by an assortment of broken marble panels, cracked vases and other carefully labelled antiquities, leaving nowhere to sit.

Hands in pockets, Asplin began to pace, pausing at the front window from time to time, staring balefully at the emptiness below and at the lethargic traffic beyond the tram stop. Two giant drays, loaded with wooden barrels, slowly appeared, drawn by plodding horses, as if they had been pushed into view by some

18

malevolent deity who was determined to remind my colleague of the world's usual indifference to anyone in a hurry.

'It isn't like him to be late.' Asplin, speaking half to the world outside and half to me, tried to be fair. 'Not like him at all.' The speaker left the drays to their lumbering journey and turned to confront me. 'But it's still a damn nuisance.'

Ted James, the elderly porter seated at the gatehouse desk did his best to console us. A former steward with the Levant Shipping Line, a friendly chap who had finished up in Athens many years ago in the wake of a failed marriage and a period clerking for a ferry service to Hydra, Ted James had lost none of his essential Englishness. After a quick bout of token throat clearing, he made his opening bid. Some tea and a biscuit perhaps? When this was refused – Asplin's veto disposing of the offer before I could get a word out – the elderly gatekeeper cast about for another diversion. Some further chat about the fragments on the bench led to him picking up and passing to me a large, handsomely framed sepia photograph. This had just been delivered to his desk in the usual way by a local picture-framer, the porter explained.

A team of archaeologists were standing in the foreground of the print at the foot of a ruined tower, most of them in white shirts and trousers, faces shaded by straw hats, almost like an Oxford boating crew. A cluster of local workers could be seen further back, some with shovels and wicker baskets in their hands. A dark-suited gentleman in a Panama hat stood at the centre of the picture, one hand on an ebony cane as if to steady himself, the other resting on the shoulder of an attractive young lady with a parasol. The tiny plaque beneath the photo said simply: *A Visit to the Mavros volunteers at Pergamon.*

'Taken before the war,' Ted James declared, as I studied the picture. 'Mr Mavros and his daughter at one of the sites.'

My interest quickened, for it wasn't so long ago, while travelling in the Aegean before the war that I myself had served as a 'Mavros volunteer' and enjoyed some happy furloughs under canvas at a couple of diggings. But I didn't remind Ted James of this. Under Asplin's tutelage in recent months, I had learned never to reveal by word or gesture what part of a conversation was thought to be of particular interest. If an agent or informer felt that something they had said was crucial they were inclined to skew their narrative in that direction.

What had by now become an instinctive sense of discretion scarcely mattered on this occasion, for Ted James, pleased to have an audience, was running onwards. 'I got to know a number of them,' he informed me. 'The pick of the Mavros volunteers. My regulars. And fine young fellows they were too. Looking in on me occasionally as they came and went. Brimful of chit chat about where they'd been, what they'd found. Keen as mustard they were.' He slipped me an old codger's wink. 'And keen on the daughter too.'

I realised with a pang of remembrance that I knew exactly what he meant. The Mavros daughter, the shapely figure beneath the parasol, entranced the volunteers at every site she went to with her father, and like many others I had counted myself as one of her admirers. But, again, with the garrulous Mr James beside me, I kept my memories to myself. Not being one of his regulars, the best I could summon up in answer to his quip was: 'Keen as mustard? Can't blame them for that.'

Ted James retrieved the photograph, examined it for a moment, and put it back on his desk. 'Yes, that they were. A fine bunch, his volunteers. Coming and going from season to season. Some numbered among the fallen by now, I expect. At Gallipoli, or on the western front. One at least that I know of.'

'But not Peter Mavros,' I murmured. 'He's still safe and sound.'

The central figure in the photograph, face half in shadow beneath the brim of his Panama, was smiling at the camera, looking pleased with himself – a ringmaster on a mound of rubble, a handsome, bushy-eyebrowed raconteur with something almost reckless in the spread of the mouth and in the way he gripped his cane, determined to talk up whatever was found in the overgrown amphitheatre at Pergamon, or in the ruins around him.

I couldn't claim that my previous acquaintance with the smiling figure gave me any real advantage in my conversation with the porter. A newcomer couldn't be in Athens for long at that time without having heard of Peter Mavros, or to have seen him out and about with his wife and daughter, hobnobbing with friends at the Panhellenion Café, or chatting to parliamentarians on the front steps of the Grande Bretagne Hotel. Tycoon, art collector, a sponsor of various archaeological ventures, he and his family circle were generally understood to be amongst those supporting King Constantine's preference for the Central Powers.

'No, not Mr Mavros,' Ted James assured me with a chuckle. But as that might have seemed too familiar the former steward quickly pulled himself into line and threw in an extra and more suitably bland remark. 'He's done a lot for us here at the School, they say.' The old fellow tapped the glass protecting the picture. 'Money for excavations and so on. And not just pieces for his private collection.'

I had imagined that these observations might be of interest to Asplin, for he went to the Panhellenion almost daily as a means of 'keeping his ear to the ground', and over the past few months had set about becoming acquainted with many of those who frequented the place. The best way of concealing what one does, Asplin had often told me, is to splash about in public and to joke about one's alleged activities – as if there's nothing to hide. One can then dive deep behind the scenes.

It was for this very reason that Asplin, when he heard of my previous link to the Mavros family, pressed me to tell him more. I obliged by mentioning the local man's background as an engineer trained in London and Berlin, his years of amassing riches in South America before returning to Athens. This was more than enough to satisfy my ever-impatient leader. He immediately sallied forth to introduce himself to the influential Peter Mavros, under the pretext of seeking further sponsorship for the British School. But even as Asplin hurried off I knew that everything I had just said sounded false. The fact was that largely due to my affection for the local man's daughter, Anita, I had, on the last occasion I served as a Mavros volunteer, fallen out with her parents. I was therefore pleased to find, this morning, that Asplin had too much on his mind to take an interest in the porter's ruminations.

'Yes, yes, of course,' Asplin left the window to join us at the desk. 'Mr Mavros and so forth. The School's supporters. They're very important.' That said, he held up a hand to end the small talk. 'Please excuse us Mr James. My friend and I – we have to confer in private.'

A few seconds later, with Asplin still gripping my elbow – the projection he had utilised to lever me outside – the two of us were on the steps to the gatehouse door, conferring in the shadow of the overhang.

Asplin aimed a finger at my jacket, probing for the concealed index card. 'My notes may have misled you. What he said was more than just a sly hint.'

I must have looked blank, for Asplin stopped fingering my jacket and came straight to the point. 'Cy Lapides! His talk about a forthcoming offensive. It sounded like the same old rumours, true, but he sounded definite. That he was on to something big. A bold new plan to surprise the Central Powers.'

'Okay. But what does he want?'

'He's after the best price he can get for it. Or so I assume. From the Germans if they paid him to go looking for it, or from us to prevent it being passed on to Berlin. Which may be why he's scared. He's double dealing and fears he might be caught out.'

Asplin dug into the pocket of his own jacket and a moment later was beckoning me inwards to inspect the note Lapides had sent him, scribbled on a menu card bearing the blue crest of the Penhellenion Café, a card that had been torn in half. 'You can sense it in his tone – 'Please, I beg of you. We must change tomorrow's meeting place.' Tears the card in half in the usual way so he can match his half to mine when we meet. A sure sign he's trying to protect himself.'

I studied the card's ragged edge and the handwritten script beneath the printed list of drinks and foodstuffs. Further down, close to the point where the card had been ripped in half, it looked as though the same pencil had been used to create a rough sketch of that part of the Aegean leading to Constantinople and the Black Sea. Between the jagged configurations representing Greece on one side, Turkey and other parts of Asia Minor on the opposite shore, there were various specks to represent the Cyclades and other scatterings of Greek islands.

But before I could look closer Asplin had retrieved the card, and shoved it back in his coat pocket. 'Which still leaves the question of what our esteemed visitor Lieutenant Commander Furnell knows about all of this. If GHQ in Alexandria is planning a new offensive we should know about it by now.'

'Should we? It's not exactly counter-espionage.'

'That's what they can't seem to grasp at GHQ. A secret plan doesn't stay secret for long. As in this case, it seems. Which puts the onus on us to prevent it being passed onwards to Constantinople and Berlin. Unless Furnell and his cronies at GHQ are trying to keep it away from us.'

The time had come to voice the thought I knew to be lurking behind these irritable observations. 'Because GHQ doesn't trust us?'

'Because they like to keep things to themselves. I sometimes think that the only way we can find out what's going on in

Cabinet or the high command is by cables to C. And he takes an age to reply. By which time things have moved on.'

Asplin had spoken feverishly, but with some justification. Like an ever-cheerful street conjurer, Whitehall kept plucking odd surprises out of its battered hat. But that meant, in the absence of any clear policy at home, those at work in Athens and Salonica were left to figure out what to do as best they could.

'So if there is a plan for some new attack,' I conjectured, 'we'll have to prise it out of Cy Lapides?'

'Apparently so.'

'And without much to go on before we test him. Although it may prove easier than we imagine. If he does have a secret to sell.'

'And if he's willing to sell it.'

Any further words of advice or consolation suddenly became superfluous. Our car had appeared and was heading for the parking space beside us. 'And here, at long last,' I ventured, 'is the man to take us to him.'

'And about time too.' Asplin raised a protective hand to his eyes as he stepped into the sunlight, watching the miscreant's approach.

The car pulled in and came to an abrupt halt. To my surprise, the figure sliding out from behind the steering wheel was not the driver I had become accustomed to over the last few months. On this occasion, Alexis Brusa was clad in the pair of mechanic's overalls that he sometimes slipped on while cleaning the car or crawling under the chassis to examine its innards – a baggy, grease-stained garment that covered him up from the soles of his thick boots to the stubble beneath his chin.

Toby Asplin wasn't interested in what his driver was wearing. With one foot on the running board already, Asplin was clambering into the back seat of the vehicle. 'This simply won't do,' he called out as he settled himself into the upholstery and gripped the leather loop by the side window, waiting for me to join him. 'Where on earth have you been?'

'Traffic!' Brusa waited until I had closed the door behind me, then returned to his place at the wheel. 'Bad traffic all the way here,' he flung over his shoulder, revving the engine.

That was the only explanation he gave for his tardy, mechanic-suited appearance, and a few streets further on, as we bumped along behind a steam-tram headed for Constitution Square, then a line of donkeys burdened by rugs and clattering copperware, it was an explanation that seemed convincing. Certainly, as Brusa sat there, upfront, staring ahead, sounding his horn impatiently, squeezing the rubber bulb again and again like a man who was being sorely inconvenienced by the ways of the city, he looked keen to regain lost time by cutting through the hubbub around us. Although, I had to admit, this was how he generally looked while driving – slightly agitated, but tough. Ready for the fray.

I hadn't heard Asplin give any directions as to where our driver was to take us. It struck me as we pushed ahead that Brusa seemed to know the route he was following, edging past the tram, slipping down a side street to find his way to a broader avenue, using short cuts. But as Asplin didn't seem inclined to talk, still brooding about the matters we had just discussed, I decided to sit back and simply let things take their course. The mayhem at our destination came as a shock.

* * *

Brusa parked in a side street close to the meeting place, then pushed ahead of us on foot around a corner and down a narrow alleyway, leading us swiftly to the front entrance of the dilapidated premises in which our room was situated. Disconcerted to find a group of locals gathered there, we eased past them to reach a low arch that took us to the inner courtyard. Here, at the foot of the stairway ascending to the upper floor, we were confronted by the landlady and a cohort of her friends, a caterwauling miscellany of black-skirted harridans who seemed to identify us immediately as the cause of their distress, milling about, flapping their hands, this way, that way, as if the chorus line of a Greek opera in full voice had been suddenly thrust to the front of the stage without knowing what was expected of them or what to do next.

Much of their clamour was incomprehensible, but the sturdy landlady at the centre of the pack was known to Brusa and me from our recent negotiations, so I managed to quell her cries and gesticulations sufficiently to find out what was amiss, piecing the story together from her disjointed answers to my queries. The end room on the upper floor. The door was open. She had found a body by the bed. A man. She made a plunging motion to portray the knife in his throat, rippling fingers for the runnels of blood. She had run out to send for the police. But when she came back another man was there. That man!

As I followed the line indicated by her outstretched arm and accusing finger my gaze was drawn to a figure at the veranda rail on the upper floor, leaning against it, quite still, surveying the commotion beneath him as a bystander on a railway footbridge with time to kill before his train came in might contemplate the hustle and bustle on the platforms below.

It was our visitor from GHQ in Alexandria: Lieutenant Commander Arnold Furnell. But on this occasion dressed not as a British naval officer, but as a civilian, protected from the cold by a shabby overcoat.

Furnell must have taken account of our puzzled upward looks, for he raised a gloved hand in a kind of half-wave, or half-salute. This was followed by a beckoning gesture as he straightened up and left the rail, pointing then to the door behind him. We were to join him there. And quickly, his semaphore said.

'What the hell is *he* doing here?' Asplin was already surging through the throng of noisy women to mount the steps, two at a time.

I told Brusa to hold back the women and to send up the police once they arrived. By the time I reached the end room on the upper floor Furnell and Asplin were through the door. A moment later, alongside Asplin, I was staring at the lifeless expression of the man we were supposed to meet. It was a chilling sight: his body in its blood-streaked clothing slumped against the iron bedstead, his pallid face partly obscured by greasy shoulder-length hair, his gap-toothed mouth and slack jaw underpinned by the hilt of a knife.

Like Asplin, I was in no mood to thank Furnell for his attendance, but it certainly came as a relief when, decisively, he dragged a blanket off the bed and covered the body: this man from Smyrna whose death had been foretold.

'So much for Cy Lapides.' Furnell made a final adjustment to ensure that the corpse was shrouded entirely, and stepped back, his rugged, seafarer's face expressionless, his lips scarcely moving. 'Whatever Lapides knew, he won't be telling your lot about it. Nor anyone else.'

This was too much for Toby Asplin. He returned to his first thought but this time with an even greater display of anger. 'What the hell are *you* doing here?'

'Doing my duty. Keeping track of things.' Furnell's solid stance and unflinching look made it clear that he didn't feel obliged to explain himself and was unlikely to do so. 'You told me you were meeting Cy Lapides, so here I am.'

'How so?'

'By quizzing your driver.' Furnell jerked a thumb at the courtyard. 'Brusa.'

Asplin was thrown off balance by this gesture. It left him trying to work out when exactly he had given Brusa the relevant details: the time and place of the meeting. Abandoning the struggle, he tried another tack. 'So when did you get here?'

'A few minutes ago. By which time the body had been discovered.'

27

'The body of a man you had met before,' I interposed. 'Or so I've been told.'

'Correct.' Furnell gave me a shrewd glance of appraisal. 'I met him at GHQ in Alexandria not so long ago. He gave his name as Cy Lapides and described himself as a businessman from Smyrna. He wanted a letter of introduction to the British Legation here in Athens. To facilitate the importation of certain goods, or so he said. I can't claim to know much about him.'

This wasn't enough to appease Asplin. 'A letter! You checked his background, I presume? Made inquiries?'

'Others did.'

'So why do you think he wanted to meet us?' I asked.

The thick-set naval officer, unbuttoning his overcoat slowly, gave me a guarded look. 'I can't say.'

'Meaning what? You know, but you *can't* say?'

Asplin jumped in to support me. 'Or you won't say?'

Furnell laughed a little at this. 'I can't say because I don't know what exactly he came here for. I can read morse code but I can't read minds.' He glanced at the shrouded body. 'I repeat. I met Lapides once or twice. That's all. I didn't stick a knife in his throat if that's what you're driving at. I've only just arrived.'

Asplin had begun to pace. 'Just arrived. Easy to say. But there's the rub. The police will soon be here and it's bound to come out that we have connections to the dead man. You in Alexandria. Me at the Penhellenion. Followed by a pre-arranged meeting at a room rented to a fictitious tenant. Who can probably be traced back to Brusa – a driver from the British School.'

'That depends ....' I reminded him.

'Yes. Yes. Of course.' Asplin knew what I meant. The inquiry would be sharper if the Palace police took control, for they were always keen to embarrass the British. On the other hand, the City police were all for Venizelos, and knowing of Asplin's backing for the Lion of Crete, they would be more likely to accept whatever Asplin told them.

'This is war time.' Furnell, standing there with folded arms, voiced his familiar credo. 'What we tell the police will be nothing more than we think they need to know. I suggest we begin by telling them that this room belongs to Cy Lapides and he invited us here. I further suggest that we leave right now. The longer we stay here, the worse it looks.'

* * *

So we left that sombre room, cold and empty, but for its shrouded occupant, and with Furnell leading the way set off along the veranda. For a fleeting whimsical moment, upon hearing the door click shut behind me, I felt as a prisoner might upon being liberated from his soiled, claustrophobic cell. The vista of blue sky above the courtyard shone with a quiet brilliance. The cluster of geranium pots at the foot of the stairs, the leaves and red petals radiant in the morning light, seemed to float upwards to greet me: a bouquet brought to the beholder as a tribute to the world outside, a little gift. And even the complaints of the landlady's friends, railing against the stalwart Brusa as he stood on sentry duty before them, came to me as if from afar, like the to and fro of workaday voices in a busy marketplace.

It ended quickly, the moment of respite. A small contingent of police were shouldering their way into the courtyard, and it was clear that their leader, who was accompanied by the distraught landlady, had been asking questions of the one who had brought him to the scene and he would soon be looking to us for answers.

The man in charge, a burly figure in the uniform of the City Police, signalled to one of his coterie to assist Brusa in keeping the women off the stairs. That done, he beckoned, and quickly lined us up beside the nearest veranda post as if we three – Furnell, Asplin and me – were about to undertake a special mission.

Asplin caught my eye and smiled faintly. He knew the officer in charge – Detective Theo Diakis – and, more importantly, he was aware from investigations in recent months that Diakis was loyal to the City police, and could be regarded as an ally. I wasn't so sure. Right now, even as the English-speaking detective in his guttural accent invited us to gather round, it seemed to me that he was less friendly than usual. The detective's subordinate, a young fellow with a firm grip on his baton and the look of a man who would like to use it, had sidled in to join his boss, staring at each of us in turn, suspiciously, angrily.

'I have spoken to that one.' Diakis glanced at the landlady who was being kept away from us by another of his men. 'I know a little, but here I must speak to you. Three visitors, suddenly appearing! So what is this I say to myself? Where does it fit?' He shrugged. 'I am so busy, but we must talk.'

I had little doubt that the speaker knew of Asplin's link to the British intelligence services for in various minor ways he had cooperated with us from time to time, but he listened impassively as Asplin went through the motions of telling the investigator what we knew, and how we came to be here – the man from Smyrna's initial approach, an arrangement to meet at his lodgings. To sell artefacts to the British School, presumably.

The Greek detective had lit up a thin black cheroot while this story was being told. He took a small puff as Asplin finished off and examined his smoke with a slight frown, although it wasn't clear whether this was due to what he had inhaled or to what he had just heard. 'His lodgings?' The smoker was still studying the glowing end. 'None of you know him but you come to his lodgings, eh? Do you all confirm it?'

'We do.' Furnell hadn't bothered to introduce himself, but his tone suggested that he was speaking for us all.

Diakis turned away and muttered something to his companion. Quick to respond, the young fellow stuck his baton under his arm and dug into his pocket, producing a scrap of folded paper. He handed it to his boss.

The rental slip!

I felt a twinge of apprehension, then worse, as the piece of paper was shoved towards me, the signature on the bottom line displayed. This wasn't Brusa's handiwork, the scrawl of a man posing as an out of town worker. It was *my* signature – that of Robert Kaub – an archaeologist (supposedly) employed by the British School of Hellenic Studies.

'Diakis showed the piece of paper to the others as a lawyer might to a jury, before turning back to me. 'I will have to talk to you about this. But first we go to the room.'

He hadn't asked for an explanation, which was just as well, for now, in a panic, I had suddenly recalled that, yes, this was one of the occasions when, inadvertently, I had wrapped up the negotiations by signing the rental slip myself, a scrap of paper that usually meant next to nothing, but could now be used against me.

Perhaps because he sensed my agitation, or seeking to patch up a flaw in Asplin's story, Furnell butted in. 'This man from Smyrna. Cy Lapides. He insisted that we find him lodgings. Before we talked.'

The detective greeted this with a crafty smile. 'I know he was from Smyrna. We have been watching him for several days. He goes to the marketplace. He is buying maps. He is asking people about roads and possible water supplies for encampments to the north of Smyrna. Perhaps he asked too many questions and lost his way?'

Diakis laughed a little at his own joke, then used one hand to roll imaginary dice. 'And all the time his gambling debts are piling up, eh?'

The joke over, Diakis faced us squarely in order to bring the discussion to an end. 'You must remain here while we go to the room.'

We watched the two policemen mount the stairs and proceed to the doorway at the far end of the veranda, leaving a faint puff of smoke behind them as they disappeared from view. Three or four policemen were still hanging about by the entrance to the courtyard, but with little to do, now that the landlady and her friends had been moved on.

Asplin and Furnell found places for themselves on a bench by the entrance and sat there calmly, waiting for the detective and his offsider to return. Having just been identified as the nominal tenant of the room in which the body had been found, I didn't feel inclined to join them. Their aplomb annoyed me. By glossing over the extent of our prior knowledge, a series of half-truths had become a lie – that the room belonged to Cy Lapides – and that lie had then been quickly exposed by the presence of my name on the rental slip, although, admittedly, my companions had no forewarning that I had signed this damaging relic of our deceit.

It was true, in a general sense, that reading minds wasn't like reading morse code. But as Asplin, the former barrister, well knew, for he had explained the rule of evidence to me many times, when a lie is told out of fear of the truth or to conceal a crime it can be taken as an implied admission of guilt. The lie lays bare the workings of the mind in question and can then be used by the police or, later on, by a cross-examiner in court, to condemn the suspect.

I gripped the veranda post, cursing the rental slip, my stupidity in signing it. And I cursed myself for going along with the story that had just been put to the detective, a version of our dealings with Lapides that left me entangled in a web of prevarication. I was no murderer, but here I was with a body in my room: the body of a man I had never met, a pallid wretch who had not

32

only managed to get himself killed in whatever game he was playing but had left behind a thicket of loose ends. Spies who double-crossed their employers to cover their gambling debts were thought to be fair game for hired assassins, and it was by no means unusual for one death to be followed closely by another. The King himself could vouch for that. The ruffian who assassinated King Constantine's father was found dead a few days later – pushed from a prison window before he could name his fellow conspirators.

Risks of this kind weren't what I had bargained for when I was sent to Athens. Far from it. Brought up in Sydney, I had achieved some early notoriety in my own country as the author of a Federation Ode read aloud at the inauguration of the Commonwealth of Australia. This achievement pleased my parents and supported my claim to be a poet when they backed my proposal to study at Oxford – an approval that led to vanity and even induced me, after a year or so, to quit my college and wander abroad in the Aegean as some latter-day Byron. I explored Cyprus, lived on Rhodes, and served briefly as a 'Mavros volunteer' on several archaeological sites. Inevitably, I finished up not as a hero in Arcadia but as an impecunious part-time teacher at the Tilly Institute in Berlin, bereft of nearly all but my last pair of trousers, a passable knowledge of various languages, and a sober realisation that it takes more than a poem to create a country, more than approval to make a man.

So I knuckled down as a teacher and managed to improve my linguistic skills. I was under instruction from my father – a barrister in Sydney – to seek out my Kaub relatives in Germany, which I promised to do, but my secret wish, underpinned by my travels and the companionship I had enjoyed at diggings in Asia Minor and on Crete, was to persevere in building up my reputation as a writer. The war had put an end to all of that, forcing me out of Berlin, back to England, where the skills I had acquired were quickly snapped up by the powers-that-be in Whitehall and put to use.

My ill-fated stint at Oxford – a matter of chagrin to my bewildered parents – proved useful eventually. It turned out that Asplin had quit the city of dreaming spires too, without a degree, when the chance arose to join his uncle's chambers near Lincoln's Inn. This meant that he was inclined to characterise premature departures of any kind as proof of 'dash', a quality he applauded but which, for my part, I wasn't sure I actually possessed.

Nonetheless, as I hunched up against the veranda post, struggling to make sense of our brief encounter with Detective Diakis, this bond between Asplin and myself, rooted in youthful misadventures, in what we had both failed to achieve at Oxford, was more than enough to excuse an outburst.

'We've compromised ourselves!' I rounded on the two figures on the bench. 'We'll be tripped up by what we've said. Best to lay out what we know about Lapides. His hints about a new offensive. The threatening gesture. The lot. It fits in with what we've just heard from Diakis about maps and water supplies, and that way we'll keep Diakis on our side.'

My tantrum didn't shift them. Furnell and Asplin were against me. These were matters for the intelligence services, they contended, not the police. Besides, no accusations had been made. We weren't under suspicion, and Diakis could be relied on not to press the investigation too far. He was for Venizelos. He could be trusted.

'Can he?' I queried. Even Asplin would have to accept that things had changed in recent months. If the recent Allied thrust at Suvla Bay and Anzac Cove had crushed the Turks and opened the way to Constantinople, Venizelos might well have brought Greece in behind us, sensing an Allied victory. But the August offensive at Gallipoli had failed, and the transfer of troops to

Salonica had failed too. Which left our friend Venizelos out of power, his supporters wavering, the King against him.

I pointed to the room upstairs. 'For all we know Diakis and his men have crossed over to the King's side. They could be looking for ways to favour Baron Von Kessell and his crew, not us.'

'Don't be ridiculous!' Asplin snapped. 'Theo Diakis will be with Venizelos to the very end. As he should be. I know him. I've talked to him. And if indeed there's some new offensive afoot on the Smyrna coast he won't be changing sides until he knows the outcome. Although, with winter coming on, it seems more likely that the forces at Gallipoli on both sides will simply dig in and sit tight for the time being.'

I was conscious that Arnold Furnell had remained silent, but as I turned to him, I realised that his eyes were fixed on the veranda above. 'They've seen enough,' he grunted. 'They're coming down.'

The visit to the crime scene had evidently borne fruit. Diakis, closely followed by his offsider, was holding what seemed to be a white handkerchief in one hand as he hurried towards the stairs. When he reached ground level he stopped to plant the butt of his cheroot in a geranium pot, then straightened up, and made his way towards us.

* * *

'We have found these,' the Greek detective informed us. 'In the pocket of the dead man. But nothing else, apart from a few coins and bank notes. The last of his money, I am thinking.'

Diakis pushed his findings towards us. In the palm of one hand he had what proved to be a square of white tissue paper containing an old, roughly-shaped coin, Roman perhaps, and it bore the imprint of a sombre face in profile. He held a torn card in the other hand, and it struck me immediately that this resembled the torn portion of the Penhellenion menu Asplin had shown me at the British School.

35

Upon closer inspection this turned out to be so. On the side presented to us by Diakis I could make out what seemed to be the lower part of the sketch map I had seen previously, a portion of the Aegean below Greece, including a crudely shaped outline of Crete. Upon turning over the torn card the police officer was able to show us a note in block capitals made by the same pencil: CYZICUS–ARISTIDES / BY THE KING'S GRACE THEREAFTER.

I glanced at Asplin. Our earlier disagreement had left me unsure as to what he was prepared to disclose and as to whether he would be willing to produce his half of the menu card. But he did so. And without hesitation. Possibly because of my plea for greater candour in dealing with the police, or perhaps (and more likely) his curiosity had overwhelmed him. Without any objection by Diakis, he removed the fragment from the detective's hand and fitted its ragged edge to his own portion, displaying then, quite proudly, what seemed to be an entire card, with a sketch on one side and the strange inscription in block capitals on the other.

'What's it mean?' Asplin asked, impatiently, as we all peered at the inscription. 'Cyzicus hyphen Aristides.' Still holding the pieces together, Asplin turned the card to and fro as if trying to shake a meaning out of it. 'Code? Or gobbledegook? Or what? In his pocket, you say?'

'With this coin wrapped in tissue paper,' Diakis confirmed.

'Perhaps an alias,' I ventured. 'Cyzicus. Another name for Cy Lapides?'

'It means nothing to us.' Furnell scowled at the coin in the tissue paper as if it were some worthless curio being held out to him by a hawker. 'Find the owner of the knife, that's what I say.' He stared at Diakis belligerently. 'But that's for you to decide. Your job. Not ours. We have to be on our way.'

Diakis smiled faintly, but was unmoved by these suggestions. 'There will be an autopsy, of course. And people are on their way in that regard. The cause of death. The knife. They will be closely inspected. But in my job, I find, one thing often leads to another. Sometimes just a little thing.' He placed his finger on the sketch map at a point marked 'Smyrna', then moved his finger upwards to a point further to the north marked 'Pergamon'. From there, very slowly, as Asplin kept the torn pieces together, Diakis moved his finger onwards past the Straits of Dardanelles to 'Constantinople', the city's name and a smudged dot marking the entrance to the Black Sea.

'Is it the same for some of you, what I am thinking?' he inquired. 'The card may be torn in half to match the half held by the man he is to meet. But can it be that here is some sign of what they were to talk about? Or to talk about some more? Another route to Constantinople, perhaps? The plan for a new offensive by the Allies. A secret of some value I might think. Worth enough to cover an informer's gambling debts.' He looked up and smiled at each of us in turn. 'If we know his secret we are on our way to the motive behind his death.'

'None of this has anything to do with us,' Furnell intoned. 'We were invited to a meeting. We came. But it seems his enemies got to him first.'

'First!' The police officer closed his hand over the coin and tissue paper and retrieved both pieces of the torn card from Asplin. 'I am reminded of a little thing by what you say. You came before the others, I am told. You were first to the room where the dead man lies.'

Discomforted by this, Furnell sought to improve his position. 'Yes, I arrived before the others. But only by a few minutes.'

'But you were by yourself for a time. And knowing that this man from Smyrna would be waiting in the room. A little room upstairs rented by your friend, Mr Kaub, as we now know?'

'I can't see what you're driving at.'

'I am simply doing my job. Asking questions. And there are some more I wish to ask. I am proposing that you will now come to my office to continue this.' He reverted to Asplin and me. 'I will send for you when I am ready.'

Furnell was clearly affronted by these exchanges but, judging by his expression, he was canny enough not to make a false move. 'So be it.' He shrugged. 'I will answer whatever is asked of me. I have nothing to hide.'

Diakis chuckled. 'I have heard that said so many times.' He threw back his shoulders, entirely serious now. 'And your driver will come with us. In his odd suit.'

It took only a moment for Diakis to explain what was happening to his men and for his subordinate to grasp Brusa's arm. When the latter looked to Asplin for guidance he was told to go with the police, but to bring the vehicle back to the British School as soon as possible. 'Don't waste time,' Asplin concluded. 'And find some better clothing. We can't have you looking like *that*!'

* * *

As the departing group moved away, Detective Diakis in the lead, I stared at Asplin, trying to divine his mood. *We can't have you looking like that.* The British School's car driven by a man in grease-stained overalls! Rumours of a police inquiry focused upon a room rented by a member of the School's staff! If news of this gets around, Asplin was probably thinking, we'll be in a real pickle – in Whitehall, at the command centre on Lemnos or, even worse, at the Panehellenion Café. The assassination of Cy Lapides would soon become a juicy topic, a windfall for local journalists, a boon to gossip-mongers such as the School's benefactor Peter Mavros and his raffish circle of friends.

I could understand Asplin's concern. Moreover, as the man whose signature was on the potentially incriminating rental slip, I felt a shared sense of responsibility for the mess we seemed to have created in agreeing to meet Lapides. The cover provided by the British School depended upon keeping up an appearance of normality. I knew from my contretemps with Peter Mavros before the war that the well-groomed businessman was likely to be offended not only by Alexis Brusa's dirty overalls but also, as a collector, by any suggestion that the British School might have something to do with an unusual coin being found in a dead man's pocket, especially if it became known that in the days preceding his demise the deceased had been talking indiscreetly – in places frequented by antiquarians.

The Mavros volunteers at Ephesus, I recalled, were often lectured about the need to set an example to local workers, the importance of punctuality, looking tidy, and in that regard I was not the only Australian to be reproved by the archaeological team's principal sponsor – Peter Mavros himself. He had spoken sharply to Michael Carter: a young fellow from the West Australian goldfields whose father had bankrolled a mining venture for the Athenian businessman, and thus, some years later, was able to secure a place at the diggings in Asia Minor for his naïve but good-humoured son.

When Michael, still in grubby work clothes, began chatting to Anita Mavros while her father leaned over a map at the end of a day's work, tracing the progress made since his last visit to the site, the youngster was given a blast. 'Smarten up!' Mavros commanded, although it wasn't entirely clear to me or to the other onlookers whether Michael's offence consisted of failing to participate in the map reading or of being under-dressed while exchanging badinage with the visitor's daughter. A trivial matter, true, but as I was to discover in due course one trivial thing could lead to another, and eventually, in a father's mind, to a need for discipline. So if Asplin was concerned as to how Mavros and his friends might respond to rumours of disarray at the British School, or possible wrongdoing, then it seemed to me that our leader's apprehension had to be taken seriously.

'This troublemaker Lapides!' Asplin blurted out.' Or Aristides! Whoever he is. The whole thing is spinning out of control. And it's bound to be talked about.'

'And it could get worse,' I warned.

'Much worse. An assassination under our noses. Torn menu cards. Grimy coins. Cyzicus! Code for what? There may be some plan afoot of which we know next to nothing. Smyrna! Pergamon! Constantinople! It could be a route or something like it. And right there in the other part of this wretched note. '*By the King's grace thereafter*'. Whoever jotted down that phrase seems to be reminding himself that King Constantine could be the crucial piece on the chess board. He's getting stronger, now that he's got rid of Venizelos and closed down the parliament. Which means he has to be kept on side, according to the author of the note.'

'If the King gets too strong,' I chipped in, 'his opponents will be looking for ways to pull the same trick.'

'Get rid of him?'

'It's a possibility.'

'We've got to fit the pieces together!' Asplin looked around him wildly. 'And on top of everything, they've taken Brusa! Commandeered our driver and our vehicle.'

'We'll have to find a cabbie.'

My impetuous boss was already on his way out. 'Find one for yourself. I can walk to the British Legation. I'll have to send a cable to C in Whitehall. Get some instructions. Ascertain what's going on. We'll get together at the British School later in the day.'

'Provided we're left alone by whoever murdered Cy Lapides.'

'Of course,' Asplin muttered. 'Athens being what it is right now.'

When we reached the street, with that thought still in mind, we shook hands solemnly and parted, each promising to take care, although, in Asplin's case, knowing his impulsive nature,

I had little doubt that his promise would be soon forgotten. If so, mishaps were bound to follow, the perils before us would increase, our rooms in the city would multiply.

South Dublin Libraries
www.southdublinlibraries.ie

THE SECOND ROOM

M Y SEARCH FOR A CAB HAD FAILED and now, having boarded a passing tram in a flurry, I sat imprisoned within it, beset by clanking and rattling, not knowing quite where I was heading or how to signal my stop to the clumsy vehicle that kept rounding unknown corners and veering off in unfamiliar directions. I may have appeared as calm as the other passengers, but in fact I was deeply disturbed by my glimpse of the body in the room upstairs and the questions hovering over it.

The body; the weird note. The clamour of the boxcar rumbling onwards began to sound like a repetition of the word lying at the very centre of the puzzle. *Cyzicus ... . Cyzicus .... Cyzicus ...* A mantra that seemed to quicken at the crossings, diminish on the straight. It was as if Cyzicus was our destination. As if the wheels and pistons beneath me could echo nothing else.

Until, at last, I glimpsed a line of familiar cafes, the outdoor tables attended by the usual ruck of waiters, hawkers, shoeshine boys, and the aged vendor who was always shambling about with an array of sponges and soap powders. As the tram slowed, I was pleased to see the trio of palm trees and the reassuring inscription on the pillars of the front gate: *British School of Hellenic Studies*.

Cyzicus ... *Cyzicus* ..... The ominous echo faded, and was soon lost in the grinding shriek of arrival.

I left my seat and edged forward. A queue had formed at the stop outside the entrance, a ragged cluster led by a bearded fellow with a gaudy child's kite under his arm. He stood there by the signpost, unsmiling, waiting to board. The kite with its tail-end streamers draped across his shoulders gave him the look of a street musician from another age, a dreamer clutching a huge, brightly-coloured tambourine. He and the throng behind him were so eager to clamber up that I was left having to straighten my jacket as I emerged from the crush, feet safely on the ground, pleased to have reached home base, but still baffled by the vagaries of the transport system in Athens, the paucity of cabs, horse-drawn or motor-driven.

I shivered a little as the mechanical doors snapped shut behind me. The dark tram with its scored wooden seats. That kite with its softly pulsating skin, its intimations of music from another, more exotic sphere – a different way of looking at things. *Cyzicus*. What was the link to Cy Lapides? What did the note found upon him mean?

On my way to the gate, as these questions continued to dip and soar within me, I was distracted by the sight of Ted James standing at the window of his little gatehouse. He stared at me sadly, the elderly porter, an old man afflicted by rheum and catarrh, with nothing much to do mid-morning but dwell upon the pre-war days when life at the British School was more congenial, enlivened by the comings and goings of the young men he had befriended, enriched by their repartee as they set forth on their excursions, their chit chat on the way back.

It couldn't go on forever, he must have realised: that golden era. And now, it seemed, from what he had told me earlier in the day, a good many of his 'regulars' had enlisted for other, more demanding ventures abroad. They were holed up in trenches and dug-outs on the Western Front, or gasping for air at Gallipoli, pinned down by daily gunfire, shrapnel, some of them lying in unmarked graves – cornered by forces beyond the old man's comprehension, adrift in the depths of his dismay.

So I waved to the gatekeeper, and was pleased to see him wave back, briskly, as if suddenly cheered up by my appearance. But his smile from the square of his dusty window pane came to me as if from the sepia print on his desk – a faint impression of straw-hatted good humour drawn from a time long past, a hillside far away. I could only wave again before hurrying on to reach the front steps of the main building. I had to push aside these unsettling ruminations; focus upon the dead man's note; be ready for the police inquiry.

Cyzicus. Aristides. My notion that these words might simply be another name for Cy Lapides, a denizen of the Aegean underworld, a rogue accustomed not only to concealing his purpose but also his true identity, had seemed quite likely when I put it to Furnell and Asplin.

But now, upon reflection, shaken up by the tram ride, the glimpse of a kite, a ghostly figure in a window pane, I wasn't so sure. As a poet does in worrying away at his first attempt to revisit some moment of epiphany, obsessed by echoes, the pure sound lying somewhere behind his stilted lines, I kept returning to a hazy feeling that the word Cyzicus was known to me from other days, as a place in history, or from a myth. I had to work my way through this feeling of familiarity before we formed a view as to what exactly the note found upon the body meant.

Was it anything to do with archaeological sites I had been assigned to while working as a Mavros volunteer before the war? The scraps of knowledge I had picked up in the course of my travels were now even scrappier, for I had spent most of my leisure hours in those carefree summer seasons gossiping with my fellow volunteers – enthusiasts drawn from various countries of the world – in the belief that this was the best way to improve my linguistic skills, the matter of real interest to me. To find out what Cyzicus meant, I needed help.

Fortunately, here at the British School, I could go straight to a man capable of relieving my angst forthwith – our archivist, Gerald Wray, an archaeologist well-versed in myths and legends, brimful of knowledge about ancient sites.

A former fellow of St John's College, Cambridge, Wray had been the archivist at the British School in Athens before the war. He had been recruited to Asplin's counter-espionage unit soon after the Minister at the British Legation had secured accommodation for us at the School, a temporary expedient that was put to bed in the manner of the diplomatic service at that time with a dash of disdain. 'If "Asplin's lot" run out of things to do', an under-secretary sniggered over gossip at the evening drinks trolley, 'they can interrogate the statues or decrypt the hieroglyphs on artefacts from Egypt!'

But it wasn't long before Gerald Wray, ignoring the initial badinage, had employed his beautiful copperplate handwriting to inscribe upon card after card details about the shadowy figures who crept into view as our work proceeded. Wray treated his card index system as a sacred trust and individual cards were handed over by him or his severe female assistant only to those entitled to receive them in urgent cases.

Yes, the British School's archivist was bound to come up with discerning answers to my queries, seated there at his desk in the basement, surrounded by the notes and garbled jottings delivered to him for blending into his index system.

I paused at the little table in the front hall upon which the usual leather-bound visitor's book was displayed. I filched a post card from the scattering of sixpenny scenes nearby and used a pencil from the book to replicate the enigmatic inscription: CYZICUS–ARISTIDES / BY THE KING'S GRACE THEREAFTER.

Beneath these words, I quickly created an approximation of the sketch appearing on the two halves of the torn menu card, a piece of evidence that Diakis and his sour lieutenant were probably in the course of referring to their own adviser. Thus equipped, and with the Lapides index card in hand also, I clattered down the stairs at the far end of the hall to seek out Gerald Wray and pick his brains, although I knew that I would prejudice my inquiry immediately if I used such an expression in his presence.

Having worked with Wray before the war I was well-aware that the apparently mild-mannered scholar could become surprisingly aggressive when it came to protecting things he cared about, from sites and precious discoveries to the finer points of language. At Ephesus, on the coast of Asia Minor, he was known to have employed local bruisers to guard his diggings at night from thieves and foreign interlopers. And when it came to formulating an exact description of what had been found, or the rationale for some further probe, he often became quite agitated, raising a hand in protest if infelicities were uttered by those around him who ought to know better. I had once seen him stalk off angrily when the insult was repeated.

In those days I had often wondered how Wray and his colleagues at the British School managed to work amicably with the School's principal benefactors who were, for the most part, practical men of the world – like Peter Mavros. The burly Athens-born railway engineer had left his fellow students in London and Berlin to their conventional careers and had branched out to make a fortune in far places. He had done so by laying out a railway system in Chile to service the increasingly prosperous nitrate industry, then by investing shrewdly in the industry itself. Forthright in his opinions, boisterous in his habits, he seemed to be always in a rush when he came to a site, but on the whole his backchat about maps and buried treasure didn't seem to upset the archaeologists such as Gerald Wray who trailed in his wake, pointing out the landmarks, or hurrying away to find parasols or canvas chairs for the visitor's daughter and her chaperone.

Perhaps Wray and his colleagues viewed the man who was funding them with detachment, appraising his mannerisms as if they had before them an array of badly painted gourds or the contents of a cracked sarcophagus. Or was it simply that they knew Mavros better than I did, having seen him in action when matters of substance were being discussed, aware that his gusto was used to disguise his ambition, his determination to get things done? Mavros could be ruthless. I knew that from the one occasion at Ephesus when I dealt with him at close quarters and was subjected to his wrath. But he could also be creative – by improving work practices on a site or reconfiguring the lay out of the trenches – and it was probably this, more than anything else, that the archaeologists respected.

These recollections reinforced my desire to sit down with Wray and set out what I knew about Cy Lapides and the events surrounding his death. But first I would have to force a passage past Gerald Wray's loyal assistant, Valerie Crawford. Today, as always, she was there at her desk outside the scholar's door – grey-haired, stony-faced, like an earth mother from some ancient fable.

I marched up to her briskly and came straight to the point, as if my request to see her boss as a matter of urgency couldn't be refused by any right-thinking person, not at a time like this.

I was quickly reminded by her stolid gaze that she and her ilk in offices all over the world – and probably in basement rooms like this throughout the underworld – had been trained to resist such approaches, scorning the pretensions of anyone with a claim to preferential treatment.

'My instructions are quite clear.' She pointed to the closed door in order to reinforce her assertion. 'He has a report to finish and is not to be disturbed. You'll have to wait. Or come back at midday.'

This was absurd, and I said so. I was possessed of important information, I explained. I had to see him. Forthwith!

'He's busy.'

'We all are.' I went on to remind her that intelligence work was always in a state of flux. One thing was often overtaken by another. The matter I had to raise was crucial.

'I'm sure it is.' She was on her feet now with a hand up as if to repel an advance. 'But my instructor is still busy.'

After some further toing and froing she agreed, reluctantly, to put my plea to the man himself. She wasn't slim but somehow she managed to slide through the door and close it behind her in one swift movement, without allowing me even a glimpse of the deity within.

Her defence of the report-in-progress and the skill with which she had effected her disappearance left me wondering, not for the first time, about the nature of Valerie Crawford's role within our unit. Gerald Wray was undoubtedly a member of Asplin's inner circle, for it was he, the former Cambridge don, whom Asplin had entrusted with the unit's card index system. The cards and the information they contained lay at the heart of our secretive work and it seemed more than likely that the woman serving the keeper of the cards on a daily basis was a member of the inner circle also, with a working knowledge not only of the system but of related matters such as the location of our rooms. If that were so then both she and Wray probably knew when and where the meeting with Cy Lapides was to take place.

It might turn out that Lapides had been followed back to the room and there, quite by chance, had been disposed of by his pursuer shortly before Asplin and I arrived. On the other hand, if the time and place of the meeting had been leaked to the assailant or to his confederates, then this might explain the absence of any signs of a struggle. It was an ambush – the killer was waiting for his victim.

I had no reason to doubt Wray's integrity or the security of his records. On the contrary, as one would expect of an archaeologist and former Cambridge don, he was meticulous in everything he did, and the keys with which he locked up his cards and related reports at night were attached to a steel ring that never left his person.

He would sometimes voice complaints about Asplin's methods, his colleague's tendency to rush at things, to act first and think later, but this was usually done in Asplin's presence, and in keeping with the tradition of dry wit employed by Cambridge graduates while speaking dismissively of the lack of seriousness, even flippancy, that they generally attributed to Oxford men. These mildly amusing asides didn't seem to reflect any rancour or absence of respect. The two men worked well together on the whole and Asplin always gave considerable weight to the many years that Gerald Wray had spent in Greece and Asia Minor.

Wray's knowledge of local ways had certainly proved useful but, at the same time, one had to recognise that he was more at home in a library than in the marketplace. Did this bring with it a risk that he, or his loyal assistant, had let slip some piece of information that might seem innocuous in the ordinary course of a bookish discussion but now, in wartime, was of interest to an academic friend from abroad with undisclosed ties to the enemy?

The wall opposite Valerie Crawford's desk was crowded with a cluster of photographs that looked like companion pieces to the recently-delivered print that Ted James in the gatehouse had shown me earlier in the day. They were framed in the same way and depicted various archaeological sites, including another view of Pergamon – a print on this occasion with Peter Mavros and

Gerald Wray in the foreground, the latter's gaunt figure topped off by the white, sweat-stained pith-helmet he still kept on a cabinet in the corner of his basement room.

While waiting for the earth-mother to reappear, I took a closer look at the view of Pergamon and at the next photograph in the series. This showed a group of Mavros volunteers at Ephesus and was probably taken before I reached the site. In addition to Peter Mavros – flanked by his daughter, Anita, and Gerald Wray – I recognised a number of faces including that of the young Australian, Michael Carter. They were gathered around a rubble-filled container on a tram track by the so-called 'harbour road', a thoroughfare that was scarcely visible beneath broken columns and tangled vegetation.

Some of the volunteers were holding scoops and buckets, a reminder that it was in this area, according to the stories I heard upon reaching the site, that the knowledge of ancient ways possessed by Wray and his colleagues from the British School was overshadowed by their sponsor's practical expertise.

Much of the site at Ephesus in those pre-war days had been conceded to German and Austrian Missions. In the part conceded to the British School under a sub-licensing arrangement there were certain areas still subject to the flooding and consequent silting up of the terrain that had led to the city's final abandonment in a bygone era. Sudden downpours led to a plea for help. After a hasty trip by ferry from Athens to Smyrna, then south to the site at Ephesus by road, Mavros reached the catastrophic scene. He quickly concluded that the area being excavated, which lay below the level of the floodplain, and was barely higher than the surface of the distant sea, could only be drained out with the help of a large steam-powered pump.

He called in favours, laid out *baksheesh* in all directions, and managed to get hold of a pump from the Ottoman Railway Company. This was dragged to the edge of the water-logged pit.

After cutting a passage seaward for the stream of filthy water which the twelve inch pipe was destined to disgorge, Mavros set about reducing the water level, although, unfortunately, the flow in certain areas of the pit couldn't be collected fast enough to keep the pipe free of air, and clear of mud.

In the end, because my compatriot, Michael Carter, had some previous experience of dewatering operations on the mining fields of Western Australia, Mavros put him in charge of cutting a network of channels through the foundations lying beneath the old harbour road, a stratagem that assisted the drainage, and led eventually to Michael winning the approval of his overseer. By the time I came to the site with another batch of volunteers, the area of interest to Wray and his colleagues from the British School had been walled off against the inflow, and Mavros had taken to calling the young Australian 'my heroic handyman.'

The mud mortar washed through the sieves left shards and trinkets behind including, on one memorable occasion, handfuls of hairpins, earrings, brooches and primitive electrum coins. These findings suggested – a thrill to our team – that we had chanced upon a 'foundation deposit': objects hidden by the original builders within the footings of a pedestal, a revered place upon which a god or goddess was to stand in effigy. Our work involved labour with picks, shovels, notebooks, tape-lines and cameras, often in blistering heat, and many hours of discouragement pondering inscribed stones turned upside down or defaced by lichen. But set against this were the red-letter days when the earth gave up its treasure, and this was such a day.

By nightfall, our discoveries were laid out on a length of board beneath Wray's bespectacled gaze, washed or wiped free of mud, so that even he, the former Cambridge don, pith-helmet under his arm, allowed himself a moment of exuberance as he reviewed the array with the air of a chef hovering over a tray of freshly-baked scones: 'There is always a subtle joy to be had when things like this emerge intact from hidden corners of the universe.'

Michael Carter, fair-headed, shirt half-open to the waist, a sweat-soaked handkerchief circling his sunburnt neck, was standing opposite Anita Mavros and me as these words were spoken. Amused by Wray's judicious pronouncement, and in the belief that no one else was watching, Michael winked at us and raised a grimy hand, using it to suppress an ostentatious yawn.

Peter Mavros had spent most of the day under a canvas awning with his daughter, keeping an eye on the pump, bossing about the operator of the cine camera he had brought to the site, commanding him to point his new-fangled piece of equipment at this or that. But now, either because he had noticed what Michael was doing, or perhaps because he had become accustomed to the young man's sense of humour – inferring from the smile on Anita's face that Michael was playing up to what had just been said – Mavros felt obliged to support the scholar.

'We are all adventurers,' the businessman declared. 'In our own way. *That's* the pleasure in it.' He leaned over the bits and pieces on the makeshift table, scooped up a clay seal, and held it aloft. 'We find what we care to find, and according to the strength of our caring. What say you to that, young man?'

Michael, the hapless joker, fingered his damp, makeshift cravat as though the hand used for the yawn had been somewhere in that vicinity all the time. 'Yes, you're probably right,' he conceded. 'We go hard for what we care about.'

Mavros looked along the table. 'And what does the scholar say?'

Discomforted by the query, Wray placed his pith-helmet on the table, slowly and carefully, casting about for a suitably tactful response. 'Adventurers? Possibly. That's one way of putting it. But if the instinct of a gamester be your motive in the digging trade, you will soon begin to crave winnings on every occasion. Or,

55

at least, a fair chance of them. In which case disappointment is bound to follow, and your toil will lack heart. On the other hand, for me, and for most students of antiquity, the past is forever, and thus an unfailing source of satisfaction.'

Untroubled by the ambiguity of this reply, Mavros beamed. 'So there you have it, Michael! Something to think about. Which may well change you for the better.'

'That's why I'm here.' In his usual good-natured way, the young Australian smiled back at his boss, flapping a hand at the diggings, the canvas awning nearby, the massive pump, still drooling mud. 'To pick up a bit of this and that.'

Mavros led the laughter that followed, hands spread wide in an exaggerated expression of disbelief – a mime show equal to the provocative yawn. He finished off by addressing everyone around the table like an affable patriarch bemoaning the vagaries of his family. 'This and that! Michael's impossible! I don't know what we can do with him.'

'Keep him working,' Wray proposed.

The laughter accompanying this further quip had ended the exchange and provided extra footage for the operator of the cine camera, squinting into the wooden case attached to his tripod as he wound a handle on the side, keen to record whatever seemed pleasing to his master. I could still hear an echo of that laughter as I edged onwards in order to examine the remaining photographs on the basement wall. The more I dwelt upon those pre-war days, my time as a Mavros volunteer, the less troubled I was by any thought that information from Wray's card index system or about the location of our rooms might have been passed on to third parties.

Wray was careful in what he said and in how he acted. One could, of course, be mistaken about such matters, or about his integrity, but everything I had seen of the index-keeper reminded me of how fastidious he was – a consummate professional in every task assigned to him. I had no means of knowing where exactly Peter Mavros stood in the present state of political uncertainty in Athens, but if Wray and Asplin trusted Valerie Crawford then I should probably do so too.

I returned to the earth-mother's desk in a better mood, but only to have my benign conclusion subverted immediately, for the lady in question had emerged from the inner sanctum, closing the door behind her with an ominous thud.

'He sends his regards and suggests you come back later. The index card you picked up last night can be left with me.'

'I wish to return it personally. And, as I said before, I have other urgent and more important matters to discuss.'

'He simply has to finish his report.'

'And I simply have to see him.'

'Then you'll have to sit here and wait.'

'No, I won't. I'm going in.'

Before she could stop me, my hand was on the door knob and I was through the door itself. This was the Arnold Furnell approach, I told myself grimly. In wartime you do what has to be done. And the quicker the better.

* * *

The man I had come to see was at his desk – Gerald Wray. There, bolt upright in his high-backed wooden chair, presiding over a crowded desk-top, at work on his report. The scrunched up pages scattered about him suggested that certain sections of the draft had been scrutinised carefully and found wanting.

The occupant of the windowless room peered at me over half-moon spectacles with the prim but steely gaze he bestowed upon interruptions of any kind. With a sigh, he lowered the card he had been inspecting and returned his pen to the ledge beneath his inkwell. He summoned up a facial expression that was probably

57

meant to serve as a welcoming smile. 'Ah! Kaub. What a pleasure to see you. So early and so far below ground. Barging into the rabbit-hole to suit yourself, it seems.'

'And to return your card.' I placed the index card upon his desk and cleared a space for the post card I had just completed. 'And a little extra. May I sit?'

Wray glanced at the new card warily and sighed again. 'Make yourself comfortable.' His gesture, introducing the small chair beside me, was enough to make it clear that to one accustomed by his training to review the rise and fall of empires a brief discussion could be tolerated, but not a quibble over entitlements lasting a century. 'Not too much extra, I trust.'

I showed him the words I had printed on the post card and explained the circumstances in which they had come to light – our visit to the ill-fated room, the discovery of the body, the nature of the police investigation. 'So what do you make of him,' I concluded. 'This man from Smyrna?'

Wray pondered. 'Shoulder length hair, you say? A menu card mentioning Cyzicus and a coin wrapped in tissue paper. Found at Cyzicus perhaps.'

'Cyzicus is the name of a place, I take it, not a person?'

'Certainly. I know it well, although you won't find it in a schoolboy's atlas.'

I had learnt to ignore his jibes, and did so now. 'Where will I find it?'

'In the classical texts. It appears in most versions of the Argonauts myth as an offshore island in the Sea of Marmara. It was there that Jason and his comrades in the *Argo* were set upon by a race of fierce warriors before they sailed on.'

The storyteller pushed back his chair and rose to scan the bookshelves flanking his desk. He crooked a finger, made his selection, and returned to his seat with the relevant volume, ready for the next question.

'Ah! A classical text!' I felt obliged to play along with the Cambridge don's air of patient inquiry. 'For students of any age?'

A pair of bleak blue eyes appeared above the half moons and inspected me critically. 'For all shapes and sizes.' He glanced at the book's spine. 'Montefiore's *Myths and Legends*'.

It took him only a few seconds to find the passage he was looking for. 'Here it is. The kingdom of Cyzicus. You can see what Montefiore says about it for yourself.

'I'll do my very best.'

Again, the tutor's sceptical gaze. 'That is all we can ask of anyone.'

He reached for one of the paper slips used to mark passages of interest. Before placing it on the page he read aloud as if to illustrate his earlier summary. *And so it was that the Argonauts came to an island haven where the young king Cyzicus received them gladly and had them to his wedding feast. It later fell to Hercules on watch to sound the alarm, for a race of fierce warriors came down from the hills and began blocking the harbour mouth with massive stones. Forthwith the hero's comrades rushed to defend their ship and beat back the enemy with swords and arrows.*

Wray lowered the book. 'The account of the battle and the Argonauts' subsequent departure varies from one source to another, of course, owing to the desire of many communities to claim an Argonautic ancestor or to link their region to Homeric myths.' Wray coughed discreetly. 'Conon's version, for instance, is coloured by the politics of Hellenistic Greece with the result that Cyzicus is said to be named after a son of Apollo. On the other hand, the account of Valerius Flaccus is thoroughly Romanised and devoid of local detail. For Aristides the relative antiquity of Troy and Cyzicus is assumed – owing to their proximity, I surmise – in an attempt to join the cycles of legend. But as most of the Aristidean tales tend to be far-fetched, I give little weight to his version.'

The speaker's pained expression became even more pronoun-ced. 'Regrettably, some over-enthusiastic authors in our own time, including Herbert Montefiore, seem to have accepted what Aristides and others say about Cyzicus without demur. For simplicity's sake, they would probably argue – if forced to defend themselves.'

I quickly disassociated myself from this conspiracy by pointing to the words on my postcard, an inscription fraught with complexity, surely enough to confound the apologists for plain talk, or whatever it was that Wray couldn't abide. 'Aristides,' I emphasised. 'Coupled with Cyzicus. But separated from the next phrase by a downstroke.'

I was too late. Wray had got his teeth into Aristides and was ahead of me. 'I have little doubt that the author of our note, be he the dead man Lapides or a third party, was referring to Aristides of Miletus. The context makes that clear. Aristides, known as 'the Just', famous for organising the Delian Confederacy to oppose the Persians, was a warrior shaped by the needs of Athens. I see no reason for his name to be linked to Cyzicus. On the other hand, Aristides of Miletus, the storyteller, seems to have drawn most of his tales from various cosmopolitan settlements along the coast of Asia Minor. Miletus, Ephesus. Smyrna, Pergamon, Troy. And Cyzicus. Places still peopled today by a mixture of Grecians, Turks and Armenians. It has to be said, however, that with the transference of religious sites, and the disappearance of older names and landmarks over the centuries, it is often difficult – as Schliemann found at Troy – to work out where some of the ruins are and what exactly is being talked about in the ancient texts, be it fact or myth.'

'Let's stick to fact,' I proposed.'

Wray surged past the interruption. 'Cyzicus itself, for example. Most of the sources place it in the Sea of Marmara between the Gallipoli peninsula and the entrance to the Bosphoros at

Constantinople. In some accounts it is said to be an island; in others a promontory. You may or may not recall that we tackled that conundrum some years ago.'

'I don't seem to recall it.' I was settling into my dullard's role, but with the defensive tone demanded of such a part. 'You may or may not recall that I was only a volunteer. Briefly. On Crete. Then at Ephesus'

My protest may have been noted, but it was certainly to no avail.

'About twelve years ago,' Wray informed me. 'Well before you began poking about in this part of the world, a team from the British School camped in the area. We studied the topography and certain ruins obscured for the most part by vines and mulberry trees. Overgrown walls and what remained of thoroughfares and dwellings. They were on a slope commanding a view of the Bay of Artaki to the west; the gulf of Pandermes to the east. It was there that we eventually placed the ancient city of Cyzicus – close to the modern port of Artaki, which *can* be found in a schoolboy's atlas. Our reasoning? With the passage of time, we concluded, an isthmus of marshy land had transformed an island into a promontory. And so, in substitution for what was once an outpost of the fabled city of Cyzicus, we now have the busy little port of today, communicating with Constantinople twice a week by steamer.'

My colleague's initial displeasure at my appearance had by now been entirely subsumed in the enthusiasm that always gripped him as he warmed to a subject of his choice or in which he was well-versed. This transformation would normally have been heartening to behold, but the shadow of the dead man still lay somewhere behind me, with the knowledge that the City Police might soon be questioning me about the rental slip. His use of the term 'transference' was a worry also, for this was Wray's speciality – the study of sites and cults transferred from Christianity to

Islam, as in the evolution of churches into mosques, or vice versa, as one regime replaced another.

'The move from Cyzicus to Artaki was probably related to the gradual creation of the isthmus,' Wray continued. 'And the gradual silting up of the Cyzicene ports that had shown a tendency in that direction in the early years of the Roman empire. We in our team felt sure that the decay of Cyzicus had certainly begun at the time of the earthquake when the Emperor Justinian spoiled Cyzicus of its marbles for the church-mosque of Sophia in Constantinople. Which brings us back, of course, to transference. An interesting subject indeed.'

I had to stop him before the flow of erudition became a flood. 'A steamer service!' I chipped in. 'You mentioned a steamer service. Now there's a point. A sea route to Constantinople! The indications are that Cy Lapides was angling to sell information about a forthcoming offensive in Asia Minor. A new way through to Constantinople and the Black Sea. A crucial link to our Russian allies. Which is where the sketch map may fit in, according to Asplin.'

The scholar Wray, enthused by the possibility of edging towards his favourite subject, had been enjoying a break from the war-time rigour of his card index system, but now, wrenched back to his duties, he gave a deep sigh as he picked up the postcard and examined my reproduction of the sketch. 'It may or may not fit whatever is taking shape in Asplin's mind, but it certainly fits my thesis that the person linked to Cyzicus by a hyphen is Aristides of Miletus, not Aristides the Athenian.'

'Why so?'

'Because the Milesian tales of the former are crowded with travellers on their way to Constantinople. Their misadventures and seductions, the broken hearts they leave behind them, these are paraded before us by Aristides, mostly for satire, but sometimes as a cautionary tale about places to be avoided. One way or another he provides advice about the various routes to Constantinople, by sea and through forests and mountain passes. He has a tale about the so-called 'city of mirrors', for example, where the citizens are threatened by reflections of themselves. Recent excavations in the vicinity of Cyzicus relate this description to some old walls built with stones containing veins of mica. The glinting mineral traces may well have created an illusion of mirrors flashing in the sun. It has never ceased to surprise me how many myths and ancient tales are rooted in some sort of fact, if you take a second look at the relevant texts and topography. And read between the lines.'

'So an apparently innocuous text could be used as a code?'

Wray smiled and flapped a weary hand at the array of stiff cardboard boxes containing his card index system. 'It happened in ancient times, and it happens now. Give a man a mask and he'll tell the truth. I sometimes think of each card as a chamber in a labyrinth – the name given to the maze of Minoan rooms buried beneath the Palace of Knossos. A place you do seem to recall.'

Now it was my turn to smile, caught off balance by this unexpected reminder of the season I had spent with Gerald Wray and his team of Mavros volunteers at the diggings on Crete. 'I do indeed. But what are we to make of the final words on this particular card. 'By the King's grace thereafter'. How are we to construe that phrase?'

'The answer will probably come to me while I'm having a bath. For the time being the meaning eludes me. But what doesn't elude me is the feeling that I may have come across this fellow Cy Lapides. A man from Smyrna with shoulder-length hair and a coin wrapped in tissue paper. Your description fits the man I have in mind.'

'Tell me more.'

'I was at the Penhellenion Café with Peter Mavros and one of his friends. Yesterday. Talking about the future of the British School, trying to win them back to our side, when a man fitting your description of Lapides came to the table. He and Mavros seemed to know each other but it was obvious that Mavros was embarrassed by his presence and wanted nothing to do with him. He drew the unwanted visitor aside, then sent him packing. I saw the fellow pocketing some object wrapped in white tissue paper.'

'And he saw you presumably?'

'I suppose so. I was right there at the table with Peter's friend from Chile, Guido Viscarra. When I asked about the stranger, it was Guido who called him a 'nobody from Smyrna'. Crudely. And in a way that closed off any further discussion. So we went back to talking about the British School, as if nothing had happened. I was never told the stranger's name.'

So far, I had managed to conceal my surprise by nodding attentively as the story was told, but it took an even greater effort to disguise the importance I attached to my next question, for this was a facet of the mess confronting me that I had kept from Wray. 'Did anyone in your group give any kind of signal to the stranger, before or after he spoke to Mavros?'

Puzzled by this inquiry, Wray pursed his lips and pondered. 'A signal? Not that I recall. If anything, it was him signalling to Mavros and Viscarra. Furtively, or so it seemed to me. Whereupon he made his way towards us like a mongrel looking for a feed. He whispered something to Mavros, but it didn't please the big fellow. That's all I know. I suggest you ask Mavros about it.'

'That's difficult. Mavros may have been friendly to the British School before the war, and to you in particular, but things have changed.'

'Which is why I was trying to win him over.'

'Of course. But what puts him in the German camp? His wife's influence, or because he's still angling for contracts connected to the Berlin to Baghdad railway?'

'A bit of both probably. Athenians with a foot in both camps have become accustomed to playing their cards close to the chest of late.'

64

'That's true,' I confirmed. 'But one way or another we have to get through to Mavros. Find out what he knows about Lapides. Before I'm questioned by the City Police.'

Wray picked up the postcard and studied the words, then the sketch. He turned back to me eventually with a tentative expression. 'Here's a thought. Suppose I set up another meeting with Peter Mavros, and bring you with me. As if for old times' sake.'

'That's a laugh. Since coming to Athens I've nodded to Mavros now and then, but you seem to have forgotten that when I parted company with him some time ago, during the dig at Ephesus, he sent me packing. "Get out of here, and don't come back!" That was the gist of it. Which is probably what he said to Cy Lapides at the Penhellenion, from what you've just told me.'

Wray abandoned the postcard with a shrug. 'You're still here. Which means you have to find out what's going on before it's too late. I've had various cat fights with Mavros over the years, and so has my opposite number at the German Institute, but one way or another we've always been able to patch things up. If I bring you along, he won't rake up old feuds or throw you out. On the contrary. From what I've seen of late, he'll pretend to be neutral, like everyone else in Athens, including the King.'

'Until they work out which side is likely to win. Which is what worries me about Detective Diakis and his team from the City Police.'

'Nonsense! Mavros will be all smiles. He may not give you a straight answer to your questions, but he won't fly into a rage. He'll treat you with respect.'

'Which is what Cy Lapides might have thought as he went about his business. Whatever it was. Until it was too late.'

'Lapides left his body in the room, not his business. That's still going on, no doubt. Which is why we have to act now. As you well know.'

Wray was right, of course. We had to meet Mavros. We had to find out what he knew about Lapides, and what they had talked about at the Panhellenion, on the day before Lapides was disposed of. What was the nature of their relationship?

But the prospect of visiting Peter Mavros brought with it a sense of dread.

A picture came to me of the Greek businessman in the front room of his villa near Ephesus on the day we parted company, his Panama hat with its dark blue band adrift on the polished table, the handle of his ebony cane gripped tightly as he paced up and down, looking me over with suspicious sidelong glances. On that traumatic day, at the meeting he had forced upon me, the formal welcome to begin with might have led a stranger to believe that Peter Mavros, if not pleased to see me, was prepared to be civil, willing to listen at least. But this pretence (to anyone who knew him) was far from convincing.

His manner became increasingly abstracted. His small talk ceased to make sense, the tone sarcastic, the words disjointed. Then, for no obvious reason, as if simply casting about for some diversion, a way of controlling whatever it was that seethed within him – contempt or rage, it could have been either – he paused to examine the handle of his cane, raising the silver grip upwards to the light: the profile of a gryphon's head. He studied the image, turning it this way and that, fitting the beak of the mythical beast to his forearm for a moment, before sighing deeply, wrenching it away from his arm, using the eagle-headed handpiece to hook the cane to the back of the nearest chair.

Then, with the look of an autocrat who had laid aside his quill after signing a decree, and was more than ready to enforce it, Mavros strode to the door. He ushered his tearful wife into the room. Without further ado, the powerfully-built businessman, his gaze hard and glinting, turned back to me and went straight to what he and his wife had hauled me up to their room to talk about – my trip to Smyrna with their daughter. My treachery.

THE THIRD ROOM

FROM THE BRIGHT PATCH AT THE centre of the darkened room the numbers kept coming at us, tumbling out of the screen like flashes of gunfire, the sound of the fray muffled by the roar of the huge, one-eyed projector producing the spectacle. Again, again, the flashing numerals from ten to one. Until, suddenly, there was nothing left to look at but a row of silent shopfronts, black and white signs, awnings propped over pedestrians, the odd wide-eyed people from an earlier day who went to and fro on the sidewalks with jerky steps, peering at bits and pieces on the roadside barrows, smaller now in their long skirts and black hats in the wake of a tramcar pulling away from them, left as stick-figures on the narrowing track, silhouettes against a dim grey sky in the distance.

More shopfronts appeared; another length of track. They hovered before us for a little while, these grainy city scenes, agitated by tics and scratches, until replaced, as if by a trick of the quivering light, with a glimpse of Peter Mavros on a ship deck, broad-shouldered, tucking the tails of his open-necked shirt into white trousers. He stopped short, managing a quick smile for the camera, but worried by it, not quite knowing where to look. The screen went to black. Rediscovered at the rail a moment later, Mavros was calmer now and seemed to be pointing out the main features of the port that lay ahead. Look here, his upraised cane commanded, tall-masted sailing ships, steamers, ferries, the caiques and busy rowing boats.

'Yours truly!' The businessman's voice with its familiar chortling undertone came from somewhere near me in the darkness. 'The old buccaneer. Heading for you know where. With half his shirt showing!'

Sure enough, as the wharves and jetties began to take shape, dominated by the massive French-built stone quay known as the Cordon, I could see that indeed this was Smyrna, there in its sheltered position at the head of the gulf, the pine-covered slopes of the Kadife Kale – the Velvet Castle – rising behind the city, overshadowing the mosques and minarets and church towers along the waterfront. Close up, the Cordon was crowded with locals: Armenian stevedores in long grey shirts, merchants and traders surrounded by camel trains and clumsy horse-drawn wooden wagons, or carts piled high with cotton bales and fig crates. Clusters of would-be passengers pushed towards the gangways, accompanied by Turkish porters in baggy trousers, bearing trunks and suitcases. A contingent of heavily-laden mules sidled into view.

These images were whisked away as a wooden sign appeared in a corner of the screen pointing to Belevi. A second or so later the flickering film, still afflicted by tics and blisters, was taking me back to the Mavros villa on the outskirts of that drowsy village, a ramshackle dwelling with a pile of melons by the gate, its front steps overhung by oleander and hibiscus. Then to the encampment set up nearby for the archaeologists and volunteers, to an aqueduct in the valley, to the work site at Ephesus where the camera lingered for a while, surveying the ruins of the amphitheatre, glancing at broken columns, vestiges of the roofless past. A moment later the frame was filled with Peter Mavros and his daughter, Anita, chatting to a group of volunteers at a table laid out for lunch within a grove of olive trees, picks and shovels propped against the tree trunks.

Next, the Mavros camera was there beside a gathering of villagers assembled in work parties of six, some with grappling hooks and wicker baskets strapped to their backs. A brawny fellow in a fez mouthed some words at the camera – a foreman perhaps – but a second later the screen went blank. It was reawakened by a glimpse of an arch marking the entrance to the Temple of Hadrian, and moved on from there to a partially excavated street, a grave chamber, a cluster of headstones, followed by a closer look at a piece of marble cornice with lion spouts.

Shards of pottery were thrust at the lens for inspection. These, it turned out, as the hand holding the pieces withdrew, were of interest to Gerald Wray, for he was standing close by in a pith helmet, glancing at the fragments, scratching away at his notebook, while a bunch of volunteers, seated on a wall covered with pottery fragments, looked on.

Ancient history was thought to have begun with Homer and the Trojan war, but the objects listed in Wray's notebook would show that later, after the classical age and the rivalry between Greece and Persia had run its course, the whole of Asia Minor was incorporated in the Roman empire in the form of provinces. These phases, the placement in time of structures and pottery pieces from Ephesus before it sank into decrepitude – affected by the silting up of its harbour and the coming of the Ottoman Empire – was the sort of thing that Wray and his colleagues enjoyed arguing about over lunch, much to the delight of the volunteers.

But the silent film gave no clue as to what the young men on the wall were nattering about as they watched Wray make his notes. And there was no chance to speculate, for they were quickly supplanted by an image of one of them on his knees beside the wall pumping a primus stove, tin pans and plates on a rug beside him.

'At last,' the old buccaneer in the darkness observed. 'A glimpse of a willing worker. Look at him go.'

'Michael Carter.' Sitting beside me in his straight-backed chair, Wray identified the youngster in the routine tone of a scholar who was accustomed to naming things – in notebooks or in index systems – although no one in the darkened room needed any reminder. 'The handyman.'

The stove alight now, the primus pumper looked up with an engaging grin and beckoned, as if inviting the camera operator to have some lunch too.

'More than a handyman, in fact.' Wray must have thought that merely attaching a name and description to the image was not enough. 'An all rounder,' he added. 'First up in the morning and last to bed at night.'

Mavros wasn't prepared to let this unfortunate remark float by in silence.

'That's one way of putting it,' he muttered. 'Michael Carter! He was certainly far more than a handyman. More of a ladies man. As it turned out.'

Wray must have felt the tension. He hurried on, reverting to his neutral tone, attaching a less prickly label to the next scene. 'Now here's a place of real importance, and I'm glad you've got a record of it. The ruins of the Temple of Artemis! Its whereabouts a mystery, but for an inscription tracing the route to it. From the gate facing Magnesia.'

The camera lingered on some lion-beaded gargoyles, before trekking slowly onwards to take in the massive pump borrowed from the Ottoman Railway Company, motionless for the time being, positioned with a saurian calm at the edge of what had once been a water-logged pit.

Gerald Wray, disconcerted perhaps by the continuing silence, or by this reminder of Michael Carter's crucial role in the dewatering operation at Ephesus, pressed ahead, casting about for some way of completing his commentary without mentioning the Australian handyman again. 'Ancient tales with ties to reality,' Wray stated. 'Homer born at Smyrna reputedly. Hercules at Ephesus.'

The scholar's flustered tone left him sounding apologetic, as if obliged to defend himself. 'And Troy, for example. There now seems to be little doubt that Troy was destroyed by an expedition from Greece. Was the recovery of Helen their only purpose? Not likely, according to most of my colleagues at the British School.'

While Wray pushed on, groping for evidence to support his case, other areas of the site were being presented to us – a gateway in a newly-excavated street with Doric stoa, a stone relief showing Hermes and the Ram, an arid hillside with a view towards the old harbour. And now we were being shown two lines of villagers on a partially excavated mound. They were in constant motion, the up line with empty baskets, the other on the downhill track bowed beneath the weight of baskets filled with dirt and rubble, about to be emptied.

* * *

As the images on the makeshift screen ran on, appearing and disappearing, accompanied by Wray's erudite observations, I had time to dwell upon the oddity of this film show, still astonished to find myself here in this darkened room at the heart of the Mavros household.

It had taken Wray longer than expected to arrange a visit, a meeting at which his request for sponsorship could be pursued, and it was now several days since the discovery of the man from Smyrna's body. We still had very little to go on. Asplin had not yet received a reply from his superior in Whitehall (the inscrutable C) as to whether any new offensive was planned. In the meantime, Diakis had interviewed Asplin and me about Cy Lapides and the renting of the room where the body was found.

The canny detective refused to say whether our answers were thought to be satisfactory or anything about his prior interviews with Furnell and Alexis Brusa. The only thing we could get out of him was that he was under pressure and his inquiry had to be carried through 'to the end'. He mentioned, as a matter that seemed to be of considerable interest to him, that there were no defensive cuts on the dead man's hands according to the autopsy. This suggested that Lapides had been knifed either by a professional killer, an expert, or by someone who was waiting for him. It was a fishing knife of a kind that could have been bought in the market, and may even have belonged to Lapides himself.

Diakis had said much the same thing to Furnell and Brusa apparently, and on their account of being interviewed at the police station he had accepted their denials of any involvement in the matter without demur, but reserving the right to question them further in due course.

This lack of progress, Wray contended, underlined the need to fix a meeting with Mavros without delay. Eventually, when Guido Viscarra turned up at the British School with a note from Mavros, Wray was able to dash off an acceptance and convey to Viscarra, as if in passing, that I would be coming too – as a former volunteer with a continuing interest in the work of the British School.

We had turned up at the Mavros mansion in Carnassus Square at the appointed hour. The houses on either side were of the usual whiteness and so exactly alike in their double-storeyed, flat-roofed dimensions that the larger residence between them with its massive, varnished front door and splendid windows – protected by thick iron bars – was bound to seem far more imposing, even impregnable.

Wray knocked on the front door firmly, with the air of a man who had been admitted to this household many times. I was pleased to find, upon the door being flung opened, that our host was all smiles as he ushered us into the hall. Yes, he was pleased to see us, he confirmed. He had something he wanted to show us. When I sought to clear the air by referring to our earlier association, some unfortunate differences of opinion, a parting of the ways, my words were simply brushed aside as 'a matter best forgotten'. While the initial pleasantries ran onwards it certainly seemed that he was prepared to leave our disagreement in the past.

'The volunteers!' Mavros paused to lock the door behind us. 'Funded by me perhaps, but in those days employed essentially by the British School. So who am I to complain of their escapades? Especially now, in war time, when everything that went before has been overtaken by events. Knocked sideways.'

He placed a hand on Wray's shoulder. 'But not entirely. We can start our talk about new ventures by looking at my film of Ephesus. You can tell me what we achieved. And what can be achieved elsewhere if Greece stays out of the war. What say you to that?'

'It largely depends,' Wray observed, 'on how long the war lasts. And where the battles are fought.'

'You're quite right. We'll have to rethink the way we do things. Asia Minor is out of bounds. The same for sub-licensing arrangements with the Turks or Germans anywhere. So it's probably down to mainland Greece. Or back to Crete.' He transferred his hand to my shoulder and added with a laugh: 'Unless our old friend Robert Kaub can use his German name and family connections to open doors.'

It was meant as a joke, presumably, but the underlying suggestion that I might have a foot in both camps left me disconcerted. Was his willingness to overlook our previous contretemps related to some agenda of his own? With a man like Peter Mavros one could never be quite sure.

The big fellow, still smiling affably, shepherded us into a room off the hall which had obviously been set up for the screening of his film. The curtains were closed and a single light bulb in a fringed shade cast a pale light on a projector in the centre of the room. Nearby, Guido Viscarra stood ready to act as the operator. A sumptuous divan had been pushed into position on one side of the projector, facing the screen, and two upright wooden chairs were on the other side, close to a sideboard bearing a decanter of port and a semi-circle of crystal glasses.

'So here we are.' Mavros invited us to make use of the chairs and found a seat for himself on the divan. 'And in addition to helping us get our thoughts in order about future excavations, my little film may help us get our stories straight about Smyrna. And certain other places. If you know what I mean.'

He wasn't pleased by our failure to respond.

'This police officer!' Mavros flapped a disdainful hand at the world beyond the curtains as if to encompass the City Police station and other annoyances of that kind. 'He is asking questions about this man from Smyrna who seems to be known to us all.' Our host spread his hands apart with a rueful expression and let them drop. 'The older I get the more I can't afford the time to make mistakes. The same for you, I expect?'

Our host's confessional manner suggested that we were all of one mind about the nature of the inconvenience and could be relied upon to pull together in getting rid of it, but this certainly wasn't reflected in the sharp look he gave as he waited for an answer. It confirmed my impression that in agreeing to meet us he wasn't really interested in new projects or auld lang syne. In much the same way as we were trying to protect ourselves, he probably wanted to find out what we had said to the police. His reference to my German name was possibly a way of encouraging me to blurt out what I knew. I was startled also by the notion that there might be something in the film about our pre-war excavation at Ephesus that had a bearing upon the present investigation, or upon a presumed need for orchestration of our so-called 'stories.'

The vague murmur, the benign but slightly woolly style of a Cambridge don, was always useful in deflecting unwanted questions, so Wray employed it now. 'Ah! The police inquiry. Well, the fact is that we know nothing much about the deceased person. An importer, I believe, but with little of interest to the British School by all of accounts. Let's watch the film to begin with. Time enough to talk later.'

Disarmed by Wray's scholarly manner, Mavros shrugged. 'So be it.' The sharp look had become a friendly smile. 'Lights out, Guido.' Our host turned to his dark-suited companion at the projector, a finger pointing to the overhead light, then settled into the divan. 'Let's get started.'

The projector whirred, and it wasn't long before we were on our way to Ephesus, then to the glimpses of the volunteers at work that had sparked Wray's commentary and the talk about Michael Carter that had left Wray disconcerted.

So far, it seemed to me, listening to my learned colleague, watching carefully as the camera moved from one place to another, there didn't seem to be anything at Ephesus that might bear upon the events leading up to the death of Cy Lapides, or be of interest to Diakis. Nonetheless, our glimpse of Michael Carter crouched over the tiny primus stove had reactivated my sense of foreboding. After all, it was my friendship with the young Australian, formed while working together at the site, that had led to my falling out with the Mavros family.

A place had been found for Michael Carter at the diggings, I recalled, because his father was a mining magnate on the goldfields of Western Australia, an investor who had been talked into contributing funds to a Mavros joint venture in South America. The outcome of the venture, or to what extent one partner finished up owing money to the other, was never mentioned. Michael had joined the volunteers at Ephesus, he told me, not because he was particularly interested in archaeology – he wasn't alone in that regard – but as a result of acting on his father's letter of introduction.

Michael had used the letter while making his first big trip abroad. Having seen his relatives in London, and moved on to Paris, Rome and Corfu, he had finished up in the Mavros home in Athens, ready for some adventures in the Aegean. A few days later, urged on by his father's old friend, he found himself in Gerald Wray's class at the British School, surrounded by other recruits, and in due course on a steamboat bound for Smyrna, followed by a short trip south by road to Ephesus. And that was where I had met him.

Now, as the jerky film ran onwards, with its hazy scenes, abrupt jumps from long shots to close ups, we were being shown Mavros standing on a mound of rubble, protected from the sun by his broad-brimmed Panama hat as he surveyed a ruined bath-house at Ephesus, Gerald Wray at his side like an attentive subaltern. Anita Mavros was on a partially reconstructed terrace close by, chatting to Michael Carter. They were standing close together, the two young people, and were obviously more interested in each other than in what was going on around them. When Michael leaned towards her and whispered something in her ear, she smiled, and pretended to push him away.

This is going to be difficult, I concluded, as the camera dwelt upon the group before me, bringing back unpleasant memories, reminding me of unfinished business. How could I find out what Mavros knew about Cy Lapides, without giving away too much myself? How could I persuade him to say what exactly he meant in proposing that we get our stories straight? How could all of this be done without reawakening our differences of opinion concerning his daughter, Anita?

For a moment, seized by a kind of panic, the projector throbbing behind me in the darkness, I wondered whether this was how Asplin's patron, Sir Ian Hamilton, had felt when the initial plan to capture Constantinople was scrapped. Unable to clear mines blocking the Straits of Dardanelles or to silence the Turkish guns on shore, the naval commanders had passed the buck. Within a few days, without much in the way of revised planning, Hamilton went from head of an auxiliary force required to take out a scattering of Turkish forts along the Straits to being the leader of a full scale assault – landings aimed at taking out the entire, well-defended Gallipoli peninsula.

The landings at Cape Helles and Anzac Cove had been effected, true, but at such a cost, and with such a limited prospect of success, despite several subsequent offensives, that Hamilton had now been recalled to London.

If the odds against an experienced General could prove too much, what chance did I have of breaking through our host's defences – his congenial but essentially crafty manner?

At that time, like Toby Asplin, I was fond of quoting General Von Moltke's famous dictum, a piece of wisdom that over the last few months seemed to come so readily to the lips of combatants at every level on the Allied side, as they contemplated the planning failures that had bedevilled the Gallipoli campaign and the carnage that greeted every attempt to make a decisive move: *no plan ever survives first contact with the enemy.*

I had to be ready for whatever came my way, to change direction if necessary. Above all, in the course of my own limited campaign to uncover what was going on, I had to find out whether Peter Mavros was a friend or in some other camp.

* * *

'That's enough'. Mavros, on his feet now, facing the projector, fended off the glare with a hand raised to shield his eyes. 'Let them see the other reel.'

The huge shadow on the screen behind him stood there like some henchman waiting to enforce his order, until Guido Viscarra, seated on a bar stool at the back of the room, gave the expected answer. 'Of course.'

Viscarra flicked a switch to extinguish the spotlight and used both hands to slow the two big reels riding above the projector. Like a horseman attending to his steed, he patted the machine here and there to see if it was overheated. That done, moving briskly, he parted the curtains to let in some afternoon light and turned to address us. 'A moment, please. I will have to find it.'

The dark suit and sleek black hair of our host's crony gave him the look of a Latin American dance instructor, swift and feline. His occasional, carefully timed glances never seemed to engage the other party to the transaction – as if he used them simply to signal a change of rhythm or a new step.

'The household?' Viscarra left the question in mid-air as he darted across to the sideboard and began sorting through a scattering of flat cardboard boxes.

'That's the one,' Mavros confirmed.

'At Ephesus?'

'Yes. It's somewhere in the pile.'

Mavros folded his arms, restored to normality by the kinder light from the window, the shadow behind him gone. He bestowed a reassuring smile upon his tiny audience, turning first to Gerald

Wray, then to me. 'And there's a cup of tea on the terrace at the end of all of this.' He winked. 'Or something stronger if you wish.'

'Diakis?' Wray inquired. 'Have you showed these pictures to him?'

'Certainly not. And I don't intend to. Whatever relevance they have is strictly between us. Agreed?'

'Research before conclusions. Let's see the next film.'

Wray, cagey as usual, was still playing the Cambridge don, but I couldn't help wondering whether he and Mavros had talked about some of the matters in issue already. They knew each other well from other days. I was the outsider.

Viscarra had found what he was looking for and was setting about the intricate task of attaching the new reel to his contraption and feeding the connecting strip of celluloid into its maw.

While waiting for the reel to be fitted, Mavros plumped himself down on the divan, saying as he did so. 'Mostly domestic scenes in this one. Filmed at the behest of my dear wife, but of interest to me also, of course. When you find out what people do in their homes, you find out what they think, and what is of importance to them.'

The thought brought with it a wry smile. 'Which may, of course, turn out to be unmentionable. These Turks in the vicinity of Smyrna, for example. You can see from their homes they're still nomads, adrift in what remains of the Ottoman Empire. You doubt me? The term *konak* they use for a house means simply a halting place on a journey. Or so I've been told. Visitors come. They go. Scarcely any pictures on the walls. Quilts dumped on the divans as if left behind for the next traveller. As we found at Belevi, their gardens are mostly stables and sheds, with a few wooden stools under a tree.'

Mavros smiled again. 'Unmentionable, but useful to know. It isn't hard to rent a place at a reasonable price when you know how low their expectations are. But to me and my wife, what happens in a man's home means everything, and one has to protect it.'

These ruminations weren't just small talk. I was left in little doubt by his shrewd glance that his apparently casual remarks were in some way related to my eviction from the site at Ephesus not so long ago. Was this, like his earlier joke about my German antecedents, a way of applying pressure? An attempt to find out who Lapides had spoken to before he was disposed of?

It came as a relief when Viscarra finished what he was doing and closed the curtains. The overhead light was turned off and the projector was brought to life again, throwing numbers at us, crowding the screen with another batch of silent, grainy, flickering images.

We were taken first to a gathering outside the Mavros villa. Helena Mavros, accompanied by her daughter and the latter's sombre chaperone – the 'double agent' as I later came to think of her – had just stepped down from their horse-drawn carriage. A pair of local men were unloading trunks and boxes from the back of a dray. Mavros himself emerged abruptly from a corner of the screen to wave them away. The family group and some of the senior staff from the British School began to assemble for the camera, jerking about on the front steps. They stood there stiffly for a moment, but were then jettisoned as the camera jumped ahead in time – to an inner courtyard, a few days later presumably, after everyone had settled in.

Dressed in black, with dark shawls obscuring their faces, local women, like giant moths, were flitting about an earthenware oven in a corner of the courtyard, jostling to and fro. Some were attending to the fire with long poles, or feeding the inner cavity with faggots. Younger women were standing at a table nearby, shaping dough into flat cakes, or tossing an expanse of dough from one pair of hands to another, receiving it back, and so on, until it was stretched thin. At that stage, laid on a wooden paddle, the flimsy dough was slapped against the oven's side until it was done, then lifted away. A group at another table were laying out the pieces of scorched bread in rows. It took me a moment to realise that this group included Anita Mavros, lovely as ever, smiling awkwardly at the camera now and then, as if conscious that she had been pushed into the scene by her father (as she probably was) in order to play a part to which she wasn't suited.

The women by the oven were followed by other outdoor scenes: out-of-focus human figures at the far end of an olive grove, an old man in a frayed waistcoat looking for eggs in a chicken coop, two women with wooden water buckets at a well. A moment later, there was Anita again, this time on her way to the house with a bucket. And with Michael Carter lurching along beside her, burdened by the weight of a yoke from which wooden buckets were suspended at either end. He must have been invited for Sunday lunch, for he was dressed in his best white suit.

At the back door of the villa they put their buckets down and straightened up. When she said something, Michael laughed and pulled a face. Her next remark had him dipping into her bucket and flicking some water at his fellow carrier. She skipped inside with a giggle, leaving her bucket in a puddle on the step.

As one scene followed another I was left in little doubt that, for the most part, the camera man was moving from place to place at his master's call. The dining room and other parts of the house were examined briefly, but I was soon reminded that the premises were generally in a state of disrepair, and sparsely furnished, as he had suggested in his earlier observations. This had annoyed Mavros, I recalled, the inefficiency of the place. So it wasn't long before we were being shown cracked tiles and broken downpipes, gashes of light between ill-fitting shutters.

The villa's sanitation was organised in a simple way. One followed the line of an open terracotta conduit across a paved patio to its origin in one of the stables, behind a shoulder-high

83

wall. Any woman of the household who saw a female guest going in that direction would come out to offer a copper basin for the washing of hands. Men were left to fend for themselves. All of this was captured by the camera.

It could hardly be thought surprising that the three principal women in the Mavros household – Helena Mavros, her daughter Anita and the latter's humourless chaperone – joined the volunteers for only a week or so at a time before returning to Smyrna to catch the ferry back to Athens. Our host's wife, Helena, a refined but melancholy woman who never looked at ease in her husband's company, came scarcely at all, which probably explained the making of the film before us – her husband's attempt to record a supposedly enjoyable excursion undertaken by the entire family, a demonstration that he cared about his household.

I was reminded by these scenes also of our host's practical cast of mind. The gutters, the downpipes, the sanitation, the aqueduct in the valley, the paving of the old streets, these were matters of real interest to him. Both here at Ephesus, and at the Palace of Knossos on Crete, I had observed him listening attentively to everything that was said by those showing him around. Much of what the scholars and archaeologists were on about flowed from their own sense of what was important – the way in which the architecture and related art could be traced back to ancient myths, or to the social mores of a particular era – but it was obvious to me that Peter Mavros was equally interested in the layout of a site and the way in which it must have functioned in order to serve the needs of its inhabitants.

This was understandable. Like so many employees of the British Consular Service who had spent most of their working lives in the Levant, Mavros's parents, resident in Athens at the time, had sent their son home to England for schooling. Peter's later training as an engineer in London and Berlin had equipped him to improve railway systems in far places when he began working for the Antofagasta Railway Company in Chile, and it was undoubtedly this – his background in engineering – that left him with an abiding interest in how things worked in practice, from streets and drains in old cities to mechanical devices in the modern world.

Not surprisingly, when his railway and mining investments in South America fell away following the decline of the nitrate industry, obliging him to draw upon his practical skills in new ways, he managed to patent several inventions that were highly thought of in London including an ingenious system for train lighting – a dynamo suspended one-sidedly and driven from a railway carriage axle by strap and pulley was so arranged that, when a certain pre-determined speed was reached, the strap slipped and there was no further increase of output by the dynamo.

He was proud of his ingenuity and of his success in turning his inventions to account. He once showed Michael Carter and me a clipping from *The Times* of London in which he was described as 'a renaissance man.' At the same time, it pleased him to point out, straight-faced, but unable to suppress the mischievous imp hopping about inside him, that the photograph below the article had him standing at the entrance to his house at Richmond on the Thames, framed by two large gates of decorative iron work. These, he claimed, had been seized on his behalf from a cathedral at Lima by Chilean troops in the War of the Pacific – a seizure worthy of a so-called renaissance man!

Having replenished his finances, it wasn't long before Mavros had moved beyond the railway companies of Great Britain in order to exploit his inventions in the colonies and on the continent, a fresh start that took him back to his birthplace eventually, not only to please his wife, for she too was born in Athens, but also as a convenient base from which to move into the manufacture of rolling stock for central Europe and the Balkans, and to pursue his passion for archaeology. The pre-war German scheme for a Berlin to Baghdad railway seemed a perfect fit.

His ingenuity wasn't confined to inventions. Soon after my own return to Athens to join Asplin's lot, I heard rumours that the Berlin to Baghdad venture was still afoot. Mavros was said to have invested in the scheme and was now so heavily indebted to Viennese bankers that he was left with no option but to support the Central Powers. On the other hand, according to Asplin, so long as Greece remained neutral it suited Mavros to have it put about – as an ingenious rumour to the contrary – that his wife's connection to the family of King Constantine lay behind his inability to speak in favour of the Allied cause.

I didn't know what to make of these contradictory rumours. For myself, recalling my own dealings with Mavros before the war, I surmised that after his immersion in the turmoil of South American politics at the turn of the century, Mavros probably preferred to sit on the fence, ready to jump either way, as the circumstances dictated. That was how he had made his first fortune in the nitrate industry, or so he had once boasted to Michael Carter and me while showing us his clippings, and it therefore seemed likely that if fence-sitting had worked for him in other days, he would probably follow the same strategy again – he would wait until he was better placed to predict the outcome of the war.

A waiting game, the merits of masterly inaction – gambits of this kind intrigued him, and was the sort of thing he used to talk about at Ephesus. The hours he had spent humouring the leaders of the German mission while moving pumps and generators across their portion of the site. The countless cups of tea he had consumed while persuading influential advisers in the Sultan's entourage to override restrictive conditions imposed by the Director of the Imperial Museum. Mavros clearly enjoyed the cut and thrust involved in getting what he wanted and it pleased him to revisit his successes in the company of uncritical young admirers.

In the evening, after work, he would sometimes have a few of us back to his villa at Belevi. There, in the courtyard, drinks in hand, our stools and chairs in a semi-circle around a fire in the old oven, we would sit and gossip, listening to his stories, thumbing through the book of clippings he brought out now and then, a tome used to illustrate an anecdote or propound some theory of his own dressed up as universal wisdom. On other occasions, we would play cards or chess, the board illuminated by smoky lanterns, the faint but constant cicada sound hovering in the darkness beyond our patch of light.

Michael Carter and a post-graduate student from Mainz in Germany, I seemed to recall, were the only players among the volunteers who could match Mavros at chess, although Gerald Wray was rumoured to have beaten him occasionally.

At the chessboard, Mavros was always good-humoured, but he liked to win. If, unexpectedly, he lost a queen or some other important piece at a crucial moment, he was inclined to call a halt. In such a case, under the guise of being obliged to attend to a household chore or to join the archaeologists hunched over their maps, he would delegate one of the volunteers to play on his behalf, an arrangement which usually lasted until the game was over. By then, of course, it was time for the rest of us to look around for a lantern and return to our encampment.

'That's it,' Viscarra said as the film ran out, bringing my reverie to an end.

The projectionist crossed the room to throw open the curtains. That done, with a weary flourish, he invited us to take in the scene outside: the jumbled rooftops, the distant Acropolis, the Parthenon on its plateau – a domain above the city, but still part of it. Somnolent in the last of the afternoon light.

'The sunset.' Viscarra's announcement was made as if by a spruiker to a half-empty music hall while pushing a painted backdrop into place.

Like a drummer at his cymbals in the pit, Mavros did what he could to lift the moment. 'Time for some refreshments! A little nip perhaps!'

The fanfare over, our host struggled up from his seat on the divan as if rising to take a bow. He stood there, flexing his legs for a bit, nodding and beaming, but with the flushed look of an old stager who knows what has be done in order to keep an audience happy before he and his offsiders start drumming up business in the next town.

'A hair of the dog to help us get our thoughts in order,' our host proposed, stretching out a hand to help Wray to his feet, leaving me to do as I pleased. 'Some lubrication to keep us on track. And to remind us that we don't have much time left to work out what we have to do.'

* * *

We were taken upstairs to a terrace on the top floor overlooking Carnassus Square. Down there, as in the amber sky, the day was coming to an end, but gradually: as if not quite willing to let go. Shutters had appeared on the front windows of a jeweller's shop directly beneath us; a few feet away a street trader and his two sons were still hard at work behind their sacks of produce, filling brown paper bags with scoops of olives, walnuts, rice, chips of bacon, hard and dry. They took possession of the notes and coins handed to them with scarcely a glance, provisioning the leather pouches on their money belts.

On the far side of the Square a shop selling carpets was still open for business but, already, with a couple of lanterns gleaming within its inner caverns. Not so for the tailor in the shop next door. He was closing up, flapping his hands at the women seated outside his premises, insisting that they lock the hoods on their sewing machines and bring in the half-clad, faceless dummies stationed beside them.

Street photographers on the marble concourse at the centre of the Square were dismantling their little stands, binding the legs of their tripods, folding up the flimsy chairs upon which their customers were expected to sit, mute as a tailor's dummy, assuming an expression of paralysed delight, while the passing traffic hooted and brayed. Most of the smiles were on the faces of the hawkers, fluttering about nearby with their trash-crammed trays, poised to swoop when the flash went off.

After a while, the cacophony from the streets below as cars and trams and mule trains moved about seemed entirely natural, a fitting accompaniment to the patchwork of rooftops and grubby white walls surrounding us. It struck me, as I turned away from the parapet enclosing the terrace, that this raucous, nightfall symphony contained as many random threads as the events of recent days and the puzzle created by the demise of Cy Lapides. Who killed him? What secret lay behind his death? We needed answers to these questions in order to get on with our work.

A cluster of chairs had been pulled up to a low table at the centre of the tiled enclosure. For a moment, I feared that upon the appearance of the promised refreshments we might be expected to sit out here in the cold as the light waned. But no, having invited us to take a look over the side, our host, as if he were an Eastern potentate affording visitors a glimpse of his realm, ushered us indoors to a book-lined studio adjoining the terrace. In here, warmer and more comfortable furnishings awaited us – Persian rugs, richly-embroidered armchairs, a mahogany sideboard displaying wine glasses on a silver tray, and a bottle slanting out of an ice-bucket.

89

Mavros took charge of the ice-bucket and invited us to sit. He held the bottle up to the light. 'A glass of Dekeleia, gentlemen?'

This might be Athens, but our host's tone established that his intention was not to initiate a Socratic dialogue enriched by dissent. His earlier proposition – a cup of tea – had been found wanting and could now be safely forgotten. 'Dekeleia?' he repeated. 'Those in favour? Motion carried. That's done, then.'

He passed the bottle to his associate. 'Which was always hard to say at meetings of our company in Antofagasta. One of the dustiest places on earth, and swarming with all sorts of hard-to-please shareholders. Whisky and beer drinkers, the lot of them. As my good friend Guido well knows.'

Viscarra reached for the corkscrew by the tray. 'Dusty, but profitable,' he reminded his mentor with a truculent edge to his voice. 'Good enough for you in those days.'

'For a while. But after a while things run down.' He watched as Viscarra went for the cork with the spiral end of his instrument. 'Which can sometimes leave a man in a tight spot. Like a hero of old.'

When the cork popped out, Mavros turned to face us and smiled as a hero might, renewing his earlier attempt to create a mood of fellowship, a means of dealing with a common enemy. 'This Detective Diakis. He's been talking to people at the British School, I gather. And having done so, it isn't long before he's on his way here and talking to us.'

Our host's final few words certainly included Viscarra, who was pouring some wine into each of the four glasses, but did his summation go further? Did his related gesture embrace others in the household – his wife and daughter perhaps?

To find out where he stood, I would have to probe. 'In the Athens of today,' I commenced, 'what Diakis puts to one person may not be as forceful as the questions asked of another. And what he does with the answers may differ too.'

'Of course.' Mavros seemed keen to humour me, but without giving away too much. 'Which is why we who are essentially on the same side should work together to keep him pointed in the right direction.'

'Essentially?' Wray, the former don, felt obliged to press for clarity. 'You say we are 'essentially' on the same side. What does that mean exactly?'

Mavros paused to receive a glass from Viscarra, then sat back, studying the receptacle and its pale contents like a chess player weighing up his prospects. He had aged since I had last seen him at close quarters on the site at Ephesus, but his mane of greying hair, the shrewd dark eyes and commanding brow, still left an impression of strength, the look of a man capable of sudden but resolute action.

As he continued to ponder, twisting the stem of his glass cautiously, pursing his lips, it came to me that our host might be possessed of information not presently known to us, but of great significance. That he was weighing up whether to divulge what he knew.

He took a quick sip from his glass and found a place for it on the small table beside his chair. His hesitation, the look of a chess player, had vanished. He had obviously drawn back from whatever it was he had been minded to say and was now inclined to pursue a different course.

'I say "essentially" because a man of my background is bound to favour the British side. I have friends in all quarters, true, and at the Palace.' Mavros waved a hand towards the terrace as if to signify that somewhere out there could be found the place he was referring to. 'But when the chips are down in a time of crisis, I can be relied upon. It is therefore disconcerting, even hurtful, that your colleague, Mr Asplin, in his naïve rush to support Venizelos and various friends of the former Prime Minister, is willing to spread rumours about me. For that reason also, I say "essentially". I favour the Allied cause, but I do so quietly and with discretion. Taking care as to whom I deal with, and as to how I express my support.'

Our host let this thought settle before retrieving his glass for another sip. 'This fellow Cy Lapides. Everyone knows he's been working for Baron Von Kessell, along with Carl Bessen and the other German agents. At their so-called import firm. But knocked about by gambling debts, it isn't long before Lapides starts sneaking up to others. Making a nuisance of himself.'

'Looking for what?' I asked.

'A higher price for what he knows.'

'Which is?'

'Probably nothing. It won't be the first time an informer has tried to inflate the size of his dowry.'

'He was running a big risk if he had nothing to sell.'

Mavros shrugged. 'I for one kept him at arm's length. Do you think his betrayals of his original paymaster went unnoticed? Not likely. If you need a suspect, I told Diakis, look to Carl Bessen and his cut-throat friends. They loathe Lapides. And they know how to sweep up what they don't like and leave it in a dustbin. *Der Eiserne Besen,* they call their leader. The Iron Broom! But is that enough for Diakis? Apparently not. The good detective has to look at every little thing, he claims. Which is why we have to talk. In case Diakis ignores the obvious and starts looking in some other direction.'

'What direction might that be?' Wray inquired.

This brought a cagey expression to our host's face, the look I had noticed earlier when he seemed to be balancing one thing against another, weighing up whether to speak frankly. 'The old coin found upon Cy Lapides? Have you seen it?'

Wray played for time by taking a sip from his own glass. 'No. I haven't seen it.' He glanced at me uneasily. 'I have a hunch I may have seen it from afar when Lapides approached you at Café Hellenion. The day before he died. I saw him holding something.'

'That's all you know?'

My colleague glanced at me again. 'A coin of the Roman period, I'm led to believe. Bearing a ruler's head in profile.'

'A ruler's head on each side, in fact – the ancient King Cyzicus and Lucullus.' Pleased to be in the tutor's chair for a change our host pressed on. 'Lucullus, you may recall, was the Roman general who took on Mithradates – that tenacious renegade from the Black Sea.'

'I know who Lucullus is. But not having seen the coin we are speaking of, I can surely be forgiven for not knowing that his head is upon it.'

Untroubled by this show of impatience, Mavros released another dart. 'Well, then, you'll know that Lucullus defeated Mithradates at Cyzicus.'

Wray thought about this for a moment before conceding the point. 'That is so.'

'The Mithradatic siege that failed. At the city mentioned in the man from Smyrna's note. Or so it seems from what Diakis showed me.'

'Again, not having been questioned by Diakis, I haven't actually seen the note itself. It mentions a king, I'm told, but without naming him.'

Mavros pointed downwards. 'You've seen a film of findings made at Ephesus. When you put all these things together, does it occur to you that you may in fact have seen the coin in question? Not simply from afar, but close up? At Ephesus.'

A silence fell as Wray pondered, taking even more time than before, although it wasn't entirely clear to me whether this was because he genuinely didn't know the answer or because he was looking ahead to where the questions might be leading. 'The film showed certain fragments. Shards of pottery and so on. But no coins that I can recall.'

'But were coins found?'

'Yes. They were. By us and by opportunists at the site. I'm not disputing it. But I would have to check our log books to see exactly what.'

'By some of the volunteers? Michael Carter, for example?'

Wray put down his glass and raised his hands in an irritable gesture. 'Without checking the records and seeing the coin found upon Lapides for myself, I am simply not prepared to say whether it came from Ephesus, or who might have found it.'

Mavros turned to me. 'Can you say?'

I parried the question. 'I recall some coins and ancient seals being found at Ephesus. Amongst other things. Bits of pottery and so on. When Diakis showed me the coin found upon Lapides it didn't strike me that I might have seen it before.'

It was hard to tell what Mavros was getting at, but his next remark made things clearer. 'I felt obliged to tell Diakis that I had several coins of the same kind in my collection. I did so to cover myself. I had to say also that there could be coins of that kind at the British School. So you can see the risk. Will our busy detective ignore the Germans and start looking in our direction?'

Wray dealt with this emphatically. 'Before we take our discussion any further, we have to see the coins in your collection. If you're suggesting that I or any of my colleagues may have had secret dealings with Lapides, or anything to do with his death, you're barking up the wrong tree. I deny it.

The chess player moved quickly to repel this thrust. 'With or without denials, we're all at risk in war time. The quest for truth is often outweighed by shifting alliances. The needs of the moment. That's all I'm saying. If that's your wish, and simply to refresh our memories, I'll dig out some of the coins found at Ephesus, including a coin corresponding to the dead man's piece. As you rightly imply, the more we know, the better placed we are to protect ourselves.'

'And to find out what it signifies,' Wray insisted. 'If it's a Roman coin minted in the imperial period to honour Lucullus, a famous general, I would expect to see a profile of a Roman emperor on the reverse side, not the ancient King Cyzicus. Although that may depend upon where it was minted, and whether from silver, bronze or electrum.'

Mavros raised a despairing hand to block the flow. 'Things like that may be of interest to you. To a pragmatist, like me, it comes down to this. Can the coin be used against us?'

Our host turned to Viscarra. 'You know where my special collection is. Bring up the two trays from Ephesus. Right away.'

* * *

I followed Guido Viscarra downstairs to a room on the second floor and waited while he produced a bunch of keys to unlock the door. My role – ostensibly to act as an extra pair of hands, a tray carrier – had been assigned to me as an afterthought. Or was it simply that Mavros wished to take advantage of my absence to review the situation with Gerald Wray in private? To ask him what Asplin was doing about the assassination of Cy Lapides. Whether Asplin knew of any plan for a new offensive by the Allied forces.

The big fellow disliked Toby Asplin, that was obvious, and having seen me in the latter's company at Cafe Hellenion from time to time, he probably thought of me as being too close to Asplin to be relied upon, quite apart from the shadow cast by our previous disagreement at Ephesus. So be it. One way or another we seemed to be momentarily united by a concern about Diakis and the focus of his investigation. There was still a chance that further information about the Lapides coin would help me to establish whether Mavros was on our side – as he claimed to be – and whether he was genuine in seeking to blame Baron Von Kessell and his thuggish underling Carl Bessen (the so-called Iron Broom) for the Lapides murder.

Having found the right key, Viscarra opened the door to let us in. The room we entered, perhaps the largest in the house, may have once been characterised as a gentleman's private library, but it now resembled a gallery in a provincial museum. It was crowded with display cases, pedestals bearing marble busts, tables loaded with figurines and ancient vases, several damaged by cracks and fractures.

A magnificent writing desk with a half-opened scroll top occupied the corner of the room nearest to the door. The presence upon it of a handsome inkstand and a spread of blotting paper – a creamy expanse bordered by hand-tooled leather margins – indicated that the desk's original purpose as a place for attending to correspondence and invoices hadn't been entirely forgotten. Within the niches of a large revolving stand nearby various exotic masks were exhibited. The weird slit eyes and square-faced look of these apparitions singled them out as relics from Mexico and South America, utterly unlike the images around them.

A table opposite the desk was dominated by a cluster of vases and alabaster drinking vessels from the Aegean. A terracotta sarcophagus stood nearby with a front panel depicting the deceased at a funeral banquet, attended by his loving family. In accordance with a well-established tradition of the Roman era, the stone relief was meant to embody a dignified and enduring image of the one destined to be destroyed by the ravages of time. This was made clear by the salutation set out in English on a plaque beside the scene. *Oh Minandros, son of Meidias, why are you walking the most painful road that has no return, leaving sad tears for your sons, and your wife Moschian lamenting?*

Further on, two small gravestones were propped against the wall, resembling stones I had often seen during my sojourn on Cyprus. They were of a kind, or so I had been led to believe, found within crypts and sacred places throughout the Roman empire, and presented a less idealised version of the final moment.

In this case, according to the plaque attached to the nearest of the two stones, the deceased had quit the world with a flourish, leaving behind a jaunty epitaph: *I have escaped. I am in the clear. Goodbye, hope and fortune. Play your tricks on others.*

The shelves in the room were laden with a miscellany of artefacts including a couple of wooden looms and some lengths of tapestry. In a far corner, by the main window, were various reminders of our host's life as an engineer in far places, and later as an inventor. These included a miniature locomotive and several model bridges. A tin sign was hanging from a hat stand that proclaimed in thick black lettering streaked with rust: *Ferrocarril de Bolivia: Official del Servicio Rurrenabaque-Reyes.* Leaning against the stand, partly obscured by several walking sticks and a black umbrella, was a strip of railway line, about one yard long, mounted on a wooden board. The plaque beneath the sample said: *Kalgoorlie-Boulder Loop Line Extension 1905.*

As I crossed the room to take a closer look at these mementos I was drawn to a framed photograph on the wall. A group of dignitaries in top hats were standing behind a handsome steam engine with an escarpment of mullock dumps in the background. These odd exhibits seemed out of character when contrasted with the splendid pieces from the Aegean occupying the greater part of the room, but the rusted sign, the plaque and the sepia print in this corner were obviously of personal importance to the collector.

Viscarra had gone straight to a line of glass-fronted cabinets mounted on shelves adjoining the desk. He took a quick look over his shoulder and noticed my interest in the mementos by the hat stand. With a sudden tango step (or something like it) he back-pedalled smoothly to finish up beside me. 'The goldfields of Western Australia.' He tapped the photograph. 'But you won't find the man you are looking for in this one.' He used two fingers to imitate a pair of scissors. 'They snip the ribbon, but he is gone by then. Or so he tells me.'

'Which man are we speaking of?'

The scissors became a two-fingered pistol pointed at the ceiling. 'Our friend upstairs.'

I glanced at the list of names beneath the photo but the inscription was tiny, faded, and hard to read. 'I was looking for someone else – the father of Michael Carter. An important man in that part of the world, I was led to believe. A friend of our friend.'

Viscarra pouted. 'I see him once in Antofagasta, that man. All talk. He is nothing. And I hear his son, this Michael – the handyman – came to our friend's home in Athens and caused trouble. But we don't have time for that.'

Viscarra sashayed back to the line of little cabinets, obliging me to slink after him like a novice forced off the dance floor by a new and more intricate rhythm. I watched as the dapper Chilean examined the first cabinet and began pulling out the display trays, each marked 'Ephesus'.

The coins and tiny seals were laid out in rows on thick black velvet. In agreeing to go downstairs and assist Viscarra I had assumed, as he must have done, that we were to return with two trays only, for that was the number mentioned by Mavros – but here were ten. And coins of various shapes and sizes mixed up with other collectables.

Viscarra beckoned. 'Can you see what we are looking for?'

I came in closer as he worked through the trays again. At a first glance, I couldn't readily identify any coin resembling the piece Diakis had shown me in the courtyard, after the body was discovered. I said so. Which prompted Viscarra to slam shut the last drawer.

'The coins he wants. They must be somewhere else.' My dark-suited companion pushed away from the cabinets and made for the door. 'Wait here while I ask him.'

Left alone, and with time to spare, I turned to the next cabinet. In this case the trays were marked 'Pergamon.' I couldn't help wondering whether some of the pieces in these cabinets had simply been purchased on the black market, although Mavros maintained that they were his own findings. Was he telling the truth? Without Wray to assist, I had no clear answer, but was inclined to remind myself that Mavros, the 'renaissance man', was given to telling stories that might or might not be true – even at the front gates of his fine house in Richmond where it might be thought that nothing turned upon the truth or falsity of the tale.

The first tray contained only a few roughly-shaped pieces. Principally of interest to me were squares of tissue paper arranged in two piles. Each white square, about the size of a handkerchief, must have been put there to be used for display if one of the objects had to be shown to a visitor, or possibly to separate one precious coin from another if several coins were passed to a purchaser.

Tissue paper of such a kind was quite common, but this could well be where the square of paper wrapped around the Lapides coin had come from.

Troubled, still pondering what to make of it, I was disturbed by a faint movement somewhere behind me, so I pushed the tray back into place quickly, not wishing to be caught out, and closed the cabinet's glass panel.

Embarrassed, I turned to face the newcomer. My sense of guilt was so acute that I might as well have been found stuffing my pockets with coins.

My disquiet intensified. There, in the doorway, had appeared Anita Mavros, our host's beguiling daughter. She stood there in her long-skirted cotton dress, loose at the waist but revealing the shapeliness of her body, the curve of her breasts.

Had she seen me at the tray? Snooping? Perhaps not. For she greeted me with a smile so warm and friendly that my look of apprehension must have seemed bizarre.

Slow to recover, I smiled back, but uneasily. I hadn't seen her at close quarters since our trip to Smyrna in that summer before the war, and I had no reason to believe that she would think well of me.

I didn't know what to say and could only manage a faint rehearsal of her name. 'Anita!' I stepped away from the cabinet, placing a hand on the nearest table to steady myself. She was so slim and so perfect, surpassing even her mother's dark-eyed beauty. As always, the liveliness in her expression seemed to speak of some inner felicity. And just by standing there with one hand raised lightly to the brooch on her pale blue walking jacket.

She left the doorway and sauntered towards me, softly, casually, as if fascinated by the one before her. She laid a hand upon my sleeve, and let it drop, a touch that left me with a sense of awkwardness, a feeling that made me avoid glancing too frequently at her slender waist or the line of her bosom.' 'So here you are,' she murmured. A slight frown, a look of puzzlement, replaced her smile. 'And after such a time. The man from Smyrna.'

I knew what she meant, of course. She was echoing a description that I had applied to myself towards the end of our trip, but the term that I had tossed off facetiously, in a moment of bravado, had come back to me now not as a little joke between us, but in a slightly ominous whisper, as if, since we had last met, it had taken on some extra meaning, and with the passage of time had become a gambit devoid of irony: the point of entry to a secret language.

Why had she come? What did she want? That she seemed pleased to see me was both unexpected and gratifying. But it was disconcerting too. Yes, I had been one of her admirers, on Crete, and at Ephesus, but from afar. It wasn't until our trip to Smyrna that I had actually spoken to her at any length.

That short, ill-fated trip and its aftermath. She was back in Athens by the time the axe fell, so I couldn't be sure what it meant to her, and nor did I know to what extent she had been affected by her parents' condemnation. Yet, here she was, treating me as someone special by every look and gesture.

I must have muttered some reply, for with another smile and her lovely eyes still fixed upon me, she added this: 'I knew you were here. So I waited.'

For some reason I felt obliged to play up to the scenario she had created – the magic of the long-awaited reunion – and blurted out the first thing that came into my head. 'Chose your moment, I take it.'

'Exactly.'

'So here we are.'

'True. But in my case not where I would like to be.'

The conversation, strange to begin with, was now well on its way to a realm of unreality, a place all too often bedevilled by misunderstandings and cross purposes. I had to find a way out of the maze before I was compromised by the plans of those around me, as had happened when I agreed to go with her to Smyrna.

'We have been watching your father's films,' I said, trying to keep things on an even keel. 'About Ephesus.'

Her warmth, the yearning that seemed to go with it, wasn't meant for me. I had grasped that by now. It was for what I represented. Steadied by this realisation, the need to extricate myself without causing a commotion, I drew her attention to the display cabinets. 'And now we are looking at coins found at Ephesus. To remind us of those days.'

The bright, slightly excited manner with which she had greeted me initially, her conspiratorial air of expectancy, gave way to a look of anxiety, as if she too had become concerned about the incongruity of our exchanges, and now, at last, had rediscovered the urge that had brought her to me.

'Michael found some valuable coins.' This remark was thrown in as if she were speaking to herself. 'Several coins,' she added, in the tone of an acolyte praising the work of a master craftsman.

'Cleaned up with a weak solution of hydrochloric acid and a special cloth. Remember that? And polished.'

I was still in the maze and unclear as to what exactly she was looking for, but I had to scramble out of it before Viscarra came back, which could be at any moment.

'That's the sort of thing we were talking about.' I sounded a nonchalant tone. 'What was done with things found on the site. The cataloguing et cetera.'

I knew of her deep affection for Michael Carter. It had become evident as the summer season at Ephesus ran on and she spent more and more of her time with the young Australian. It lay behind the misunderstandings that had led to my eviction from the site. But this wasn't the right time or place to be talking about her feelings.

'He gave me a coin as a keepsake.'

'Michael was a hard worker and a good-hearted fellow,' I confirmed in a neutral manner. 'Helping your father sort out the flooding problem. Manning the primus stove and so forth. Which is why he was called the handyman.'

She raised a hand as if to quell any further attempt on my part to deflect the flow of her recollections. 'My father loved him too,' she assured me. 'Although he would never admit it. He knows that now.'

The silence that followed these words lengthened as I struggled to respond. Should I keep trying to change the subject, or was she after information? Some insight about what had happened at Ephesus? Or bearing upon more recent events? The Lapides coin perhaps? I had little to offer. Her father had sent me packing after the trip to Smyrna. I had heard nothing of Michael Carter since that time.

I was about to quiz her when Viscarra suddenly reappeared. Annoyed by the scene confronting him, he stalked inwards. For a moment, I feared that he was about to seize poor Anita by the shoulders and bundle her out of the room. Instead, he paused beside her in order to rap out what he must have thought was sound advice. 'You will have to leave us be. Your father is at work with this gentleman. He and his friend. Upstairs.'

She kept her eyes on mine, scarcely noticing what had been said. But something in his voice must have left a mark, for she retreated, breaking away from us, the two men, with a hurt expression. Whatever she had in mind to say when she entered the room had been abandoned. If she had been hoping for some news of Michael Carter from a visitor who had once been close to him, the hope had vanished.

She looked so downcast, turning away, that I almost followed her – to make it clear that upon leaving Ephesus I had ceased to have any further connection to those at the site. That I was here in Athens on war duty.

I couldn't do so, not with Viscarra there, trying to acquaint me with what he had just been told upstairs, his fresh instructions.

The rush of contradictory thoughts and emotions had left me bemused. When I asked Viscarra to repeat what he had just said, he held up his bunch of keys, very slowly, a few inches from my face, and waggled the metal objects, to and fro, as a hypnotist might do in bringing his vassal back to the surface. 'The locked cabinets! You know what I am saying? You understand? That is where we were meant to go.'

I nodded, trying to look diligent, but conscious that our quest for the coins had now been well and truly eclipsed by the mystery of Anita's appearance, her attempt to communicate. What had happened to her romance with the young Australian after I left the site? What bearing did my actions have upon the affair? I watched quietly, but with indifference, as Viscarra swept aside a curtain by the hatstand to reveal a line up of display cabinets similar to those we had looked at before. He began sorting through his clinking key bunch, trying each lock in turn.

For myself, I could think only of what Anita had said and of what I had failed to say. My thoughts kept drifting back to the afternoon Peter Mavros came to my tent in the encampment at Ephesus. He drew me aside, using his wide-brimmed Panama hat to slap away the flies as he passed on his instructions. Tomorrow morning. At first light. I was to accompany his daughter and her chaperone on a trip to Smyrna. His wife was insisting that an early start be made so that the two travellers could get back to Athens on tomorrow's steamer. I was to stay with them at all times until they were safely aboard.

He looked me in the eyes and gripped my hand. He trusted me, he said. As if we had just committed ourselves to a solemn pact.

* * *

The road to Smyrna was in poor condition, dusty, scarred by wheel ruts, fractured by seams and fissures, a threat to wayfarers taking that route for the first time, no doubt, but probably not to the experienced local man who had been recruited to act as our driver. A taciturn fellow, he stood patiently beside his car in the dawn light as Anita and her parents emerged from the door of the Mavros villa and came down the front steps. She embraced her father, kissed her watchful mother, and surged past me in order to clamber into the back seat of the vehicle.

The chaperone in her long black dress, a severe expression on her face, stepped forward to offer a gloved hand to each of the parents. That done, she joined her charge in the back while the driver and I took our places up front. The farewells had been said but that wasn't enough to prevent Peter Mavros having the last word. He came in close while the driver revved the engine and spoke to me directly: 'Straight there and back!'

I nodded, but without being sure what he meant. Not that it mattered because the car had suddenly lurched away from him as the driver let out the clutch, and we were on our way. The possibility of any further talk was lost in the roar of the engine. And very soon, once outside the old gate overhung by hibiscus, the driver, without any sign of alarm or displeasure, set about manoeuvring through the rifts and pot-holes that kept appearing as we clattered along, following a track that led for the first half mile or so through low outcrops of limestone.

The driver told me his name was Josip, but did so reluctantly. I was secretly pleased that he fended off any further attempts to start a conversation, not even bothering to turn his bearded face towards me as he dredged up a few guttural responses to my first few questions. We drove in silence after that which left me free to dwell upon the changing colours of the ancient terrain, the ravines and stony hillsides that seemed to be constantly confronting us, edging towards our narrow thoroughfare as if to close it off, but only to be thwarted at the last moment by the appearance of a cutting or some other escape route – a stone bridge or even a few old houses coming at us out of the gloom to signify that as people lived here in these parts there must be a way through.

We gradually overtook a line of camels. Their claim to most of the rutted thoroughfare was signalled by the tinkle of their head bells and the mellow tone of the larger bells slung beneath their fetlocks: music with a strange unearthly resonance. The camel driver in his grimy turban brought them to a halt as we approached. Crowded together, the huge shapes stood there at the roadside, chawing and ruckling and blowing forth their froth, as our flimsy vehicle struggled past.

We came then to a tavern with a brushwood roof covered over by a layer of earth from which weeds were sprouting. Here we stopped for coffee and flat bread sweetened with honey. The food stalls adjoining the central mud-brick structure were thinly-stocked and the carts pulled up nearby were drawn by donkeys with toast-rack ribs and mangy hides. Their owners, garbed in threadbare waistcoats and baggy harem trousers, haggled with the stallholders, jabbering furiously as they fingered the meagre offerings. It looked to me as though the purchasers were paying for what they bought by exchanging comestibles – eggs, beans, dates, onions, pomegranates.

There were other signs of deprivation, but on the whole these left me unaffected. The sun was up by now and the sky was clear. I emptied my cup and strolled back to where the car stood waiting by its shadow. The road ahead seemed full of promise.

Anita had been entrusted to my care – for that is how I thought of it – if only for a day! Like a number of the volunteers I had been entranced by her visits to the site. At the villa I was always willing to attend to any task she asked of me, principally as a means of continuing whatever scrap of conversation had preceded her request. Nonetheless, like most of my fellow volunteers, I had to accept that there was only a slim chance of getting to know her better. She had been spending so much time with Michael Carter in recent weeks that it seemed as though the rest of us scarcely existed. He was always there, at the villa, under one pretext or another, delivering a bowl of figs, fixing a gutter, or – even worse from a rival's point of view – yarning companionably with her father.

But now, at her father's command, here I was: chatting over coffee, helping her into the car as we resumed our journey, talking freely about the excavations at Ephesus, the majestic landscape we were passing through. Heartened by all of this, a mile or so further on, I told Josip to pull over. A moment later I was drawing Anita's attention to some old ruins and pointing out, beyond them, an apparition in the distance – a line of snaggle-toothed cliffs snarling at the sea.

The mysterious coast of Asia Minor, I declared, was a lure for the Greeks in Trojan times. Stories about the riches of the region may have prompted the siege of Troy. After all, I reminded her, as we stood beside our car, the Argonauts had recently made their way through the Straits of Dardanelles to the potential riches of the Black Sea, access to which was controlled by the Trojans. With stories like that to intrigue them the Greeks were bound to set forth.

I made it sound as though I was well-versed in every aspect of Homer's vision in *The Iliad*. I rushed on to tell her that, according some accounts, an early method of collecting gold dust from the rivers of the Black Sea region was to lay sheepskins in a shallow part of the watercourse to catch the particles, a method that had given rise to the legend of the golden fleece. Is that really so, she inquired, somewhat doubtfully? I assured her that it was. Myths illuminate reality, I contended, but not quite sure on this occasion whether I was quoting the studious Gerald Wray or marketing some invention patented by her father.

My enjoyment was tempered to some extent, of course, by the knowledge that Anita was leaving the site at Ephesus, and without there being any indication as to whether she would be coming back. The presence of Anita's chaperone weighed upon me also. This dour lady of a certain age was skilled at sitting or standing perfectly still with hands clasped at waist level, while directing disapproving glances at everything around her. I had to accept, as the billows of dust and occasional milestones rolled away behind us, that Anita, try as I might to amuse her by pointing out this or that, was not her usual, cheerful self. This too I attributed to the pursed lips and parchment hands of the lady in black beside her.

Scuttlebutt at the encampment in recent weeks had suggested that Anita would soon be sent home to Athens because, in her mother's opinion, she had become too close to Michael Carter. Several of the volunteers claimed to have overheard conversations in which Anita had been reproved by one or both of her parents. When I put this to Michael himself, reminding him as a fellow

Australian that the easy going habits in our own country might be frowned upon in this part of the world, he assured me that there was no need to worry. He had been ticked off by Anita's mother once or twice, true, but he and Anita's father had much in common – the same way of looking at life, an appetite for knuckling down and doing what was needed. Enterprise!

Any disagreements, Michael went on to assure me, always fell away. They were simply brushed aside, dumped in a bin marked – to use his words – 'of no importance'. He followed this with a rambling account of his father's trip to mining works in Peru and the weeks Peter Mavros had spent on the West Australian goldfields in the course of a reciprocal visit some years later.

Michael had spoken with such confidence that I almost managed to believe him. But my doubts lingered. It was quite possible of course that he had misjudged the situation entirely, unaware that the emotions swirling around him were more strongly held and complex than he could have imagined. The closer we came to Smyrna, the more these darker thoughts were forced upon me.

We climbed through sombre pine woods to the summit of a pass, beholding Smyrna in the distance, a gypsy encampment on the slope below. It consisted of a huddle of black tents, sooty fireplaces and yapping dogs. A contingent of would-be vendors laden with trinket trays and bolts of richly-embroidered cloths ran out to accost us, but we managed to evade them, and rattled downward to the valley.

On the outskirts of the city, as we passed a mosque that had once served as a Christian church, I turned to acquaint the two passengers in the back seat with Gerald Wray's interest in this holy place, another example of 'transference.' I was surprised, even shocked, to find Anita with a handkerchief to her eyes and the chaperone appraising her with the grim, dispassionate gaze of a warder.

At a loss, not sure what the matter was, I pressed on, telling them that Wray and I had visited this mosque not so long ago – admired its golden dome, the mosaics within. Transference, I informed them, is characterised by the movement from Christian church to mosque in many parts of Asia Minor. Structures such as this one drew upon and were enriched by two great traditions of religious monotheism ....

The signs of distress before me were now so plain I had to stop. The chaperone was quick to censure. She told me in effect – her tone fraught with the loathing generally reserved for pedants who leave their drivel in the wrong place at the worst possible time – that I had said more than enough on a subject of no interest to anyone. She patted Anita's knee with a gloved hand as if to reassure her ward that the flow had been turned off.

I should have yielded gracefully and turned away to keep my eyes on the road ahead, a chaotic route thronged with carts and wagons and peasant farmers on their way to market. Unfortunately, Kaub by name, and with the combative instinct of distant teutonic forbears in my nature, I couldn't retreat. There was something about the chaperone's manner that had touched a Wagnerian chord within me, a perverse desire to subject my audience, such as it was, to another and even more tedious repetition of my initial theme. So I held her gaze and began again.

'According to Gerald Wray,' I asserted, summoning up about the only facet of my mentor's scholarship that I could remember, 'no story is more widely circulated in these parts for the glorification of a holy place than that the building in question occupies the site of a pagan temple. This in turn demonstrates the complexity of cultural life in areas notable for a mixing of religious doctrines and a degree of co-existence over many centuries.'

The deities must have been listening in. I had sinned against them by muffling the music of the spheres with verbiage. I was thus condemned to the pedant's usual fate. One half of my audience – the chaperone – sought to fend off any renewal of the offence by saying: 'Enough!' But far worse, the other and more attractive half, the maiden I had been trying to impress, raised both hands to her face unable to hold back a flow of tears.

The chaperone, still affronted by the stench of book learning, incited by Anita's sobs, raised her little bamboo fan and struck me on the shoulder, calmly and deliberately. 'For shame! Look at what you've done!'

We completed what remained of the journey in silence. The narrow streets leading to the Cordon became increasingly congested as we approached the waterfront, edging between houses that at times seemed dangerously unbalanced, the latticed windows of the upper storeys overhanging the ground floor rooms, supported as a rule by curved joists springing from the lower level that looked in need of strengthening. Fortunately, Josip managed to find a parking place by the water's edge, directly opposite a giant signboard that read: *British and English Bible Society.*

Smyrna's claim to be a cosmopolitan trading centre, notable for a degree of autonomy within the crumbling confines of the Ottoman Empire, was borne out by the surrounding scene. The Cordon was swarming with mules and camels bringing merchandise to the gangways of the outgoing vessels. Crates and bales were being unloaded from the ships recently arrived, creating piles of merchandise heaped along the wharf, providing loads for the drivers of battered lorries and horse-drawn drays.

On the pavement beside us an old hunchback with one arm in a sling was selling dates and roasted nuts, supplemented with sticks of *simit* – the large ring-shaped biscuits sprinkled with sesame seeds. A line of shabby stalls led away from him offering cheap trinkets and an array of baskets and poorly-fashioned leather goods. A knife-grinder, with his grindstone on a clumsy barrow, stood at the end of the line, flashing a cardboard sign at the passing crowd, pointing to a sharpened knife lying on the stone, but attracting little interest. All of this was being observed by various groupings of shoeshine boys and the usual ruck of newspaper readers and idlers in the cafes by the quay.

It was a colourful scene and in the bright light of the afternoon sun seemed safe enough. So I left our driver with the two women and set off briskly on foot to locate the ferry to Athens and to pick up some information about the time and place to board. Still unsettled by my foolishness, my absurd persistence in the face of the chaperone's rebuke, I felt relieved to be out and about, doing something useful, comforted by the flow of workaday activities on all sides, a feeling of well-being enhanced by a recollection of my recent weeks of comparative solitude at Ephesus.

A series of inquiries brought me eventually to a blue kiosk marking the relevant embarkation point. This was manned by an overweight ship's purser with a drooping moustache and a ticket clerk with watery eyes. They were seated at a table bearing the name of the vessel I was looking for. Sluggish at first, but stirred into action eventually, the purser pointed out the gangway reserved for first class passengers and went on to acquaint me with the boarding procedure.

I headed back to the car feeling a little better. Along the way, I had to fend off the blandishments of various hawkers and the eager cries with which they sought to detain me. 'This way, effendi!' Or simply: 'Ingilhiz! Ingilhiz!' As if they knew something special about me. Perhaps they did. I didn't imagine for a moment that my ramblings about holy places, my foolish attempts to pass on what Wray had told me about the mosque, were the sole or even the principal cause of Anita's tearful outburst, but I somehow felt responsible for her distress. It was now painfully clear that she was sorry to be leaving Ephesus and that her wish to remain had gathered strength as we went along. The fact was that in my enthusiasm to please her I had failed to read her mood and had

111

made everything worse. I had little doubt that she thought less of me than she had at the beginning of the journey. The only way I could redeem myself, I reasoned, was by ensuring that she and her companion boarded the ship in good time and by getting their luggage safely stowed away.

Within a few minutes these thoughts had evaporated. The driver and his two passengers were standing by the car, but with a fourth person beside them – a scruffy looking fellow in a woollen jersey with his back towards me. I pushed through the flow of pedestrians, the customers at the little stalls, and as I reached them my initial apprehension became a fact. It was Michael Carter, turning towards me now with a huge smile and a slightly mischievous look that must have been passed on to the girlfriend he had come to see, for Anita was smiling also, gleefully, any vestige of her earlier tears now swept away.

It came to me in a flash that Michael must have left the encampment yesterday afternoon, hitching a ride to Smyrna on the truck bringing supplies to the encampment. Her excitement, her joy, suggested that this was done without forewarning. She had been taken by surprise and was revelling in the unexpected appearance of the one she had been yearning for.

Anita was clearly not the only one who had been taken by surprise. The chaperone's little fan was hard at work in the vicinity of her warder's face. The lady herself took a few steps towards me with the air of one who expected me to assist her in dealing with the crisis. I sensed her alarm, and could foresee immediately that the scene I had chanced upon was bound to have repercussions, but this realisation was outweighed by Anita's enthusiasm, and finally displaced by the acute recollection of the chaperone's peevish fan batting my shoulder. If it came to taking sides, I knew where I stood.

I reached them, breathless, and after drawing Michael aside to quiz him about his movements – a quick exchange that simply confirmed my earlier surmise – I gathered everyone together and presented my findings about the Athens ferry.

'It sounds to me,' Michael chipped in, after I had rounded off my summary, 'that we still have plenty of time.' He turned to Anita with a breezy smile. 'Am I right in that?'

'Plenty of time to spare,' she confirmed. Then, with a saucy look, she ventured an aside I had heard her use before, at the villa, when the rest of us were chatting or playing cards. 'Time enough for a short stroll.'

'There will be nothing whatsoever of that sort,' the chaperone declared. 'Do you hear me?'

At this, I saw an opening, my chance to make amends. 'The driver will take the car and the two ladies closer to the embarkation point. From there we can present the tickets and carry your luggage aboard. That will give us plenty of time to solve any difficulties in a manner satisfactory to all parties.'

It was apparent from the way the chaperone was eyeing me that she viewed this little speech as simply another example of my odious circumlocution, but as my proposal seemed to be aimed at shepherding people in the right direction, or so she must have reasoned, it was worth a nod of approval, and that she gave – but warily.

I could see that my emphasis upon the word 'difficulties' meant something else to Michael. He knew me and he could sense that I had some plan afoot. He caught my eye and nodded too. He smiled at Anita again. This was good enough for her. So I finished up, as I had intended, escorting the two women back to the car.

I gave the driver a quick description of where he had to go, what he was to do with the luggage, and found my way back to Michael's side.

As we set off on our short walk to the embarkation kiosk I told him what I had in mind. I could see no harm in my stratagem, my plan to confer upon the young couple an hour or so for a final stroll, a moment in which to say their last farewells. And it was a plan that seemed so easily effected. Simply a matter of getting them aboard and amidst the jostling of suitcases and boxes allowing Anita to return to shore in order to retrieve a supposedly forgotten item while I monopolised the chaperone's attention.

On that fateful afternoon, while striding along the waterfront, the good-humoured young Australian beside me, my friend of recent weeks, I thought of myself not as an agent of misfortune setting in motion a dire pattern of betrayal, a breach of my promise to Anita's father to keep her safe, but simply as a kind of urbane benefactor, a cosmopolitan attuned to the ways of the world, a man from Smyrna. Which is how I described myself to my companion, in a moment of vainglory, as we pushed towards our destination, chatting happily, knowing that he would probably seek to amuse Anita by mentioning my quip. Not knowing that I would never see him again.

'A man from Smyrna is a handyman too,' I ventured with a friendly smile. 'He's there to fix things up. That's why people use him.'

* * *

We peered at the trays marked 'Ephesus' that Viscarra and I had brought up from the library downstairs and at the coins, seals and tiny clay tablets laid out in rows on the velvet inlays. While Viscarra topped up our wine glasses with Dekeleia, Peter Mavros edged his chair closer to the low table at the centre of the studio, a large magnifying glass in hand in case it was needed.

Our host completed his inspection of the display by picking up a coin from the top row of the second tray. 'There it is.' He placed the old coin in the palm of one hand and used his glass to magnify the image. 'The coin Diakis showed me – found upon Cy Lapides – was like that.'

Wray took the coin and held it up to the light of the pressure lamp beside his chair. 'Bronze,' he declared. 'King Cyzicus on one side. Lucullus on the reverse. Their identities verified in each case by the encircling inscriptions.' He lowered the coin. 'I can't recall having seen such a coin before. And it certainly doesn't conform to our present view of the matter.'

'Doesn't conform?' Mavros retrieved the coin and used his glass to magnify it again. 'It's just an old coin.' He used his glass to expand a couple of other coins on the tray before him. 'There are plenty of others like it. Which is the message we have to get through to Diakis. You can buy coins like this all over the place. On the black market. Or in the Plaka. Lapides could have picked up a coin like this anywhere.'

'That's not what I meant,' Wray protested. 'You will know from Diakis that police spies were watching Lapides for several days before he was knifed. He was buying maps. Gathering information about camp sites and routes to the north of Smyrna. Because this seemed to fit with the sketch map it struck me that the coin might fit too – another coded reference to a route to Constantinople via Cyzicus and the Sea of Marmara. Some new offensive perhaps. Was this the secret he was trying to sell? Yes it was, according to my colleague at the British School, Mr Asplin. Could it be, I wondered, taking account of the description given to me, that the coin was minted in the so-called "alliance era" under the Roman emperor Antoninus?'

'Antoninus.' Mavros laid the magnifying glass on the table between the two trays with the air of a medical practitioner who feels obliged to let the patient ramble for a bit. 'And why would you be wondering that?'

'Under the rule of Antoninus certain comparatively autonomous cities on the outskirts of the Roman empire – Ephesus, Smyrna, Pergamon, Cyzicus – combined to oppose the influence of Constantinople. This link and the route connecting these cities was of interest to Asplin.'

'Asplin!' The speaker's grimace suggested that, as he feared, the patient before him was not only coughing up outlandish theories about his health but, worse, a spray of virulent germs. 'Yesterday's man!' Mavros declared. 'Since his principal supporter, General Hamilton, was sent back to London.'

Wray ignored the interruption. 'But I see now it simply doesn't fit. Precious coins in the imperial period, even in the provinces of Asia Minor, were always minted under the authority of the emperor. I would therefore expect to find Antoninus on one side of the coin, even if the intention was to honour the city of Cyzicus by singling out some heroic figures in the city's history. But in this case – no emperor. Just Cyzicus, the legendary King, and Lucullus: a famous Roman general who ended a siege of the city by defeating Mithradates.'

'What about less than precious coins?' I interposed.

For once, Wray seemed genuinely impressed by my contribution to the debate, although, so far, the debate was mainly with himself. 'A point well made. In the case of mints operated by the large and more autonomous provincial cities, bronze coins were usually excepted from the normal rule. Bronze coinage was issued by authority of the Senate. Moreover, as the Mithradatic siege, took place shortly before the imperial period, I'm inclined to hold, all things considered, that a coin minted to honour Lucullus must have been brought out well before the alliance era. It can't be regarded as a coded reference to a new offensive, quite the contrary.'

'Anything else?' Mavros inquired, a sarcastic edge to his voice.

'Only this. As Ephesus was the commercial centre of Asia Minor at the time, it can't be thought surprising that bronze coins from neighbouring cities to the north were circulating in its vicinity. Gold and silver coins are mostly found within the region where they were minted. Not so for bronze. They have been found at sites quite distant from their place of origin.'

Wray's sage expression was now replaced by a searching look. 'So there you have it. A line of thought about the Lapides coin.'

His look suggested that someone in the class was supposed to venture a few thoughts of his own before closing the discussion with a summary. Emboldened by my previous intervention, I had a go. 'So Asplin's theory doesn't stack up.'

Wray winced. 'That isn't quite the way I would have put it myself. I am simply saying that, upon close analysis, we can't necessarily presume that the map on the menu card, or the coin found upon the victim, show that Lapides had been talking to someone about a new offensive or a route north from Smyrna to overrun Constantinople. Likewise, we can't readily infer that this is what he intended to talk about with anyone willing to pay for his secret. For all we know, these were simply bits and pieces found in his pocket of no particular significance. The coin might be just some private memento.'

My earlier summary had been found wanting, but now a fresh idea came to me, a way of winkling out what Mavros knew. 'A keepsake? The coin was wrapped in tissue paper. As if it had some special importance.'

'Possibly,' Wray conceded. 'Or it might have been held as a means of identifying himself to a contact or a fellow agent. Someone who knew where the coin came from.'

'That's what Diakis seemed to think, until I put him right.' Mavros pointed to the busy street outside. 'Go to the market, I told him. A coin like that is quite common and I for one don't keep wads of tissue paper. But he kept on. Forced me to admit, eventually, that I have a sizable coin collection. A fact well-known to him and his circle of police informers. They keep an eye on who's buying what, he claims. So we have to work together to convince him that coins like this are everywhere. Lapides could

117

have bought and sold a dozen coins of that kind. He may have had it on him as a sample to entice the British School into dealing with him.'

I was troubled by this speech. Our host's lie about not keeping wads of tissue paper could be excused in certain circumstances – as an aside about a detail that didn't really matter. But in the context of his other remarks, all of which revealed, in one way or another, a desire to stymie the police inquiry, the lie could be regarded as an admission that Mavros had something to hide. This wasn't just any old coin. There were indications (to me at least) that it had been found at Ephesus in the course of excavations before the war by a team from the British School – a team sponsored by Mavros. Further, as evidenced by the note on the menu card, the Cyzicus coin seemed to be related in some way to the victim's attempt to sell an important secret.

Cy Lapides had approached Asplin, widely rumoured to be an agent working for the Allied cause, like a number of others at the British School, but he had then been struck down, possibly by an assassin hired by our enemies, and before he could give Asplin a clearer sense of what he had to sell. If the allegations about our host's difficulties with Viennese bankers were true, it might turn out that Mavros was minded to mislead the police. By doing so, he would not only be diverting attention from himself, but protecting his German friends, and in a way that might lessen his financial pressures.

Mavros claimed to be 'essentially' on our side, and in our presence he had suggested that German agents were probably behind the assassination of Cy Lapides, but was that what Mavros had said to Diakis? Or was it simply a story for us?

Wray must have been thinking along the same lines. Before I could remind Mavros that downstairs he had a cabinet drawer loaded with squares of tissue paper, Wray spoke up, as if merely ruminating, but soon showing that he was alive to a flaw in our host's argument. 'It seems you told Detective Diakis that the coin in the victim's possession may have come from a collection held by the British School. Diakis knows that the murder took place in a room allegedly rented by an employee of the School, immediately prior to a meeting arranged by another employee – Mr Asplin. From our point of view, all of this looks bad.'

Mavros nodded vigorously. 'That's my point. It suits everyone to emphasize that coins like this are freely available. Cy Lapides was just a drifter. A man of no importance.' Our host put one hand on top of the other. 'Close the file, we tell Diakis. We don't have time for this. Greece is on the brink of civil war.'

'If Lapides knew something important,' I pointed out, 'we at the British School could hardly be expected to ignore his death. We have to help Diakis find out who killed him and why he was killed. To sweep it under the carpet would be a betrayal of the Allied cause.'

'Betrayal!' Mavros threw up his hands in a disbelieving gesture and turned to Viscarra for support. 'Did you hear that Guido? He speaks of betrayal at a time like this. Armies are in the trenches, the King and the former Prime Minister are at each other's throats, and there's a risk of a lot more bodies piling up. And he speaks of betrayal like a schoolboy on the playing fields of Eton. As if any small deception amounts to treachery. Disloyalty to a cause.'

He turned back to face me. 'In most cases loyalty is simply a failure of nerve. From mining to warfare, if a man clings to the same old path it gives out. Betrayal is transformation. A means of breaking the mould. Without betrayal you can't put what you learn to use. Even the so-called victim of betrayal – the friend, the partner, the country – knows deep down that what was there for a while won't last forever. Something new is bound to be put in its place. I've lived my life by recognising these realities. Although I accept that one will never become a hero by voicing such ugly truths.'

The longer he spoke, the more I became enraged. The small deception I had perpetrated in the final hours of my trip to Smyrna with his daughter – a deception that left his daughter on shore with Michael Carter for an hour or so of freedom – had been greeted by an entirely different set of sentiments upon my return to the Mavros villa at Belevi. There was talk of betrayal then, but not as another word for superior understanding. The chaperone's note, sent back to the villa with the driver, complained of my misconduct and much else. It was thrust in my face aggressively as Mavros stalked up and down the sombre dining room in the presence of his tearful wife and myself, denouncing my breach of faith, my lack of integrity, my treachery.

'You may not become a hero,' I told him, 'for the simple reason that you might, instead, be called a hypocrite – a man who professes one thing but thinks and does another.'

This gave him pause. Slowly, deliberately, he put the coin back in its place on the velvet inlay and pushed the tray aside. 'You have in mind our altercation at the villa?'

'I do.'

'When I sent you away?'

'Sent me packing with a flea in one ear and a lot of hot air in the other. Without listening to my side of the story.'

He laughed, but now slightly abashed. 'I had to appease my wife.'

'Not much of an excuse. Not for a man who complained of betrayal then, but sees merit in it now.'

Viscarra took a step towards me. 'You are not to speak like that.'

His help wasn't needed. The old buccaneer from the film show was back on deck. 'In that moment of excitement at the villa,' Mavros exclaimed, eyes aflame as he put his case, 'I betrayed myself! It was the only way to keep the peace. My wife became hysterical when she read the chaperone's note. We didn't know where the young man was. He hadn't come back to the camp and

120

for all we knew he was on the ferry to Athens with our daughter. What else could I do?'

'So I was sacrificed to keep the peace? For some piece of minor foolishness. For breaking the mould.'

'You weren't the only one. When Michael Carter came back from Smyrna a few days later, I made sure he left the site.'

'Left it for where?'

'To return to Australia.'

'Which didn't please your daughter, I imagine.'

Mavros stared at me long and hard. 'We kept in touch with him, but that's all gone. He won't be coming back. She has her own life to lead now.'

'This is all very interesting,' Wray chipped in, 'but it still leaves the loose ends trailing. What do we do about Diakis? Can we ourselves find out what secret Lapides had to sell?'

Mavros was still staring at me and paid no attention to what had just been said.

Wray pushed back his chair and rose to depart. 'For myself, I think we should answer whatever questions are put to us by Diakis and the City Police, frankly and fearlessly. On the basis that we at the British School having nothing to hide.'

Now, at last, Mavros turned to deal with Wray's line of thought. 'I wouldn't be so sure of that. In war time you never know what people are up to or what can happen to them. Even to a man from Smyrna.'

There was something about our host's reply, his ominous tone, the looks passing between he and Viscarra, that forced me to round off our earlier exchanges. 'You say Michael Carter won't be coming back. What happened to him?'

Mavros had been about to rise, but my question left him with his hands at rest on the arms of his chair, brought to a halt by indecision. 'He went back to where he came from. Worked for a while. Enlisted after war broke out.'

'And then?'

Our host sank back into his chair as if unable to make any further effort. 'He and his fellow Australians were sent first to Egypt, then to Gallipoli.'

What remained of the answer was slow in coming; the voice subdued. 'I kept in touch with him. By letter. At one stage, when it seemed his duties would take him to Lemnos, it looked as though we might see him again. But no. The news reached us only a few weeks ago. He was killed in action.'

South Dublin Libraries
www.southdublinlibraries.ie

THE FOURTH ROOM

I CAN STILL SEE THE SPONGE-MAN ON HIS evening round, a shambling figure beyond our gatehouse, working his way along the tram stop queue, looking out for custom in the falling light. His boots and shin-pads are layered with sponges. Aprons made of sponges cover his thighs. His tunic, a breast-plate of dry sponges, sits hard and chain-mail grey upon his chest. An old helmet heaped high with sponges teeters upon his head. He beseeches the would-be passengers to inspect his body, touch the offerings, explore their pockets for the price.

He is trying to win them over: the people waiting their turn. With smiles, with gestures, he lurches along the queue, importuning the bystanders, the silhouettes beneath a tram stop roof on rusted poles. He raises his lumpen arms and flaps them slowly like giant wings – a wing-spread made of sponges stitched together. But his eyes are never smiling. He can't speak, his tongue nothing but pink flesh cut down to a bobbling cork. It glistens when his mouth tries smiling. It does what it can to speak on his behalf, jerking about incomprehensibly at the prospect of a sale. If the time comes to sever a sponge from his breast-plate, he saws at the stitching with his knife and tears the grey husk from his chest, pocketing the price with a croak of gratitude.

When a tram comes in and departs, removing his customers, he will wander across to the cafes on the far side of the street. I can see him standing before the people over there, from one nightfall to another, uplifting his nobbled, sponge-weighted wings, flapping them ineffectually, before moping along to the next table, hands held out in a mute reproach as patrons pay for something hastily, any coin, relieved to see him lumbering onwards, this flightless, earthbound spectre, marketing his remnants of the sea.

The Sponge-man is always there. He was there before the war. He was there, on his evening round, when I stepped down from a tram and passed through the front gate of the British School as a Mavros volunteer. He was there upon my return to Athens to join Asplin's lot. I had looked into his sad, unsmiling eyes from time to time while waiting for a tram to bear me away. I had bought some of his sponges when it proved impossible to withstand his imploring gaze, the speechless mouth.

In the bright, summer seasons before the war, while moving about the city, Michael Carter and a good many of his fellow volunteers had probably faced the Sponge-man too and dug into their pockets for drachmas. A sponge? Why not? Water was available and baths were taken as a matter of course.

What would Michael think now, I asked myself, if he were still alive?

I had come to the right place to ponder this and other questions, standing here at the front window of the gatehouse, the day after our film show at the Mavros home, still saddened by the news of Michael's death.

126

Ted James, the British School's elderly porter had kept in touch with his 'regulars'. Yes, he had sent cards and letters, he told me proudly, got replies. The letter from Michael's friend was a case in point, so tragic, but things in it worth knowing: a bait that had brought me to the window, letter in hand, to find out what the old man meant. Whether Michael had nurtured some hope of seeing Anita again.

My first quick reading had numbed me, left me staring blankly at the street, conscious that I would have to read the letter once more, but slower this time. So I left the Sponge-man to his melancholy toil and turned away from the window. I eased myself into a seat opposite the porter's desk and steeled myself to go through it again.

Michael's friend opened with the part they had played in the initial landings at Anzac Cove in April – the confusion on the narrow beach, the slaughter. He went on to portray the hardships that followed as the Allied forces dug in and settled down to their ongoing attempts to reach the Turks on the heights above and break through. He spoke of the lack of food and water, the heat, the flies, the dysentery, the snipers, the inconclusive engagements, the mounting casualties, the constant fear of death.

The great offensive in August, he said, aimed at capturing heights to the north of Anzac Cove, and further north at Suvla Bay, had added to the initial gains but in the end left another stalemate – the Turks still held the crucial hills and ridges. It then became apparent that cooperation between the British forces at Suvla and the Anzacs couldn't be effected so long as the strip of beach connecting the two sectors was open to lethal Turkish fire, from Hill 60 and a hill called the Scimitar. This led to the bringing in of the British 29th Division from Cape Helles to make a fresh assault upon the Scimitar and to General Birdwood in the Anzac sector assembling a mixed force to attack Hill 60.

The ragged handwriting of Michael's friend ran on, edging now, at last, towards the moment he couldn't soften, but felt he couldn't avoid, for this was why he had written.

The men of our battalion were manning trenches at Sikh's Post to begin with and along the slopes of Damakjelik Bair. In the heavy fighting that followed the first assault a number of us were moved from place to place. Much of the confusion was brought about by the nature of the landscape and a mistaken belief that the main Turkish trenches were on the summit of Hill 60 when it turned out they were on the forward slopes. The sight lines were obscured by a patchwork of tangled undergrowth – saltbush, wild thyme, camel thorn, and here and there stunted olive trees and dwarf oak covered with small acorns. Much of this, of course, was torn apart when our artillery started bombarding the hill above us, a torrent of explosive shells being poured into what was thought to be the Turkish position.

We were some distance back at that stage but we saw a chance to hit the enemy. From a certain point one of our machine guns could fire into a Turkish communication sap down which reinforcements were being moved, two abreast, during the Anzac attack. The length of the trench was soon filled with Turkish bodies, dead or wounded. Blocked like that, it wasn't long before a large circular patch on either side was covered with dead Turks, the ones who had tried to get past the obstruction by scrambling out of the narrow channel.

None of this was enough to displace the Turks or to counter the losses they inflicted. A renewed assault on 27 August was preceded by bombardments in the usual way, but to less effect. They probably served only to alert the enemy that we were about to attack. When the lull came and the whistle blew, Turkish machine-gun and small arms fire was very quickly tearing into the Australian line, cutting men down like scythes to a khaki crop. Michael Carter was beside me as we left the trench, the next thing he was flat on his face, shot through the head. It was an inferno. For those of us who made it back it seemed like murder, and worsened by the noise of the wounded where we couldn't get to them, groaning throughout the night.

A bit of ground was captured but the summit and the tiers of trenches on the slopes below remained in Turkish hands. The Scimitar and Hill 60 were still in their hands when we shipped out of the Cove on 13 September for rest and recuperation on Lemnos: that godsend of an island where the doctors and nurses are. We were 900 strong at the beginning of the so-called great offensive and about 200 when we boarded the ship. As to our fellow West Australians – the 10th Light Horse has virtually ceased to exist. It was down to 200 men after the charge at The Nek and down to 63 after the battle at the Hill. The British casualty rate, I believe, was much the same.

I have done my best to let you know what happened, but trying to keep it short. If Michael had lived to reach Lemnos, and got together with his friends, a clearer picture would probably have reached you by now as to what we've been through and as to what the future holds. For the moment at Gallipoli its back to stalemate, so I'm writing to you on Michael's behalf before we are sent to the front again. I have written to his parents separately.

So there it is. Most mornings, for a few more days at least, a group of us limp along the cobbled streets, or stare at the warships in the bay and the ocean liner where the top brass have their meetings. It won't be long before we're heading back to the same old stand off with Johnny Turk. We will have to accept things as they are, no doubt, with the only change being deep inside ourselves. A welcome addition to our daily rations is a pint bottle of English ale or half a bottle of stout. These are to your taste, I imagine, from what Michael told me. Let's drink to that.

I folded up the letter and put it back on the old man's desk. He raised a hand to his mouth to suppress a faint cough, eyes on mine, waiting for me to press him further, or to ask about some of the others he had befriended – his regulars. I couldn't do so. The recently framed photograph on the wall behind him – a glimpse of the straw-hatted volunteers at Pergamon – and the story I had just taken in were more than I could endure. I pushed my chair away from his desk and departed, without a word. On this occasion the chill air on the gatehouse steps felt warmer than the porter's room. Until the Sponge-man in the distance turned to face me.

* * *

A new offensive! The need for fresh intelligence! Toby Asplin wanted action. He was sick and tired of the dithering, he told me. In Whitehall. In Athens. At Gallipoli. The time had come to shake things up, take the plunge, rattle the enemy.

If that's what Asplin thought, I told myself, it was probably what Lord Kitchener and his colleagues on the War Committee in Whitehall were thinking too, an approach that would inevitably be echoed by commanders close to the front as they pored over maps and charts on their liner in the bay at Lemnos.

To Asplin, the question was not whether a plan existed but rather: what was in it? If Cy Lapides knew what was going on, had he sold the secret to others? The note on the menu card? *By the king's grace thereafter.* Was Lapides dealing with the Palace before he was murdered? Had he approached the Turks or Germans?

My superior's agitation was understandable. Diakis and his sour lieutenant, acting on the information provided by Mavros (or so they claimed) had turned up at the British School to inspect the academy's coin collection and question Gerald Wray. They left empty-handed, but let it be known that the investigation was still proceeding. They had put the menu card to an informer who

130

had witnessed the assassination of King Constantine's father. They had interrogated hirelings linked to Baron Von Kessell and in the course of doing so they had searched Carl Bessen's import agency situated in a warehouse near the British School.

Carl Bessen. *Der Eiserne Besen.* When the German operative threatened the police officers with a crowbar as they began rummaging through the cupboards in his back room, exposing the livid scar on his forearm to show what could happen to anyone who crossed The Iron Broom, they had been obliged to summon reinforcements, although, in the end, it became clear that the cupboards contained only propaganda pamphlets, nothing of any relevance to the murder investigation.

As far as we could make out, wherever he went, Diakis was presented with alibis, or met by denials. He let slip, possibly to help us, that the denials were concerned essentially with the circumstances of the Lapides death. His inquiries hadn't uncovered any further information about the deceased's activities in recent weeks.

On top of this our 'esteemed' visitor from GHQ, Arnold Furnell, was proving irksome. He had made it clear that, before he completed his review, the intelligence services in Athens were not to communicate with any other branches of our own organisation, in Salonica or elsewhere. We were not to contact any naval or military commands in the Aegean, except through GHQ at Alexandria. Our cables and telegrams had to be encoded in the cellar at the British Legation in Athens which left us with an incomplete control over staff permitted access to the system.

Infuriated by these restrictions, Asplin continued to communicate direct with C in London in an effort to obtain further and more detailed briefings about current plans and priorities. The flow of information from that quarter continued to be not only slow but scant, and with every utterance being qualified by ifs and buts, blurred by an overlay of warnings about security provisions and the need for confidentiality.

It emerged, as best we could divine, that there were different views on the War Committee and in Cabinet. Lord Kitchener, at the apex of the high command, believed a landing well to the south of Smyrna, at Ayas Bay near Alexandretta, where the railway line connecting Palestine and Baghdad ran close to the coast, would not only draw Turkish troops from Gallipoli but serve to restore British and French prestige in the region. Hamilton's replacement, General Sir Charles Monro, saw merit in blocking a Turkish advance on the Suez canal, subject to getting the troops out of Gallipoli. The naval leaders were divided, but certain of them favoured a fresh assault on the Straits with battleships and cruisers. This would be followed by landings at the Bulair isthmus to cut the road supplying Turkish forces on the peninsula, a bold stroke which would pave the way to Constantinople.

To me, and even to Asplin, although he was loathe to admit it, these alternatives sounded too vague to be described as a specific plan, a secret of the kind foreshadowed by Cy Lapides in his initial approach to Asplin at the Panhellenion. The torn portion of the menu card found upon Lapides, the inquiries he had been making in the days before his assassination, all of these pointed not to any of the alternatives filtering through to us from C in Whitehall, but to a plan involving landings and encampments on the coast of Asia Minor, north of Smyrna, and leading ultimately to Constantinople via Cyzicus. We didn't know what to make of it. It was hard to work out what to do next. We knew that with bad weather coming on a decisive move of any kind would have to be made before the Allied troops at Gallipoli dug in for winter.

One afternoon, while Asplin and I were vetting the cables, seated on the porch fronting Asplin's little cottage in the grounds of the British School, groping for a lead of any kind, our feeling of paralysis accentuated by the withered leaves scattered beneath the surrounding plane trees, a reminder that winter was on its way, we noticed Gerald Wray by the gatehouse. He waved and hurried towards us. Breathless upon arrival, the tie beneath his starched collar askew, he took a moment to compose himself, before speaking in a rush.

He had come straight from the Panhellenion Café, he told us. On the first available tram. His news? We had a chance to capture the German mail! It was due to leave the German Legation with a courier tomorrow evening. Their usual courier had been struck down with a fever. His replacement was a compliant Austrian called Gustav Gelin – a simple kind of chap who was to catch a train north to Larissa where he would be met by the German network's local contact. Gelin would then be supplied with a horse to take him further north to Berat on the border. He was to hand the mail to the senior officer at the first Austrian outpost.

Having got all of this off his chest, Wray summed up. Our best course would be to stop the courier before he caught the train. This would be easy to do because his orders were not to leave from Athens but to take a carriage to Sepori a few stops further on. The roads would be deserted at that hour. The whole operation would cost us about 6,000 francs, covering the informer's fee, a payment to the courier's fiancée who was in on the plan – unbeknownst to the courier himself – and a hire charge for the carriage and pair of horses required to take the courier to the Sepori railway station by a route suited to the seizure.

Asplin was excited by what he had just heard and was obviously adding one jigsaw piece to another as Wray completed his tale. 'The German mail! Yes. If the Baron was dealing with Lapides, he's bound to be keeping Berlin posted. About the man from Smyrna's movements. His ghastly fate.'

Wray nodded. 'That's what the informer seemed to think. Which is why the Germans can't wait for their usual courier to recover. He says their sending maps and plans to Berlin. Various reports.'

Asplin was on his feet now, pacing, keen to get started. 'This fiancée. What's that all about?'

'She's the sister of a man known to our informer. She knows her beloved would never betray the Central Powers, but she wants the money. So the plan is for her to invite her lover to a farewell supper before he sets off. We'll have our carriage standing by on a cab rank at the end of the street. When the unsuspecting Austrian leaves the table and calls for a cab he's whisked away to a quiet location where our confederates, dressed up as police officers, carry him off in their own car, supposedly for questioning.'

'I like the sound of it.' Asplin turned to me. 'We can rustle up some uniforms presumably. For Alexis Brusa and one of his friends?'

'Probably,' I agreed. 'But who's behind the plan. Can the informer be trusted?'

Wray adjusted his spectacles and looked a little beyond us as he often did when forced to dwell upon some aspect of the matter in hand which might prove important. 'The informer comes to us from Guido Viscarra. I spoke to the informer separately, of course, but they seem to know each other.'

These ruminations brought Wray to his next point, for which he looked to me for support. 'Guido Viscarra says that he and his employer are on our side.'

'*Essentially* on our side,' I murmured

Asplin, unsettled by Wray's report, my *sotto voce* aside, wasn't in the mood for nuance. 'His employer? That's Peter Mavros you're talking about. Which puts the whole thing in a different light. A man with an eye for the main chance, and so on. And with a wife in the king's corner.'

'If the rumours are to be believed.'

Asplin began pacing again, thinking aloud. 'Yes, the rumours. But the truth is we're always working in the dark. Can we trust any of our informers? Not in my experience. What's to be lost if we take a chance.'

'The money,' Wray observed.

'Of course. But there are ways of getting it back.'

'Remember the hessian sacks,' I cautioned him. 'The big risk is another damaging controversy. Plus the risk of damage to life and limb. If it's a trap. If we walk into an ambush.'

These last few words, I perceived, far from deterring my superior, had simply acted as an incentive to proceed. 'We can handle whatever they throw at us,' Asplin countered, defiantly. 'Time is the enemy. Whatever the risks, we have to do it, and do it fast.'

* * *

Our rooms in the city included a small office on the second floor of an old building overlooking the harbour at Piraeus. The dilapidated room – held in Brusa's name on this occasion – formed part of a ramshackle establishment that looked like a warehouse from the outside but, within, pursuant to an eccentric process of reconstruction over many years, a process reflecting the penny-pinching habits of its owners, smelt of bad drains, creaked in response to the slightest movement, and generally resembled the interior of a convict hulk at anchor – replete with gloomy landings, narrow walkways and rows of padlocked doors.

For all its faults, the building was fully occupied, its various tenants working busily by all accounts to service the needs of the shipping industry and its acolytes – marine insurers, commission agents, salvage contractors and the usual array of opportunists masquerading as export/import agents, willing to handle merchandise of any kind.

We had taken the office space some months ago in order to keep an eye on the German consul at Piraeus who was, according to our informers, engaged in the supply of benzine to German submarines at secret coves along the Grecian seaboard, but as this was difficult to prove our room was now being used principally as a place to keep track of things on the waterfront and to distribute funds to our agents and informers.

To call our room an office was probably too kind. Like the rest of the building, it was malodorous and damp. It was to an ordinary office as vinegar is to wine. The furniture consisted of an obese desk standing squarely in the centre of the room, attended by a couple of badly-upholstered chairs. The faded red regalia of these attendants matched the frayed appearance of the sofa in the corner, one end of which was held up by a pair of bricks.

An archaic typewriter had been left in charge of the desktop, displaying, above its little amphitheatre of slender metal keys, a sheet of blank paper which must have been pushed into place in an attempt to create an office-like air of prospective diligence. The faintly jaundiced appearance of this single, empty sheet left one fearing for the health of the typist who had rolled it into the machine and not entirely surprised that it didn't seem to have been touched since.

Nonetheless, the squat black typewriter, reinforced by a leather-bound ledger laid beside it, was probably enough at a first glance to give the room the look of an office, or at least, putting it another way, an office in this particular building. On the whole, principally because of its position close to the harbour, the room suited our plan to intimidate the courier and persuade him to hand over the mail.

We had ticked off the preliminaries without difficulty. Our informer, upon receiving half the agreed fee, had lined up a horse-drawn cab and compliant driver. Brusa and his accomplice, posing as policemen, were to apprehend the Austrian and bring him to our room, keeping up the pretence that he was under arrest. Once we had satisfied ourselves that Gustav Gelin was indeed a courier, that the mail in his possession was authentic, the informer was to be paid the rest of his fee. The courier would then be escorted to the waterfront for removal to a yacht waiting in the harbour. From there, he would be delivered to a cove south of Athens where, within a few days, if all went well, the unsuspecting Austrian would be reunited with his mercenary lover, for she had family and friends in that vicinity.

There was much to suggest that things would go well. Wray had taken Asplin to meet the informer. He seemed better than most, according to Asplin, and specific as to matters of timing and the way in which the mail was to be carried – implanted in two small cushions. And he had certainly proved useful in working out the details of the plan. When I pointed out that we had been let down by apparently reliable informers before, my caveat was brushed aside. It was a risk worth taking, Asplin continued to affirm. We had to find out what our German counterparts were saying to their masters in Berlin and to their Turkish allies. He lifted the flap of his overcoat to reveal his Sam Browne belt and the holster containing his Webley .455. We had to act, he said. We couldn't afford to wait.

So here I was in our creaking room at Piraeus, with Gerald Wray at my elbow, waiting for the courier to be marched into our presence with his cushions. Asplin was out there in the darkness, hiding on the wharf with the yacht's skipper's, waiting for a signal from the front window of our room.

It was getting late. The lantern on the desk would give us enough light to scan the mail and give the signal to proceed if we reached that point. Our informer was in the taverna next door with a crowd of locals, listening to the accordion players, staring at the couples on the dance floor, waiting impatiently for our call – to come upstairs and collect his final payment.

The dingy glow of the lantern flame made the room seem a little warmer than it was – far warmer than the wharf outside where Asplin was situated, keeping the cold at bay with a scarf and heavy overcoat. But how much longer would we have to wait?

The questions, my underlying doubts, kept surfacing. We were here because of an informer brought to us by Guido Viscarra? Could an informer with such a backer actually be trusted? Or was the informer dancing to the tune of others? Had he gone looking for a higher price and sold us out?

'No plan ever survives first contact with the enemy.' I had quoted General Von Moltke's dictum to myself more than once over the last half hour, but to say it aloud to Wray at this uncertain moment seemed fitting. 'They should be here by now,' I added. 'For all we know, the usual courier shook off his fever and is on the train to Larissa. Minding his pregnant cushions.'

Wray, seated at the desk, staring at the typewriter as if the blank sheet upon it represented the final distillation of its working life, nodded sagely. 'Yes, he might be. Leaving our man Gustav Gelin to finish off a quiet supper with his loving wife-to-be. If, indeed, either of them actually exists.'

For once, I was ahead of Wray. He had been dragged along to assist us, reluctantly, and owing to the haste with which the necessary arrangements had been made, without an index card to underpin his appraisal of those involved in our venture. In my case, in the course of equipping Brusa and his offsider with fake uniforms, I had managed to satisfy myself that Gustav Gelin and his canny fiancée did exist. Brusa had seen them in the Plaka, gazing into each other's eyes, walking hand in hand.

I crossed to the window and took a peek at the harbour front below. Fishing boats, ferries, yachts, steamers. The only movement was in the golden reflections from the lights ashore, quivering faintly as they crossed the water. Not surprisingly, there was no sign of our confederates – Asplin and the skipper.

Our skipper. The mere thought of him was enough to darken my mood. He and his disreputable vessel had been scavenging along the Grecian and Levantine coasts for years, picking up more contraband than licensed cargo by all accounts, renowned for defying customs officers and rules of port wherever he went. For all we knew it was only a matter of time before the authorities caught up with him and an arrest warrant was nailed to his mast. *Not now, please,* I urged the sea-god Glaucus as I stared at the scene, by no means sure that the ancient deities had any influence over what might happen at Piraeus on a night like this, or over what was fated to happen anywhere else for that matter.

Tables and chairs belonging to the taverna adjoining our premises were laid out in a square of light directly beneath me, resembling props on an empty stage. The gas lights and the little stoves around the deserted dining area, left with nothing to warm, were burning down, submitting themselves to the cold that was keeping everyone indoors. Further along, a group of drivers in coats and gloves were standing in a huddle by their brazier, the faint shapes of horses and carriages behind them.

There was no sign of our man Alexis Brusa and his Sunbeam, but this didn't surprise me, for his instructions were to park in the alley behind the building and use the stairs at the rear in bringing the courier to our room.

Then, at the very moment I turned away from the window, the door was flung open. Our informer stood before us, a lanky, wild-eyed shyster in a grubby jacket, one hand still gripping the door handle. '*Der Eiserne Besen!*' he gasped. 'Carl Bessen and his men. They must have been tipped off.'

'What do you mean?' I snapped.

He pointed downwards. 'When Brusa got to the alley, a car pulled up behind him. They blocked his way in here.'

'So where is he now?'

'He got to the bar where I was waiting.'

'With the courier?'

The informer nodded. 'Brusa and his friend. They've got the courier with them at their table, holding tight to his cushions. He's so frightened he won't budge. Brusa filled me in when I brushed past him, pretending to knock a plate off his table. He told me to get you before Bessen makes a move.'

I glanced at Wray. 'Get Asplin here with the warning signal. I'm going down.'

With the informer clattering along the corridor behind me I headed for the stairs. 'We'll go to the front door,' I hollered over my shoulder. 'Where's Brusa now?'

'Sitting amidships. Bessen and his men are at a table by the back door.'

'Armed?'

'I can't say. They'll have knives, at least.'

As we dashed outside, into the cold, the informer gripped my arm and brought me to a halt. 'I can't be seen with you. The courier is here as I promised. So I want the rest of my money.'

I pushed away from him. 'You'll get your money when we get the cushions. And find out what's inside them.'

I could hear the fracas before I reached it. The hubbub swelled as I pushed in. I found the bar in a state of upheaval. The accordion players were cowering in a corner, seeking refuge from the struggle around them. I could see Carl Bessen at the centre of the fray, a huge muscular fellow grappling with Alexis Brusa.

Brusa was doing his best to shield the Austrian courier. Our driver's companion, in a police uniform also, was throwing punches at the ruffians attacking him. The assailants lunged and circled, lurching into the table and chairs nearby, yelling at their opponent. A good many of the taverna's regulars must have decided to join in, swinging their fists and crashing about without caring who they hit, the chaos thickened by their shouts and curses.

The slightly-built Austrian, terrified by the mayhem, the onslaught, kept backing away from the commotion, cushions under his arm.

I knew what I had to do.

I waded into the medley, arm raised to ward off blows. Coming from behind, I snatched a first cushion from its keeper and managed to get a grip on the second. But now, the little Austrian, strengthened by hysteria, held the remaining cushion tightly, as though his life depended on it, screaming at me, trying to push me off with his free hand, quash the attack, his cries for help contributing to the tumult.

I got the better of him, wrenching loose the tightly-held cushion, fixing the two trophies under my own arm as I reeled away, gripping the fabric. I was about to make a run for it when I found myself facing Carl Bessen, knife in hand, coming straight at me. The Iron Broom!

I stumbled backwards to get clear of the oncoming blade. I kicked a chair at him, but he simply bumped it away and kept coming. When I scrambled behind an overturned table he was at me again, the blade drawing him onwards, sharp and metal-bright.

My German foe made a beckoning gesture with his free hand, urging me to hand over the cushions, give them up. As if to convince me that I would pay dearly for it if I didn't do so, he raised his free hand again, but this time to draw a finger across his throat, a quick slashing movement, accompanied by a wicked smile. And with the other hand, the knife-hand, sleeve rolled to the elbow to expose an ugly scar, he kept thrusting the blade at me, this way, that way, looking for a hit, searching for blood.

I tightened my grip on the precious cargo as I scrambled away, but fearing, ever so intensely, that I had no answer to his threats.

With no other weapon to hand, I was about to use a cushion to block his blade. The moment passed. For my assailant had

141

suddenly been set upon by two newcomers. The larger of the two grabbed Bessen by the wrist and wrenched his arm with such force that the German was disabled. His knife fell to the floor with a clatter, leaving him to his fists.

My protector, I realised, disguised as a fisherman, was our swarthy visitor from GHQ, Arnold Furnell. His ally, equipped with a knife of his own, was Guido Viscarra, the glinting blade in his hand raised in a fierce gesture to prevent any interference with Furnell's attack.

I didn't hang around to learn the outcome of the fray. I had what we wanted. I made for the front door, still holding the cushions, not knowing what had happened to Alexis Brusa or the Austrian courier, unable to predict what might happen next in the battle going on behind me.

At that moment, Asplin appeared in the doorway, right in front of me, shouting furiously. 'Get upstairs and check it.' He surged past, eyes afire, keen to play some part in the brawl, adding only: 'Don't wait.'

So I left them to it and stumbled on to reach the warehouse door, the stairs to take me back to our room. I raced upwards in a fit of mad exertion. At the top I found Wray peering at me from the doorway of our room at the far end of the corridor. Still fearing pursuit I raced towards him.

It wasn't until he had closed the door behind us and got me seated at the desk, that I could, at last, get a few words out. 'The cushions!' To make room for them on the desk I pushed the old typewriter aside. 'We have them. But we've had to fight.' Breathless, I made a fist to make sure he understood. 'A fight, still going on.'

My agitated appearance and portrayal of the turmoil below left Wray unmoved. 'It would be odd if things did run smoothly.' He adjusted his spectacles and picked up the first of the two small cushions. He examined its crimson cover and squeezed it here and there, tentatively, like an absent-minded uncle testing the potential of a well-wrapped Christmas present. 'One way or another, it seems. We're making progress.'

Without further ado, Wray reached into his pocket and produced a penknife. He slit the seam of the cushion and dipped his hand into the flock stuffing. Still the uncle, with a look of slight surprise, he extracted an oblong bag of light oatmeal-coloured Holland sewn up with string. 'What have we here?'

An address was attached to the bag by four blue wafers, each embossed with the Imperial Eagle and accompanied by the words *Kaiserliche Deutsche Gesandtschaft in Athen*

'The Imperial German Legation in Athens.' Wray showed me the inscription and went quickly to the words that followed. These established that the package was an urgent communication directed to the German intelligence officer at the courier's destination. '*Eilt sehr! An den Deutschen Nachrichten Offizier, Monastir.*'

'Monastir?'

'Close to Berat.'

'So far, so good. Everything the informer said seems to be falling into place.'

'Shall I cut the string?'

'The sooner the better.'

Inside the Holland bag there was a brown envelope heavily sealed and addressed as before. Inside this again were a number of smaller envelopes sealed with red wax bearing imprints of the German eagle with wings uplifted. Some of these were addressed to the Ministry of Foreign Affairs in Berlin but one, the largest in the envelope, was addressed to the Admiralty.

With a few deft strokes Wray disembowelled the other cushion, observing, as he did so, that he preferred the floral design of its cotton cover to the lurid crimson hue of its twin. He brought forth from the stuffing a bag made of waterproof paper. When he opened this up a number of private letters for various addresses in Germany spilled out.

We gathered up the private letters, shoved them to one side, and inspected those that were principally of interest to us.

The envelope addressed to the Admiralty contained maps of various parts of the defences along the Suez canal and elsewhere in Egypt. One or two of them were marked up with rough sketches of soldiers in different uniforms, depicting the defenders, presumably. The letters to the Ministry of Foreign Affairs were lengthy and as this wasn't the best time or place to work through them in detail we skimmed them hastily.

They covered a wide range of matters including various proposals to bring in King Constantine on the side of the Central Powers. They intimated that the Allied troops in Salonica were incapable of mounting an offensive in that area of conflict, and would be of little use to the Serbians.

The last letter in the sequence was of the greatest interest to us. It spoke of information being gathered by Baron Von Kessell from sources in Athens and elsewhere. It addressed the possibility of a new Allied offensive in Asia Minor as a means of breaking the impasse at Gallipoli. The French were thought to be involved and, on the British side, Lord Kitchener was said to be supportive. One of the sources in Athens had been silenced but a further and full report was being prepared.

With no other piece of paper close to hand I dragged the squat black typewriter across the desk to reach the yellowing sheet poised upon its roller. Wray found a pencil for me and I began scribbling out a translation of the crucial passage. *From reports received here in recent days it seems probable that further strong attacks will be made on the Dardanelles as an element of the new strategy, or as a diversion, in conjunction with a landing in the Gulf of Saros or on the coast of Asia Minor. It will be well to economise ammunition, and this should be put to the Turkish command accordingly.*

Wray listened attentively as I read my rendition of the passage to him, but his approval was cut short by a commotion in the corridor. The door burst open to admit Asplin followed by Furnell. They took in the scene before them at a glance. With the eagerness of hounds cornering an exhausted fox, they went straight for the wreckage of the cushions, the documents nearby. Wray and I were momentarily as of much of interest to them as the stuffing strewn about the desk top.

Asplin grabbed the nearest piece of paper, which happened to be the translation I had just completed, and scanned it feverishly. 'Yes, indeed. Pure gold!' He looked up, triumphantly. 'We've done it! Blocked them! For the time being at least. But in English. Which surprises me.'

He glanced at the other side and gave it to Furnell. 'In English. On a scrap of paper,' Asplin mused. 'That's odd. There could be more in this than meets the eye.'

To block his leap to some wild conclusion, I told him where the paper and the words upon it had come from, but he, like Furnell, was only half listening. I retrieved my translation with a view to saying a few words about it, but their eyes were still gleaming, fixed upon the treasure trove of letters, maps and envelopes.

'Worth fighting for,' Furnell declared in his rasping seafarer's voice.

This brought Asplin to a halt. 'And worth paying for. Where's the informer. He'll be wanting his money.'

Before Asplin could dash off in some other direction I asked him what had happened downstairs.

'The brawl?'

'Of course. I had to leave before it ended.'

'You did indeed. Well done.'

It was Furnell who gave me what I was looking for and typically in a few short words. 'We got rid of them. But they got hold of the courier and took him with them. Poor devil. For all we know he'll finish up like Lapides.'

Shocked by this, Asplin remonstrated. 'He didn't betray them knowingly. They'll look to his fiancée.'

Furnell shrugged. 'Perhaps.' He pointed to my note. 'The main thing is you've got what you wanted.'

Wray had been watching these exchanges silently but now felt obliged to keep us on the straight and narrow. 'We can't really say we've blocked them. Bessen will report back to Baron Von Kessell.' My colleague's gesture encompassed all the bits and pieces on the desk. 'They may have lost the bulk of it, but they can send the gist of it to Berlin by cable.'

This didn't seem to trouble Furnell. 'Let them. But now you know what they're thinking. And you've got proof that Lapides was on to something of real interest to them. Which should be enough to keep Diakis off our backs. All of which comes at a good time.'

'What makes you say that?' Asplin demanded.

Furnell hesitated before responding, glancing at each of us in turn, as if weighing up something known to him but not to us. He must have decided that we could be trusted with the answer he was about to give. 'Lord Kitchener is on his way to the Aegean. To review the situation at Gallipoli. When he gets to Lemnos he'll want to know not only what the naval and military high command makes of the current impasse, but what the enemy is thinking. That's why I decided to keep an eye on things tonight. To make sure the operation worked.'

Asplin stepped in smartly to head off any criticism. 'Which it did.'

'But only just. With help from me and Guido Viscarra.' As he often did, much to Asplin's annoyance, Furnell chuckled softly at his own joke. 'At the start by finding the informer, and in the brawl that brought the operation to an end.'

Asplin could scarcely contain himself, blurting out as the best he could manage in a fit of rage: 'I hope you're not getting too close to Viscarra's boss. This fellow Mavros. What do you know about him? He's in the King's camp by all accounts and can't be trusted.'

Furnell waved a hand at the desk top where the typewriter stood like a little castle besieged by a mish-mash of paper and cushion stuffing. 'We're living through a time of trickery where nothing can be trusted. Nothing! Which means we have to work it out for ourselves. And do what we can.'

* * *

Asplin hurried downstairs to pay off the informer while the rest of us bundled the documents into separate bags and cleared up the room. When Asplin returned we left the building by the back stairs by which time Viscarra had appeared with a car to take Furnell back to the city. The rest of us piled into Brusa's Sunbeam, having stowed the document bags in the back of the vehicle. We watched as Brusa bent over the crank handle, and a moment later we were on our way.

It was late, but as we rattled along the gloomy road Asplin insisted that he be taken straight to the British Legation. He had to send a cable to C in Whitehall. He had to find out more about the Kitchener trip. He went on to tell us more than once, affecting the air of a barrister who has been forced to endure the vagaries of an arrogant judge, that he didn't feel insulted by Furnell's manner, no, not at all, far from it: one was simply amused by the man's presumption, the way in which he let sophistry serve for common sense, preconceptions for intelligence, he was bound to come a cropper, bite the dust .... and so on. I knew of gallows humour, but Asplin's tirade as the car ran onwards was humour reeking of the tumbril, the guillotine and the head-filled basket.

We dropped Asplin off at the front door of the Legation and pushed on to the British School. Once there we carried the document bags down to the safety of Wray's basement stronghold to be looked at in more detail in the morning. It was only then, by the light of an oil lamp, that we allowed ourselves a moment to talk about the ups and downs of the evening, the crucial passage I had translated, the missing pieces of the jigsaw.

It was gratifying, we agreed, to learn a little more about the so-called new offensive, but Furnell's sudden appearance with Viscarra seemed eerie. It was equally upsetting that Carl Bessen and his men had found their way to where the courier was to be divested of his cargo. The Austrian, Gustav Gelin, by all accounts, lacked any knowledge of what was afoot. This could only mean that Bessen and his men had been tipped off by the informer – playing a double game perhaps, as informers often did – or possibly by the fiancée, or even Viscarra.

As to the last possibility, we reasoned, there were related questions. How did it come about that Furnell and Viscarra were communicating with each other so freely, an association which almost certainly suggested that Peter Mavros was involved? And why was it that Furnell seemed untroubled by the notion that Berlin might soon be told about some new offensive, a plan being hawked around to the highest bidder by Cy Lapides before he was disposed of? *They can send the gist of it to Berlin by cable. So let them.* Furnell didn't seem to care. And throughout the evening, in the aftermath of the chaotic brawl, he had talked as though what we were doing was an operation that might seem important to us but wasn't necessarily the matter of principal concern to him.

'It all comes back to something we've talked about before,' Wray ventured, calmer now that he was seated in his usual chair, the cardboard boxes containing his card index system close to hand. 'The coin and the menu card found upon Cy Lapides. We've talked about the notation. The likelihood that the card contained a veiled description of what had been put to Lapides, or of what he was seeking to achieve.'

'True enough. Cyzicus-Aristides / By the King's grace thereafter.'

'That's what the notation said. But the coin in the Mavros collection, we concluded, a coin matching the dead man's piece, couldn't be regarded as a coded reference to a new offensive. It symbolises the defeat of Mithradates at Cyzicus in Roman times. That made me think more deeply about the notation on the card.'

'So where did your thinking take you?'

'We concluded, safely in my view, that in ancient times, long before the Roman empire, Cyzicus was an island city, now an isthmus, ruled by a king of that name. It was there that the Argonauts were set upon by a race of fierce warriors from the hills. Before they sailed on.'

'Correct. You found a passage to that effect.' The book in question was still on his desk so I touched the cover. 'In Montefiore's *Myths and Legends*.'

'I did. And I've looked at the passage again. Copied it out, in fact.' He opened the book and extracted a sheet of paper bearing his seamless copperplate handwriting. 'I've marked the part of special interest, because it may help us to understand the Lapides note.'

He laid the sheet of paper before me with a finger upon it to identify the important part.

It later fell to Hercules to sound the alarm, for a race of fierce warriors came down from the hills and began blocking off the harbour mouth with massive stones. Forthwith the hero's comrades rushed to defend their ship and beat back the enemy with swords and arrows. But worse was to befall Jason and the Argonauts at this place. When the Argo ventured forth again, a storm forced her back to shore by night. They were then attacked

by the young King Cyzicus and his followers who mistook them
for marauders. Jason, equally confounded by the dark, drew his
sword and slew the king. When the dawn came the Argonauts
were stricken with remorse and remained ashore for the funeral
rites of those unhappily slain. Until, at last, Rhea, the dead king's
heavenly attendant, appeared and sent the Argonauts a fair wind
for their departure, but without their brave companion Hercules,
who had left them to go his own way.

I lowered the sheet to find Wray gazing at me thoughtfully. 'And so they departed,' he said. 'Resuming their journey to the Black Sea, their quest for the golden fleece.'

'It troubles you? That passage?'

'It interests me. As ambiguities always do in the course of acquiring fresh intelligence. Asplin seemed to think that the phrase 'By the King's grace thereafter' was a reference to King Constantine, the way in which he might use his authority to support the Central Powers. It has come to me in recent days that the Lapides note may in fact be referring to King Cyzicus, a king unhappily slain by the Argonauts.'

Wray pointed to the sheet again. 'By the grace of the king's attendant, a fair wind was then provided and the Argonauts sailed on. To me, it doesn't sound like a new offensive in Asia Minor. It sounds more like the assassination of a monarch, with his grace and favour being exercised thereafter by his attendant.'

'The King's Prime Minister? In this case the Lion of Crete – Venezilos?

Wray shrugged. 'Perhaps. One way or another, on this interpretation, the effect of the king's death was to assist the Argonauts on their way to the Black Sea, via Constantinople. But that isn't all.'

'So what else is troubling you?

The assertion that the hero Hercules went his own way. It may fit in with something else I've heard. From Peter Mavros, this time.'

'Namely?'

'I understand from what Mavros happened to let slip that the British commanders have a habit of meeting on an ocean liner moored in the bay at Lemnos which is being used as a communications centre.'

'I've heard some mention of it.'

'The ship's name is *Aragon*. It was formerly a South American liner which was then commandeered for the Allied war effort. Mavros and Viscarra know various members of the crew. The meetings with Lord Kitchener will probably take place aboard the *Aragon*.'

'That could well be so. But where does it fit?'

'Hercules, a hero famous for accomplishing labours that were thought to be impossible, is said to have gone his own way after the landing at Cyzicus. As if to accomplish a special mission.'

Wray watched me as I folded up the sheet and stuffed it in my pocket. 'Put shortly,' he said. 'I think we should find out whether King Constantine will be invited to the meeting on the *Aragon*. His father was assassinated, not so long ago. The same fate may be awaiting him.'

THE FIFTH ROOM

THE WARDROOM OF THE *ARAGON*: a space enclosed by polished wooden panels and photograph-laden walls, images evoking an elegant pre-war existence, an age when the mahogany table at the centre of the room and the lush blue carpet underfoot served commercial needs, a vision defined by the whims of a constantly rotating cast of well-heeled travellers. To casual observers, when the ship was launched, the new century must have seemed bright with promise, a place for shipping lines to send forth their splendid steamers in pursuit of weather-proof destinations, on quests for the golden dividends foreshadowed by their glossy booklets.

To more experienced observers, such as seafarers and shipping agents, one age probably looked much like another. From a print above the bar, a bearded figure in a handsomely-braided Argentinian uniform – the first captain of the ship – bestowed a weary gaze upon the scene before him, as if resigned to the notion that in the sea-lanes of the world the fate of a ship like this was always a matter of chance. It could be used for years by trans-Atlantic passengers or be sent to the depths by an iceberg. It could be taken over by socialites for genteel cruises to the Caribbean or be commandeered by ministers of a foreign power for moving troops to the Aegean. It might even, as had proved to be its fate for the time being, become a British 'Communications Centre' in the bay at Lemnos: an aid to the Gallipoli venture.

At that end of the wardroom, the former captain, imprisoned by the gilt frame containing his image (now flanked by two union jacks) was the only indication of the ship's South American antecedents. The photographs on the other walls were mostly of stately ocean liners or members of the British royal family. Here and there, the sepia prints were accompanied by caricatures from *Punch,* and there was even a reproduction of Lord Kitchener's familiar recruiting poster, the pointed finger and the sombre, moustachioed face reminding the onlooker that *Your Country Needs You.* This portrait, attached to a panel opposite the bar, looked out of place and had probably been put on display in recent days – as a talking point to mark his Lordship's visit to Lemnos.

My companion for the time being, Lieutenant Commander Arnold Furnell, was at the bar, ordering drinks, standing there with his naval companions, straight-backed, sure-footed, although the swell that had been with us throughout the day created a need for care – for me, if not for those around me in the room.

Back in uniform for his meetings with the top brass, Furnell, from the moment we had left the picket boat earlier in the day and struggled up the ladder to reach the deck, seemed to be in his element, moving about the ship with confidence, pausing now and then to acquaint me with the daily routine aboard a naval vessel, mentioning the 'pipes' and the traditional orders which were (as he correctly divined) something of a mystery to me, as they probably were to others bemused by the ways of the 'silent service'.

This was a world, I had discovered, in which – more so than in the army – salutes and brisk commands were made and reciprocated with such frequency that it became difficult at times for a layman like myself to keep track of who was giving the orders and who was undertaking to perform them. The puzzling language, the ever-present swell and the profusion of steel ladders, alleyways, hammocks and hatches below deck made everything about the place seem like a threat to one's head. My sense of estrangement was accentuated by the constant bustling to and fro along the narrow corridors, for the comings and goings suggested that everyone was purposefully employed, they had specific tasks to perform, and this at a time when my own duties were less than clearly defined.

Kitchener's review of the situation at Gallipoli, according to Furnell, might involve the interrogation of Turkish prisoners-of-war on Lemnos, or on the mainland. This meant that I had been brought from Athens to assist the Maltese interpreter usually relied on by the top brass – Damaso Montiele – but the exact nature of the assistance was still up in the air. The two of us had spent most of the day in the cafeteria used by the ratings and midshipmen, on call, available if required.

As the hours went by we were left with nothing to do but sit there, drinking tea, venturing out occasionally to peer through a porthole or watch the passing parade in the corridors – naval officers, soldiers, airmen, doctors, nurses, radio operators, cipher clerks. Uniforms of all colours, shapes and sizes hurried by, collecting and delivering messages, arriving and departing, scurrying up to the bridge and the map room from time to time, or heading back to shore. The miscellany included a scattering of South American stewards who had been kept on after the ship was taken over. Their uniforms consisted of stiff white jackets and blue serge trousers, outfits that placed them a cut above their compatriots in the kitchen who were glimpsed occasionally in greasy white aprons and sweat-stained shirts.

Until, at last, a message reached us that we were to join Furnell in the wardroom. Damaso, in the middle of finishing a bowl of chicken soup, insisted that I get moving right away. He would join us shortly. So I followed the midshipman upstairs, still feeling ungainly and somewhat self-conscious in my Australian army uniform, the jacket and ill-fitting trousers I had acquired after my recruitment at the centre on Salisbury Plains, but had scarcely worn since being seconded to Asplin's unit. Within a few minutes my guide had brought me to where Furnell was waiting for me outside the wardroom.

Upon ushering me into the wardroom, Furnell had immediately set about making his own contribution to the purposeful mood of the Communications Centre, unaware that this simply added to my feeling of estrangement. He began by telling me how the second-rate dining room of the South American liner had been divided into sections which were then converted into a wardroom, a map room and a related ante-chamber – a suite of rooms now suitable for use by officers of the British navy.

He didn't stop there. As we paused to admire the mahogany table and the bright lighting above it he outlined some of the other changes. The elaborate wood and plaster work fitted to much of the interior by the original owners had to be removed in order to reduce the risk of fire. The stairwell connecting what was now the approach to the wardroom to the former dining saloon – reconstructed as the cafeteria I had been sitting in all day – was thought to be a fire hazard also, with the result that the handsome wooden stairs in that vicinity were ripped out and replaced by steel steps. Most of the circuits had been rewired and the wardroom and adjoining areas – he made an expansive gesture – had been painted a 'fire-resistant cream.' He completed the narrative by taking me across to a framed photograph showing me the former stairwell in its heyday, peopled by men in dinner suits and society women in long frocks.

In the course of finding a seat for ourselves, and possibly because he was still enthused by all that had been achieved, Furnell had even introduced me to a naval officer who was seated nearby, reading a letter from home. The man in question was the Paymaster Lieutenant – called 'Pay' for short, or so I was told – who had kept track of the cost during the renovations. He looked me up and down with the peevish air of a man who has just discovered that there is further work to be done. When, in an attempt to be sociable, I complimented him on his improvements and, still being conscious of the swell, asked about the glassware behind the bar, the risk of breakages, Pay folded up his letter and told me, curtly, that at night the wardroom tumblers were placed in shatter-proof boxes, in the usual way. That said, he left us. His tone was so frosty that I couldn't help wondering whether, in addition to my uniform, my German-sounding name was the problem. I had struck disdain of that kind on a number of occasions since the war began, and not only in the Aegean.

We settled into our seats at the small table that had just been vacated while Furnell assured me that whatever Pay did was always done impeccably. This had proved to be so when the ship was being fitted out in the dockyards at Malta. It was equally true of the further work that had been done here at Lemnos. When Pay said 'jump', the workmen jumped. And he personally supervised the search of their belongings at the end of each working day to put an end to the pilfering and petty theft which was bound to occur.

I had been left to reflect upon all of this as Furnell made his way to the cluster of uniforms surrounding the bar. Pay's brusque manner and first severe glance suggested that I was definitely in the category of those who were expected to jump when told to do so, and I was left with the impression that he was surprised to find me in the wardroom at all. But that was how it was in wartime, I had to remind myself: one had to put up with things that might

159

otherwise be thought objectionable. Simple friendliness, the usual courtesies, were often displaced by more important concerns – the assertion of authority, the need for haste, efficiency. Indeed, I was still puzzled by a passage towards the end of the letter Ted James had received from Michael Carter's friend intimating that, on Lemnos, if he had survived the battle at Hill 60, Michael might have 'got together with his friends.' But in the regimented world at Lemnos it was hard to imagine who these friends might be. Doctors? Nurses? Australians from other units of the Anzac forces? Or friends from Athens?

These were questions I couldn't resolve as I watched Furnell exchanging badinage with others at the bar before picking up the glasses put in front of him and making his way back to our table.

Furnell handed me the dry sherry I had requested and eased himself into his chair, placing his glass of ale on the low table between us. 'Kitchener and the others are still in the map room.' He drew my attention to the door leading to the adjoining room. 'Been at it all day, and feel they have to keep going. Or so I'm told. So it looks like they won't be wanting any interpreters for the time being.'

Before I could press him about what they were doing in the map room, Damaso Montiele, brought upstairs by a midshipman, edged into the wardroom. Damaso was an olive-skinned, overweight Maltesian with pudgy cheeks and dark brown hair grizzled at the temples. He was kitted out in a naval uniform that looked as though it had been assembled by cadging bits and pieces from friends and sympathisers. He stood there, his wide-awake eyes presenting to those within the room an expression of bewildered astonishment, an expression that would almost certainly be equalled, or even surpassed, if Pay caught sight of him.

'I'd better get him,' Furnell exclaimed. 'Everything's haywire on a ship like this at the moment. Half the people aboard don't know why they're here or what's going on and the other half keep most of what they know to themselves.'

'I don't like the sound of that.'

Furnell was already on his feet. 'It's just the way things are. Everyone's meant to be subject to naval discipline but officers below the captain and the senior ratings have been warned not to confuse things by giving direct orders to personnel from the other services or odd bods like you and Damaso.' He jerked a thumb at the bar. 'Even the usual rules in the wardroom have been relaxed. Which doesn't please the sticklers.'

I had imagined that I would hear these sentiments being expressed in a tone of indignation. It had seemed to me initially, and as the day progressed, with Furnell popping in to the downstairs cafeteria from time to time to keep us posted, that he himself was a stickler for tradition, but there was something about the derisive chuckle accompanying his last remarks that suggested he was amused, if not invigorated, by the way things had been shaken up, and it struck me that I had heard an echo of this when he spoke of Pay's penchant for doing things impeccably.

When Pay said 'jump', the minions jumped. The straight up and down approach. This had seemed to be typical of the bluntly-spoken Furnell when I first met him in Athens, but was it just a convenient façade? I had seen him fabricate cover stories without blinking. He didn't get flustered when he was taken away for questioning by Diakis. He didn't seem to be bothered by the notion that, irrespective of our seizure of the German mail, the likelihood was that Berlin would be told about the assassination of Cy Lapides and the prospect of a new Allied offensive north of Smyrna. Everything Furnell said or did suggested a commitment to some undisclosed purpose and defined him not as a stickler treading the well-worn track but as a man of subtlety, accustomed to branching out on his own.

I laid these thoughts aside, for Furnell was on his way back to our table, Damaso trailing in his wake.

'What will you have to drink?' Furnell found a chair for the newcomer. 'They'll soon be booting us out of here, I expect. When the paper-shufflers in the map room finish whatever they're doing, and scuttle in for a quickie.'

'What *are* they doing?' I asked, but without much hope of a straight reply.

Furnell chuckled. 'Still dithering, probably. Fussing over his Lordship. Or working out what to say to King Constantine in order to bring Greece in behind us.'

'Will Kitchener meet the King here? Or on shore?'

'Not yet decided. Like so many other things. But you know all about that from Athens. Figuring out what has to be done, without waiting for Whitehall or the War Committee.'

'Can't follow?'

'No need to follow.' Furnell put his finger to his lips.' Enough said for now. Damaso?'

The man from Malta responded with an ingratiating smile. 'I will drink whatever you are drinking, sir. That will be exactly right for me.'

'So be it.'

Furnell stalked off to join the cluster at the bar, leaving Damaso and me to smile at each other, as we had been doing for most of the day.

'He would never say those sort of things to me,' Damaso remarked in a matter-of-fact tone. He glanced at the surrounding scene and at the nearest photograph. 'The wardroom! I am surprised we are included.'

'I know Lieutenant Commander Furnell from Athens. He is probably embarrassed to have kept us waiting, with nothing to do.'

'Twiddling our thumbs? Is that what we would say?'

'Something like that.' I raised my sherry glass. 'Hence the drink.'

My companion was gaining confidence. He answered this with a robust grin. 'It is more than that. I can see he has taken to you. Ha! I say to myself when the message comes. Finish your soup. Send Robert up there first to ease the way. This fellow from the British School. There is something about him which is of interest to Furnell. Our boss will probably want a moment with him for a private chat. His German name might make him useful in some way.'

'Nothing has been said of any substance. I can assure you of that.'

'That is not the point. He has something in mind for you. The little hints and looks. I can sense it. Please, you must understand. I am not annoyed by that. I am surprised to be here at all. But for you, I am sure, he wants you close by for something special. You see what I am saying?'

'I'm not sure I do see.'

'We are all in our uniforms acting our part. But it comes about after a time that some can't tell when they are acting and when they are being themselves. Do you see now? There is a kind of madness in it. Mr Pay. I have seen in Malta. Struts about with the rule book. Wants the dockets signed. And in my case even for half an hour's work. Would you want him leading you into battle?'

'So what's your point?'

'This Arnold Furnell. He is different. He is pretending also, but in a different way. He is sane. He will never lose sight of what is important and what has to be done.'

My companion leaned closer, speaking in a whisper. 'I have seen him here on Lemnos one or two times before now. He keeps quiet about what he is doing but he is listening all the time. He talks to the wounded soldiers coming in from the front. He has used me to speak to the captured Turks. But not always, so I won't be hearing too much. He should be in that room next door, the map room, telling them what to do.'

'Damaso!' I exclaimed. 'You seem to be getting ahead of yourself. The man you are speaking of may give advice from time to time, but the decisions have to be made further up the line.'

'Pah! The system!' Damaso sat back, clearly affronted by my failure to agree. 'You will see. This man Furnell knows what has to be done. He came here once with a man from Smyrna. To this very ship. I have seen them talking to one of the South American stewards. Which left me curious. I made it my business to have a little drink with the one they had spoken to.' Damaso held out two empty hands.' He would tell me nothing. But I could see the exaltation in his eyes. He sees the merit in Furnell.'

'This man from Smyrna. How did you know he was from that place.'

'The steward told me that, but would say no more.'

'Anyone can be called a man from Smyrna. Describe him.'

'Thin. Gaunt. Shoulder-length hair. Such a ruffian, I am surprised they let him aboard. But I must stop now. Here comes our friend.'

Furnell was beside us again but before he could deliver another glass to the table, Pay was upon him, stiff and commanding. 'Sorry, old boy. No time for that. The big guns are coming through from the map room. Time to pull up stumps.'

The speaker turned to face us. 'Out!' Pay said. 'You can leave your drinks where they are.'

'Give them a minute,' Furnell counselled.

'Sorry, old boy. My domain. Out!'

I finished off the last of my sherry, slowly and carefully. 'A nice drop,' I informed the Paymaster Lieutenant. 'Very warming. Which it needs to be.'

* * *

I sat beside Furnell in the picket boat as we pushed away from the huge grey hull of the destroyer and headed for shore. In a gruff, naval officer's way my companion began drawing my attention to the main features of the terrain before us – Anzac Cove on the far side of the promontory to the right, North Beach by the pier in front. He went on to point out The Sphinx and Russell's Top, and other fiercely contested humps and ridges, but at this distance from shore the well-known names and related landmarks seemed meaningless. Ahead of us I could see only a grey-green serrated escarpment propped up by ragged cliffs and dusty slopes most of which were riddled with fissures and gullies. Glass or metal within the sombre mass glinted occasionally as bits and pieces caught the midday sun.

I was reminded of what Gerald Wray had once told me – that mineral traces in the walls of a city near Cyzicus had spawned tales, eventually a myth, about the so-called 'city of mirrors', a realm where the citizens were thought to be threatened by reflections of themselves. Perhaps some vestige of the story had found its way to the Gallipoli peninsula, a spectral presence to haunt the opposing troops as they faced each other across the various body-littered battle sites, raising their fearful periscopes from the trenches to see what was being done by men just like themselves, only a few yards away.

A consequence of the stalemate, Furnell had told me, was that there had been a good deal of communication with the Turks of late. A few weeks ago, on one of their festival days, the Turks at one of the front line positions had thrown over two packets of cigarettes and a note in French saying: 'Smoke with pleasure, our heroic enemies.' The Australians threw back some bully beef. This was answered with a message on a stone-weighted stick saying: 'Bully beef, non.' So the Australians chucked over biscuits and jam. At that stage an officer must have intervened because someone in the Turkish trench called out 'Fin', and the shooting and the sniper fire from a ridge nearby began again.

This wasn't the moment to ponder such matters, for we were getting closer to shore. I was pleased (albeit apprehensive) to be here with Furnell in the picket boat, otherwise my trip to Lemnos might have seemed superfluous. I had spent a few hours in the hospital tents by the port at Mudros while Turkish prisoners-of-war were being interviewed, true, but the information obtained was repetitive and of little value.

My attempt to quiz Furnell about the presence of Cy Lapides on Lemnos some weeks ago had been brushed aside with a brusque and unconvincing reference to finalisation of a letter to the British Legation in Athens – the matter that Furnell had set in train a while ago in Alexandria. Our tiff had repercussions. Yesterday, when Lord Kitchener had set off in the destroyer to review the British position at Cape Helles, Damaso Montiele was attached to the official party, notwithstanding his earlier suggestion aboard the *Aragon* that Furnell had some special role in mind for me. Flattery or simply a Maltese sleight of hand? I couldn't be sure. But here I was, the day after the visit to Cape Helles and the entrance to the Straits, restored to favour, a member of His Lordship's party on its way to the Anzac sector, with Furnell beside me in what seemed to be a companionable mood.

We reached the pier and scrambled up the ladder to join a group of senior officers, a small assembly of jodhpurs, jackets, polished belts and boots, its status verified by a plethora of red gorget patches. When the second picket pulled in, bearing the Secretary of War himself, the official party assumed its final form. Lord Kitchener, a large ungainly figure with a blazing red cap-band towered above the surrounding uniforms. Scarlet cheeks, thick moustache, chest covered with ribbons – he was immediately recognizable as the commander of all the British and Imperial forces.

Within the group, dressed in a grey jacket and much smaller, General Birdwood hovered by the great man's side as the greetings and handshakes were completed, bringing in a French general and some of the local commanders – Generals Godley and Maxwell, and Colonel White.

'That red cap-band,' Furnell whispered as the group set off. 'There's nowhere on the beachhead or anywhere else in this wretched place that's safe from shells or snipers. For the next few hours Birdie and the others will be in a cold sweat.' As if to underline his point there was a sudden burst of gunfire on the slopes above us and the clubbing of distant shells. But Kitchener, with General Birdwood by his side, kept striding onwards, undeterred.

The risk was real, for the closer we got to the beach the more intensive the crackle of intermittent firing. It then became apparent that the tall figure and the conspicuous red cap-band was creating a commotion of an entirely different kind. The denizens of the dug-out shelters on the slopes above us must have noticed the arrival of the picket boats and the appearance of the tall figure at the head of our group. They were scrambling down the hillside to greet us, half-clad, in torn shirts and trousers. Upon reaching the beach, Kitchener, Birdie and the rest of us were surrounded by a throng of grimy, grinning faces. A cheer went up as the onlookers pressed forward to hear what the famous soldier might say, standing there between the tram tracks, looking into the eyes of each man in turn.

What would my friend Michael Carter have made of this scene, I wondered: a youngster from the West Australian goldfields. The desolate surroundings at this end of the pier had the aura of a mining camp in the desert country, replete with hungry miners, sand-bagged shafts and mullock dumps, so that the only role left for the upright figure at the centre of the crowd was that of an old-timer firing up the mob with talk about some recently-discovered nugget on the outskirts of the encampment.

Kitchener held up a hand to quell the cheering and, as he did so, my scenario vanished. The man before us was far more than an old prospector with a tall tale, he was an experienced soldier, renowned for his loyalty to his country and to his men, from Khartoum to the South African veldt. 'The King ...' The speaker stifled a cough and began again. 'The King asked me to tell you this. How splendidly he thinks you have done, for those at home in England and for the Empire. Yes, you have done splendidly. Better, even, than I thought you would.'

The local commander – 'Birdie' to those around him – stepped forward to suppress the cheer that had followed these solemn words. Time was short, he explained, with a grave expression. The visitors had to move on and see as much as they could. Lord Kitchener had important work to do. This announcement had an immediate effect. The throng of dishevelled soldiers quietly parted. We set off again and were soon trekking up the slope, with Birdie leading the way.

We had to pause at times to make room for stretcher-bearers on their way to the dressing station on the beach. These pauses gave me a chance to look around but there was little to see. The weather had eaten away the gravel facade of the rugged spur to our right known as the Sphinx. The nick-name suited the worn, pock-marked appearance of the impassive cliff face. A torn flag on the dressing station below, fluttered bravely, adding a dash of colour to the scene.

Our first stop was a dug-out with a sandbag-protected entrance and a galvanised iron canopy, weighted down with rocks and earth, providing shade. The interior was lined with ragged blankets. The makeshift bed had been built up from the stony floor with biscuit boxes. The officer living in this space produced some maps and with Birdie beside him set about acquainting Kitchener and the French General with the surrounding topography and the principal vantage points. I was brought in to assist the Frenchman but others in the group including Furnell were left to loiter near the entrance to the tiny premises, chatting quietly, listening to the gunfire. I edged out of the shelter as the group got ready to move on.

Close to the dug-out, as in other places along the track, there was a cluster of wooden crosses scattered about in a shallow depression, silent, forlorn, some dignified by a few stones heaped up at the base of the cross. Kitchener must have noticed the little burial place. When he questioned Major Howse about treatment of the wounded in the Anzac sector he was told that all transport was by stretcher, on foot, or by donkey, none of which was good for the casualty. Now that winter was coming on the usual routes along narrow tracks were becoming increasingly hazardous when wet. These tracks were crowded with men and pack animals carrying stores, ammunition, rubbish, rations, water cans, and sometimes – closer to the front – they were littered with the bodies of the fallen. Nearly every route was a target for Turkish snipers. Winter would reduce the flies, lice, and other pests, and thus the prevalence of dysentery, but the increased slipperiness underfoot would make the work of the stretcher-bearers even more difficult than at present.

Birdie must have felt that the picture being painted was too grim. 'For all our difficulties,' he asserted, 'we can persevere, and with a few more reinforcements dislodge the enemy.' His gesture embraced the beach below. 'You've heard it for yourself. The men are proud of what they've achieved. They see it plainly, as I do. To abandon the ground they've gained would be selling out their friends.' He pointed to the crosses. 'Those who have lost their lives. The ones they would have to leave behind. It would be a betrayal of all they've fought for.'

'And a betrayal of all the other lives that would be lost.' another voice in the group added. 'If we leave.'

This, I inferred, was a reference to the impossibility of withdrawing from the Anzac sector without incurring heavy losses, a complication that Asplin and others had explained to me many times. The normal method of falling back in stages was out of the question here. If the Turks noticed what was happening, they had only to thrust forward a few hundred yards from their trenches on the high ground in order to overlook and fire down upon the embarkation piers.

'Too many lives would be lost,' Birdie emphasized. 'Far too many.'

Kitchener nodded, his frown conveying his own feelings. 'I know exactly what you mean. I pace my room at night and see the boats being fired upon. Capsizing. And the drowning men. I said this to the War Committee before I left. 'Perhaps if I lose a lot of men over there I shall not want to come back'.' He straightened his shoulders. 'But for now, we had better keep moving on.'

With Birdie still out in front and the famous visitor from London behind, his red cap-band clearly visible, pushing ahead with his long and purposeful strides, we resumed our trek to the battle zone I had just seen pin-pointed on the map – Walker's Ridge. We ascended steadily, picking our way along rutted paths, through saps and trenches, murmuring greetings to the exhausted-looking Australian soldiers we met as we proceeded, standing aside for stretcher-bearers.

The next stop was at a section of trench that had been widened to facilitate diggings beneath the enemy lines. Kitchener crouched down and ventured into the tunnel for a few yards, straightening up as he made his way out of the gloom. 'How far does it go?'

'Under Abdul's trench,' Birdie informed him.

'How far is that?'

Birdie hesitated, glancing at the digger next to him. 'Perhaps we can show you.' He held out one hand and the digger, somewhat reluctantly, passed him a periscope.

Frowning, clearly not quite sure about the wisdom of what he was about to do, the British General removed his staff cap and used his sleeve to clear dust off the small glass viewing panel. He stepped on to the nearest mound and cautiously pushed the top of the periscope above the parapet of sand bags. At the snap of a rifle shot we all ducked and the periscope was sent splintering into the trench beside the mound.'

'That chap can shoot the eye out of a mosquito,' the digger remarked. 'Watch this.'

The digger stuck his battered slouch hat on the end of his rifle and, as Birdie made way for him on the mound, he raised the hat above the parapet and waited. With a swift crack the hat went into the bottom of the trench too. 'If I had my head in it,' the digger said with a rueful laugh, 'he would have drilled a hole in both.'

Birdie returned his staff cap to his head. 'This may not be the best place to show you how far our tunnel goes. Perhaps we'd better move on.' He glanced uneasily at the red cap-band beside him. 'Keeping our heads down. Crouching if we have to.'

The hint was ignored. Kitchener, far from asking for a helmet, or any form of less conspicuous headgear, simply tugged his red cap-band securely into place, saying as he did so: 'Thank god, Birdie, I came to see this for myself. I had no idea of the difficulties you were up against.' He swivelled round to address the group as a whole. 'I think you have all done wonders.'

At that moment Kitchener noticed another soldier in a dug-out to one side of the enclosure, pounding away with an entrenching tool handle at something in a metal tray. 'What on earth is that man doing?'

Birdie was looking nonplussed, so the Australian chief of Birdwood's army corps staff, Colonel Brudenell White, came to the rescue, his voice as crisp and precise as his neat moustache. 'He's making a fritter by pounding a biscuit to flour.'

Brudenell White's adjutant, Captain Alan Emery, took a closer look at what was happening and completed the description with a few brisk words of his own. 'With a dash from his ration of water, some condensed milk, a little fat from a bully-beef tin and a flame from the primus stove, he's got his fritter.'

'Hey presto!' Kitchener said.

We all laughed dutifully but left it to the unflappable Brudenell White to round off the moment as the laughter subsided. 'Better than nothing,' he responded. This drew a laugh also, but of a rather cautious kind.

By now, bemused by our presence, the soldier had stopped what he was doing, grinning upwards at us as if wondering whether to add some extra flourish to his floorshow. At a signal from Captain Emery he quickly went back to what he was doing, while the rest of us, with Birdie leading the way, edged out of the enclosure, leaving the first digger to gather up the bits and pieces of his periscope. Within a few minutes, by a dusty, semi-precipitous track, Birdie had brought his visitor and those behind him to the observation post at Russell's Top.

Here, as in the dug-out below, Furnell insisted that I be brought in close to the leading figures in the group as they were, at last, about to be provided with an overview of the topography. The French General in particular could be in need of assistance. And so it was, with hands on the parapet at shoulder height like Kitchener and those around me, I listened carefully to Birdie's description and took in the main features of the scene before us, conscious, as the others were, no doubt, that in this position we were only about sixty yards from the Turkish trenches, but protected to some extent by rising ground.

The battered landscape seemed extinct, the ground inert like the buckled carapace of some pre-historic creature, exhausted beneath the sun, and with a stoic indifference to all human activity, from the snarl of machine guns in the distance to the random crack of rifles on a ridge nearby. The desolation of the scene was accentuated by the desultory nature of the gunfire and the occasional puffs of white smoke adrift in the air, as if parts of the sky had been left in tatters.

There was The Nek where Michael Carter's fellow West Australians from the 10th Light Horse had been annihilated while running across open ground into lethal machine gun fire. Following orders. Not just once, but in several successive charges. Further away, I could see Hill 60 where Michael himself had perished. It became clear from what Birdie was pointing out that, in the other direction, lay Pope's Hill and Quinn's, Courtney's and Steele's Posts, ranged along the edges of the cliffs. It occurred to me, as it probably did to others in our group, that a determined Turkish attack along this stretch of the line might well result in the Anzac positions being overwhelmed, in which case the Turks could reach the beach below in a sudden rush.

Beyond these fiercely contested outposts, like a walled castle, lay the massive upland of the Kilid Bahr Plateau, flanked to its south by Achi Baba – the first day objective of the British landing at Cape Helles, a destination that was never reached. Near the far corner of Kilid Bahr, where the Straits of the Dardanelles narrowed, stood old white fortresses, on each side of the water. These were built by the Turks in the last days of the Roman empire, Birdie explained, and beyond them, somewhere in the hazy distance, lay Troy and the hills of Asia Minor.

I could imagine what Furnell was thinking as we looked towards the distant Straits, visualizing in not only the old, white defences but the modern forts that stood alongside them. In the course of our conversations over the last few days Furnell had acquainted me with secret information concerning these sites that had been passed to him by Turkish informers. It was the modern forts, mobile batteries and minefields in the navigable channels that had blocked the attempt to capture Constantinople by naval action, before the costly April landings at Cape Helles and Anzac Cove were undertaken.

The fierce naval battle in March that ran on for hours masked the fact – verified later by Furnell's informers – that the Turks had come very close to running out of ammunition. If the naval commanders had persisted, exploited the weakness, the British ships could have forced a passage through the Straits, and the need for landings would have been averted. But it was not to be. As three battleships had been sunk by mines, the naval attack was called off. 'That's war', Furnell had said, rounding off the story in a bitter tone. It was a tragic irony. It was an irony known at this stage only to himself and a few others in the naval high command, and probably not even to the Secretary of State for War, now standing beside me.

I glanced at Lord Kitchener: at the thick moustache and sombre, red-cheeked countenance, at the aged eyes that had seen so many conflicts. He appeared to be listening to what was being said about the savage fighting at Lone Pine, beyond Steele's Post, and about the possibility of extra German guns being used on the heights now that Bulgaria had joined the Central Powers, but I sensed that the information about these near positions was not the matter of real interest to him. His troubled gaze was still focused upon the blue of the Straits, the membrane of distant water. He stared at the scene as an interpreter might stare at a row of hieroglyphs.

It came to me then, in a moment of illumination, that the British and Imperial forces would never take Constantinople. The valour of those who had lost their lives in this place would be written off. The dead with their tiny crosses would be left behind. The able-bodied and the wounded would depart.

There was nothing of this to be found in the conversation going on around me, where the talk was still of reinforcements, the possibility of new offensives. There was even talk of getting an Anzac magazine out in time for Christmas, filled with contributions from the troops ashore, one of various ruses to convince the enemy that the Anzacs were digging in for winter, they were here to stay. To me, still possessed by what I had just divined, my intuition that the Allied forces would leave Gallipoli, all this talk was meaningless, just palaver, dross. From now on lives lost would be lost to no avail.

Furnell was at my elbow. He must have noticed some agitation in my manner, an indication of my inner distress. 'So what do you think?' he inquired softly. 'Of what we can see from here?'

'It has to end.'

He placed his hands on the parapet beside mine. 'We are of one mind,' he murmured. 'And there are others like us. Those who know deep down that a siege like this can't last forever.'

* * *

The ferry from Lemnos to Athens left early, so it was still dark as I lit a lamp in the room that had been found for me on the waterfront at Mudros and began gathering up my belongings. These included the uniform I had been obliged to wear over the last few days. After all that I had seen in the Anzac sector on the mainland, I was glad to get it into my kitbag, out of sight, for the time being at least.

It was only a short walk to the ferry quay. This meant that, after packing, I would have enough time to farewell my fellow interpreter. The canny Damaso Montiele had secured a room at the far end of the corridor – a larger room – that he had been using as his living quarters since coming to this place from Malta six months ago. He had arrived at about the same time as the *Aragon,* and had watched it being moored in the bay to serve as a communications centre.

Damaso and I had little in common, and only a scant acquaintance, but I had enjoyed his company, especially over a glass of retsina at the end of the day. He was, in a good-natured way, always brimful of gossip and ingenious speculation as to what would happen next in the Aegean.

It was impossible to tell whether his ideas were purely disinterested or in fact focused mainly upon his own advancement. According to Damaso, Furnell had a special regard for me, but it was Damaso himself, the following day, who had joined Furnell on the trip to Cape Helles with Lord Kitchener's party.

Likewise, when I first arrived on Lemnos, it was Damaso who had graciously offered me the use of his larger and more comfortable room in the hostel to which we had been assigned, on the grounds that my reputation as a gentleman and a scholar had preceded me – a phrase he frequently used and sometimes mangled. It had taken less than a few words of token politeness on my part to convince him that this was not only unnecessary but inconsistent with the usual 'first come, first served rule'. He had gone on to treat my refusal – according to his rendition of the rule – as the refusal one would have expected of 'a gentleman's scholar': a rendition that made me sound like an insignificant clerk.

Nonetheless, after our initial encounter, a brief jostling for position, we had rubbed along quite well. So now, this morning, as I approached his door, my kit-bag on my shoulder, I expected to find him snoring contentedly as he made the most of his better bed in the larger room, his sense of contentment being probably enhanced by the recollection that his handsome offer to the newcomer had been proffered with such finesse that it had to be handsomely refused.

I knocked softly and pushed open the door, but only to be taken by surprise. No somnolent hump beneath the bedclothes. No jovial face turning to greet me from above the shaving bowl, cut-throat razor dripping soap suds, a shrubbery of brushes sprouting from a mug beneath the mirror. Instead, I was confronted by an overweight, hirsute, and generally out-of-sorts Maltesian, struggling into his trousers.

'Late last night,' he growled. 'I am at the café and am told to go with you. First thing.'

'To Athens?'

'Of course. We are both to be on the early ferry. This is what I am told. Our Arnold will meet me at the quay.'

I commiserated as he began stuffing some spare clothes into a bag, unsure of what lay behind this new development. A few minutes later, with the sky changing to a faint blue and the surface of the bay becoming opal, we were on our way, trudging along the cobbled street, the fleshy figure beside me still grumbling, but heartened to some extent by my reminder that in Athens there were better places to eat than on Mudros, and he might even be allowed time off to look up some of his friends.

'That will be good,' Damaso declared. 'Yes, I have some friends in Athens. And some debts due to me. Unless the man in question sees me coming and scuttles back to Smyrna.'

'Smyrna? The man from Smyrna?'

Damaso gave me a quick, sidelong glance as if surprised to learn that I didn't know what he was talking about. 'Mr Cy Lapides.' He trailed his chunky fingers down each side of his head in an attempt to illustrate his remarks. 'With the shoulder-length hair. The one who was here with our Lieutenant Commander. I mentioned him. He is talking not just to the stewards, you see. But also to me. And borrowing money.'

'For gambling?'

Damaso gave a deep sigh. 'I fear so. But how can I refuse him when he seems to have friends in the high places. Not just Furnell, but other friends. Peter Mavros, he says. Rich and famous in Athens.'

I grasped my companion's sleeve to bring him to a halt. 'I have to tell you this. Lapides won't be in Athens, and he won't be coming back to Lemnos. He's dead. Murdered.'

My companion's eyes seemed always to be in a state of astonishment and now they widened even further. I went on to tell him, as briefly as possible, what had happened to Lapides, closing my account by mentioning that the matter was being investigated by the City police.

We began walking again, but slower.

'The City police!' Damaso muttered.

'Detective Theo Diakis.'

'The City police! The Palace police! What does it matter? None of this was said to me. And now I am concerned for my own safety. Why does Furnell not tell me all of this?'

'He may have his mind on other things.'

'Or he wants me on the boat to Athens before he tells me. Without any fuss.'

'I don't know the answer to that. You'll have to talk to him yourself.'

Damaso lengthened his stride. 'I will.'

Furnell, rugged up in his familiar overcoat, was waiting for us by the gangway. He must have anticipated some show of resistance, for he drew Damaso aside, leaving me to observe their heated exchanges from afar. Whatever was said, or perhaps the amount of money offered, was enough to appease the Maltesian. Back at the gangway, Damaso was sullen but compliant. Furnell lost no further time in bundling us aboard.

Calmer now, and having sent Damaso off to the gallery to look for coffee and biscuits, Furnell gripped my elbow and piloted me to a quiet spot by the rail. 'The news came through last night.'

The swarthy face and the shrewd eyes were giving nothing away. Did he presume that I was 'in the know' about the news in question, or was he being deliberately obtuse in order to find out how much, if anything I had been told about the matter in hand?

Asplin had been inclined to characterise Furnell as simply a bluff and none-too-subtle seaman who, somehow or other, probably due to the vagaries of war, had finished up in 'intelligence'. When Furnell had first arrived in Athens to review coordination between the various British intelligence services, Asplin had once gone so far as to characterise the visitor, in a moment of exasperation, as a blinkered ghost-hunter: the sort who tries to prove the house isn't haunted by producing a wad of photographs containing nothing but pictures of empty rooms.

The last few days had left me with an entirely different opinion.

Even empty rooms are infused with memories or delusions as the viewer fits them to some vision of his own. Furnell had a habit of asking apparently innocuous questions that led to the conversation being furnished eventually with facts and matters that might not otherwise have been disclosed. He could sense a mood and pick up details invisible to others.

Asplin might enjoy sparring with him at this hour, but it was too early for me. I didn't feel up to it. My look must have revealed to Furnell that I knew less than he did, that I wasn't hooked into some network of my own, so I threw in the towel: 'What news?'

'The meeting with King Constantine.'

'Constantine and Kitchener?'

'Exactly.'

'So what about it?'

'It will take place in Athens.'

'Where?'

'At the Palace. Which is why we have to get back there. In a hurry.'

'And Damaso?' Having played the innocent it was time to profit by the role. 'Why is he needed?' I inquired in a suitably casual tone. 'He claims Lapides owed him money. What's that all about?'

Furnell paused. After a quick glance to ensure that we couldn't be overheard, he moved a little closer, appraising me with a level gaze. 'It's about time you and I had a long talk,' he said. 'A good long talk.'

He raised his eyes to check the movements of any passengers in our vicinity. A moment later, with a slight inclination of the head, he let me know that Damaso was on his way back. 'A talk will be of use to us both,' Furnell added. 'But not right now. There'll be time enough for that in Athens.'

THE SIXTH ROOM

I QUIT THE TRAM WHEN IT REACHED the British School, swept
through the front gate, and rushed upstairs to my room. I
upended my kit-bag, grabbed my notebook and sketches, and left
the balance of the contents in a state of upheaval on the bed.
Gerald Wray! He was the one to see.

I had expected to find him in his usual position, upright at
his desk, cool and precise, hemmed in by the boxes containing
his index cards. But I was in for a surprise. On this occasion his
grey-haired assistant, Valerie Crawford, was seated beside him.
They were craning forward to study what appeared to be a set of
architectural drawings. They looked up as I pushed through the
doorway but neither seemed pleased to see me.

'Back in one piece?' Wray summoned up a cordial tone, but
left both hands outstretched to prevent the drawing before him
from rolling inwards, ready for further work upon it as soon as
I left.

'Back in one piece and with things to discuss.'

'Of course. As can often happen.'

Valerie began tapping the butt of her pencil on the desk top as she waited for me to elaborate, or leave.

Without removing his hands from the edges of the print, Wray managed to nod awkwardly at the image beneath his spectacles. 'From the cushions,' he informed me. 'Drawings to scale of forts on the Suez Canal. Valerie has done a splendid job in checking measurements and various particulars against what we know from other sources.'

I cast about for a suitable compliment, but without much luck. 'Well done,' I ventured. 'Keep at it.'

Valerie stopped tapping. Irritated by my lack of enthusiasm, she trumped my card with a blatantly unenthusiastic response of her own. 'Good to see you back, sir.' She rose to her feet and prepared to leave, pencil and wooden ruler in one hand, eyes on Wray for guidance. 'Call me if you need any help.'

'Of course.'

'We certainly will,' I called after her, but conscious that in the insincerity stakes she had bustled past me for a clear win.

Wray let the extremities of his various sheets roll inwards until they met at the midpoint with a slapping sound. He fiddled with them for a bit until he had reduced them to a manageable scroll. 'She's a good sort,' he observed, tying a white ribbon around the tube he had just created. He couldn't bring himself to go further and admonish me for getting rid of his assistant with my inept pleasantries, but he clearly felt obliged to stick up for the lady in question. 'Totally dependable, in what is becoming an increasingly feckless world.'

'That she is,' I affirmed. 'Which brings me to the things we have to discuss.'

'Which are?'

'Furnell and Cy Lapides. There's a link between them. And I have to find out what it is. Before I talk to Furnell.'

'Anything else?'

'There's a Maltese fellow called Damaso Montiele.' I touched the nearest cardboard box. 'I have to find out where he fits in. There could be something about him in your cards.'

'There could be. But before we go to the cards, I need to know what you're looking for.'

'You want me to fill you in?'

'I do.' Wray paused to polish my question. 'Context is the word we archaeologists usually employ. It helps to know the context in which the inquiry arises.'

So I pulled up a chair and as Wray listened, fingers raised to his lips in a quiet steeple, I told him what I had been doing on Lemnos and at Gallipoli, finishing up with my moment of intuition as Kitchener and those around him at Russell's Top looked towards the Straits and the distant hills of Asia Minor.

When I came to Furnell's final observation – 'no siege lasts forever' – Wray nodded. 'A curious thing to say, I agree. But not entirely surprising.'

'It didn't fit with all the talk about new offensives and reinforcements,' I pointed out. 'But that's what Furnell said – "no siege lasts forever".'

'Perhaps it does fit. As I tried to explain when we last met, the bits and pieces found upon Lapides point not so much to a new offensive as to a new endeavour of a different kind. 'Cyzicus-Aristides', the note on the menu card says. 'By the King's grace thereafter'. If, as we now surmise in construing the text, the King in question is not Constantine but the ancient monarch Cyzicus, what remains?'

I had been groping in my pocket as he began reviewing the possibilities and was now able to produce the extract from Montefiore's *Myths and Legends* in Wray's handwriting. I glanced at the sheet of paper and summarised a passage towards the end that he had touched on previously. 'The dead king's heavenly attendant sent the Argonauts a fair wind for their departure. Is that what you mean?'

'They left by the king's grace.' Wray gathered up the handwritten script and read the next part aloud. '*And so it was, after such a great ordeal, they departed. And from the waves around them as they pulled away the sea-god Glaucus rose up to say how Hercules, left ashore, was not destined to share the gaining of the golden fleece.*'

My mentor handed back the sheet of paper and proceeded to add his own gloss. 'It's describing an evacuation. A departure dependent upon fair weather. The coin bearing the profiles of King Cyzicus and the great Roman General Lucullus fits in also. It marks the defeat of a foreign interloper – Mithradates. It commemorates the ending of a siege. If these bits and pieces are regarded as part of the context, as they must be, then it strikes me that the secret known to Cy Lapides was a plan to leave Gallipoli, a secret which would, if divulged to the enemy, have terrible consequences. From what you tell me, at the first hint of any withdrawal, the Turks would press forward until they could see what was happening on the beaches below. They could massacre the men boarding the boats.'

'General Birdwood is against evacuation for that very reason,' I chipped in. 'He estimates that about one third of the troops presently ashore would perish.'

'There is so much at stake,' Wray observed, choosing his words carefully, 'that the life or death of Cy Lapides is beginning to seem inconsequential. If, indeed, he knew the secret and began to act as though he might deal with it in the wrong way.'

'And yet, from what Diakis told us, and from what we found in the cushions, Lapides let it be known in various ways, by hints, by acquiring maps, by talk about water for encampments, that there might be a new Allied offensive in Asia Minor.'

Wray shrugged. 'Look to Homer. The Greeks let it be known that they had a gift for the Trojans. A wooden horse! And thus, by a ruthless subterfuge, the siege was brought to an end. You had better put all of this to our friend Furnell when you meet him. Only he can tell you what he was doing with Cy Lapides on Lemnos, and whether he saw him again back in Athens.'

'And whether Cy Lapides was still alive,' I added, 'when Furnell came to the room where the body was found.'

'Your room, unfortunately.'

'Mine for a moment only,' I reminded him. 'By a quirk of fate.' A new thought struck me. 'Furnell got the address from our driver. Alexis Brusa. Who was acting strangely that morning. Dressed in overalls. Running late.'

'One thing leads to another.' Wray leaned forward and drew towards him one of the cardboard boxes that seemed to be always maintaining a vigil on his desk. 'In the meantime, I'll see what information we have about this brand new friend of yours, Damaso Montiele from Malta. Furnell must have brought him to Athens for a specific purpose.'

* * *

It was hard to keep pace with Toby Asplin as he strode towards the front gates of the British School where Brusa was waiting for us. The driver, guarding his vehicle, was clad on this occasion not in grease-stained overalls but in the navy blue jacket and matching trousers that served as a chauffeur's uniform. We were on our way to a hastily-arranged reception for Lord Kitchener at the British Legation, and Asplin was determined to get there early, well before the other guests. He hadn't said so, but I had little doubt that he intended to button-hole the great man and prevail upon him, as Secretary of State for War, to improve the line of communication with C in Whitehall and to take a personal interest in the coordination of British 'intelligence' in the Aegean. This was the vexed issue that Furnell was supposed to be reviewing, but seemed, by his continuing presence in Athens and neighbouring places, to be complicating – in Asplin's eyes.

Lieutenant Commander Arnold Brooke Furnell! By uttering the name in full, as he usually did, Asplin had extra syllables with which to emphasise his loathing for the visitor from Alexandria, and to hint that Furnell's review was simply a time-consuming sideshow. It had nothing to do with counter-espionage and was not likely to be of any value to Asplin's team as they went about their work.

Frustrations of this nature were so obviously to the forefront of my superior's mind that I had not yet briefed him about my trip to Lemnos or the forebodings I harboured as a result of running through the frightening possibilities with Gerald Wray. Before I took any further step, I had to put Wray's suppositions to Furnell. A reception wasn't the best place to confront him, but unless I did so the true meaning of the man from Smyrna's movements before he died and the events surrounding his death would remain a mystery. That, of itself, or so it seemed to me in the light of Wray's ruminations, might bear upon what was done at Gallipoli in coming weeks, an increasingly tragic realm haunted by misjudgements and so many deaths.

'To the British Legation,' Asplin commanded as we clambered into the back seat of the Sunbeam. He slid across to the far side to make room for me and gripped his leather loop. 'And quick smart.'

The brawny, bald-headed driver was already on his way to the wheel. 'Of course. I will go hard.'

Asplin settled into his seat as the car rumbled away from the gatehouse and bumped across the tram tracks. 'I have reason to believe that His Lordship will be in a good mood. A receptive mood, I trust. He's met King Constantine and they seem to have got on famously.'

'Was the Minister with them?'

'He was indeed. When Kitchener let it be known in a roundabout way that he saw little merit in the presence of French and British troops at Salonica, because every shot fired at a Bulgarian instead of a German was a waste of ammunition, the King was delighted. He treated this as a criticism of Venezilos whose blandishments had led to the Entente troops being there in the first place. He saw it as an endorsement of his decision to get rid of the former Prime Minister. The indications are that, for the time being at least, the Greek government will remain strictly neutral.'

'But will they come in on our side eventually?'

Asplin frowned. 'That's still up in the air as far as I can make out. It will probably depend on what happens at Gallipoli. A calamitous defeat will have repercussions throughout the region.'

'Which is what the High Command is pondering, I gather.'

'Yes. Reinforcements or retreat. In the latter case the blow to our prestige will be severe. And a Turkish victory will leave them with extra troops for a push to Suez. But these aren't the only factors. One keeps coming back to the peculiarity of the King's position.'

'Absolutely.'

Asplin was fascinated by royal genealogy and needed more than faint approval to validate his reasoning. 'Not the only factors by a long chalk. Think about it! Here in Greece the people are led by a family with ties of equal strength to England, Prussia and Germany. King Constantine himself is half Prussian and half a Dane. He is a favourite nephew of the British Queen and a brother-in-law of the German Emperor. Which brings into play a factor we can't afford to lose sight of. That fateful day two years ago at Potsdam.'

'Which was ...?'

'The moment when the Kaiser handed his brother-in-law the baton of a German Field-Marshal! And went on to award him the collar of the Black Eagle. A fateful day indeed. To his even greater delight, King Constantine was then installed as a Colonel of the Second Nassau Infantry Regiment.'

Asplin flapped a hand at the passing traffic and flow of pedestrians. 'To some, of course, these military honours may seem meaningless, simply the compliment one sovereign pays to another, but the King certainly made more of it than that when he returned to Greece. He was careful to attribute the Greek victories during the war with Bulgaria and Turkey to the principles of warfare that he and his officers are said to have learnt from the Prussian General Staff.'

We had moved from genealogy to matters I was less sure about, but I had to keep up. 'Which didn't sit well with his Prime Minister at the time, I imagine.'

'It certainly didn't. It was vainglorious and untrue. The Greek army had, in fact, been reorganised by a French Military Mission which had been summoned to Greece by Venezilos.'

Asplin was facing me now, fingering his moustache, determined to convince me. 'King Constantine would have turned aside at a crucial moment in the campaign against the Turks. If it weren't for the Prime Minister's foresight, the Greeks would never have taken Salonica! So you can see why I remain loyal to Venezilos and deeply suspicious of the Palace. My fear is that Kitchener may have gone too far in seeking to appease the prickly monarch. So as soon as we arrive I intend to talk to His Lordship about that and several other matters. What we need right now is determination and decisiveness. Not this continual wallowing in the swell, without a glimpse of the port ahead, or even of the far horizon.'

* * *

Brusa turned off the busy street and brought us to the front steps of the Legation with a shriek of brakes. We had come to a graceful mansion overlooking a large garden, shady with dark pines and the dappled light-green foliage of false pepper trees. The Minister, Sir Francis Elliott, lean and grey, was in the entrance hall with his languid wife, waiting for their guests to arrive. After a few congenial words of welcome, we left them to greet the guests bunching up behind us and mounted the marble staircase to a drawing room on the first floor. As we were ushered into the room I caught a glimpse of Lord Kitchener, broad-shouldered and still in uniform, seated by a fireplace at one end of the room, listening solemnly to those around him, most of whom were civilians.

'Some people!' Asplin hissed, trying to keep his voice down. 'The man's had a long and tiring day, and here they are like a bunch of shoe-shine boys, falling all over themselves to get at him.' He plucked a glass of wine from a passing tray. 'Some of them probably came half an hour early. It's pathetic.'

Nonetheless, obviously fearing that the queue might lengthen before he could present his own plea, Asplin, under the guise of talking to an aide-de-camp from the Chancery adjoining the Legation, began to sidle towards the fire-place. I left him to it, for I had just noticed the arrival of the man I wanted to see – Arnold Furnell, spic and span, in full naval uniform, gold braid and all. He stood in the doorway, upright, stalwart, taking in the scene quietly. He moved inwards as I approached.

'On the ferry at Lemnos,' I reminded him. 'You proposed we have a chat.'

'I did.'

'Now's the time.'

'I've only just arrived.'

'So have I. But what I have to say can't wait.'

'Nor can Lord Kitchener. He'll be leaving soon and I have to talk to him.'

'To hell with Lord Kitchener. We have to talk about Cy Lapides. And about other departures.'

Startled by this, Furnell gripped my arm with the look of a swarthy pugilist closing in for a quick body blow before the bell sounds. 'What's that you say?'

'Let's talk.'

Reluctantly, he followed me to a distant corner, well away from the talkative group at the far end of the room. We found seats by a low table. In a quiet place at last, I quickly put to him the points made by Gerald Wray – about the coin, and about the meaning of the note. To this I added my own surmise: that Furnell had in some way been associated with Lapides in a covert operation, a plan designed not to set the scene for a new offensive in Asia Minor but to facilitate the evacuation of British and Imperial forces from Gallipoli. I was minded to report this to Asplin, I said, for it looked to me as though this was an unauthorised venture which had run off the rails, as evidenced by the assassination of Cy Lapides, an escapade that could lead to disaster.

Furnell, in his stalwart way, had been listening attentively, without any expression, but at my last few words, to my surprise, he smiled. 'Yes, there could well be a disastrous outcome. Way beyond anything Asplin could possibly imagine. Which is why we needn't trouble him with it. Not right now while things are still taking shape. The fewer people who know what's going on, the better'.

'Perhaps you'd better explain.'

'I will. For the simple reason that you, unlike Asplin, can be of assistance to us. And you strike me as someone who can see things clearly.'

Furnell pulled his chair in closer and settled down to providing me with the explanation that I wanted, some of which I had inferred – with Wray's help – but with the rest coming to me as a revelation. I kept reminding myself that this was Athens: the home of the inquiring mind, the sceptical outlook. Even now, as he claimed to be taking me into his confidence, I had to be careful about believing everything that was being divulged. I would have to back my own judgment.

He began by telling me that since the failure of the August offensive and Sir Ian Hamilton's recall to London, Furnell and a small group at GHQ had been forced to review all the strategic alternatives, including evacuation, now that winter was coming on. The impossibility of a staged withdrawal, especially in the Anzac sector, made it clear from the outset that a retreat could only be effected by a process of deception which would allow for the front line trenches to be held, however lightly, until the last of the troops could get down to the beaches in one concerted movement under cover of darkness, and board the waiting boats.

All of this, he said, called for planning at various levels. The story had to be put about in regional centres such as Athens and Constantinople that the Allied forces were not only determined to stay but were planning to launch new offensives. At the tactical level, particularly in the Anzac sector, a number of ruses would have to be employed to maintain an appearance of normality in the weeks preceding whatever date was chosen for the final departure. I was told that one of the senior officers I had met at North Beach a few days ago – Colonel Brudenell White – was arranging for the Australian guns to remain silent from time to time so that, if the evacuation went ahead, the Turks by then would have become accustomed to periods in which there was a cessation of gunfire. They would have been schooled to silence.

'But will it go ahead?' I interjected.

This prompted a growl of displeasure. 'You've seen the situation for yourself. It *has* to go ahead. It's a stalemate. Unless we act decisively, there's no way through and no way out. And one dreads to think what snow and blizzards will do to our men in coming months.'

'But what about the risks involved?'

'That's the stumbling block. It's been getting in the way of everything we do. More so than any moves made by the enemy. Hamilton claimed that half our forces would be lost if we tried to leave. General Monro said one third. Birdwood's estimate is twenty five thousand lives. You can see why no one's keen to get started.' Furnell raised a weary hand and invited me to study the group at the far end of the room. 'Kitchener dreads giving the order that might lead to the destruction of many thousands of men whose endurance he has so deeply admired. For much the same reason, Birdwood is opposed to evacuation also.'

I loosened my collar. I could scarcely believe what I was hearing. I could feel the Sponge-man tearing loose a fragment of my chest. I could sense the convulsions in the spectre's throat as I tried to speak. 'Twenty five thousand lives! But you, your group at GHQ, others presumably, are preparing for it. A complete withdrawal? From the beaches?'

'We are. It has to be done, and it can be done. And if it's done in a certain way there won't be losses of that order. And in the end lives will be saved.'

We sat in silence for a moment. I couldn't bring myself to say anything else. So Furnell continued. 'The final decision rests with Cabinet. In the meantime, various preliminaries have to be attended to – on the assumption that approval will come through in due course. Hence, Brudenell White's 'silent ruse' at Anzac. Lapides buying maps and spreading stories in Athens. One or two others like him doing the same in Constantinople and Salonica. Things will be in place and ready to go once the final decision is made. If people keep their mouths shut, and the deception works, we can, in my opinion, get out of Gallipoli without any loss of life.'

'And Cy Lapides?'

'Recruited for us by Peter Mavros and his friend Viscarra. They knew him from Smyrna and have used him for some of their own dealings. He did what he was employed to do initially, and did it well. That's clear from the German mail we discovered in the cushions. By pretending to sell them British secrets, he led them to believe that a new offensive was planned in Asia Minor that would get the Allied forces to Constantinople via Cyzicus and the Sea of Marmara. Until his gambling debts got the better of him and he tried to double cross us by threatening to sell the real secret – the plan for an evacuation. He was getting too clever by more than half. He had to go'

My shocked look must have disconcerted Furnell. He filled the silence quickly. 'I didn't knife him. And nor did Mavros or Viscarra, although Mavros was mad as hops when Lapides tried to blackmail him, and refused to return the coin that Mavros had given him. No, after pretending to be an informer for the Germans, as we had instructed him to do, the Germans were tipped off about his communications with Mavros, then Asplin. They concluded he was double dealing, according to my informants, so Carl Bessen stuck a knife in his throat. That's why they call Bessen The Iron Broom. The problem is that the circumstances of Lapides' death and the objects found upon him seemed to point elsewhere – a coin obtained from Mavros, a room connected to Asplin's lot. Rented by you, in fact, I seem to recall. So you can see why I'm not keen to bring Asplin into the picture. It isn't just his fanatical support for Venezilos at a time when we're trying to keep the King on side. Asplin's too full of himself. Too certain. He rushes into things and complicates them.'

Too certain. I was having trouble adjusting to the storyteller's tale. If everything he said was true, thousands of lives could depend on Furnell's certainty that his process of deception would be enough to end the siege without loss of life. Such a process could come unstuck for a number of reasons including the risk that in coming days Diakis pursued some misguided theory of his own about the Lapides death. Furnell's stance was hard to accept. So I put a question to him about a matter that had been puzzling

195

me. Why did he seek out Peter Mavros for assistance? And, more importantly, could he trust Mavros and Viscarra to keep their mouths shut? For whatever reason – debts to Viennese Bankers, or possibly to appease his wife – the rumour was that Mavros favoured the Central Powers.

'It's a risk,' Furnell admitted, 'dealing with Mavros and his Chilean friend. But I'm sure we can trust him. We didn't seek him out. He came to us, after the death of a young Australian friend in August. Gunned down at Hill 60, apparently. Mavros feels responsible. Wants to make amends. Offered his services, money, anything to assist the Allied cause. So we took him on. An influential person with contacts in the shady world of trading in artefacts and precious coins. At arm's length if anything went wrong. He could engage a mercenary like Lapides without any risk of the man in question – this so-called man from Smyrna – being connected to British intelligence. But little did we know that Lapides was *too* mercenary. That he would strike out on his own and finish up in your room. Dead, but living on as a potential threat.'

'Like it or not,' I replied, 'the logic of the situation is that you'll have to bring Asplin in on it. If he doesn't know what's really going on he might say things to Diakis, or to others, that don't suit you. In any event, I feel duty bound to tell him. I owe him that.'

'I can't stop you. But I want you to clear it with Mavros first. For some quixotic reason I don't quite understand, he's in this thing up to his neck. You owe him something too, and to clear it with him, to look at the situation from his point of view, may well facilitate the strategy we're now committed to. Get your stories straight and work out a way to point Asplin and Diakis in the right direction. We can't afford any more mishaps. Too much depends upon it.'

* * *

The guests had assembled downstairs in the entrance hall as Lord Kitchener prepared to take his leave. His ship, the *Dartmouth,* he explained, was waiting at Piraeus and once he was aboard it would take him back to Lemnos for further meetings with his Generals. All of this was said quite stoically, with the air of a man who was burdened by duty and would rather be somewhere else. Perhaps it was this air of melancholy that prompted Lady Elliott to remark in the cheerful but at times bizarre tone of a British hostess: 'Goodbye, Lord Kitchener. I hope you'll look in and have tea with us the next time you come this way.'

As the big front door closed behind the famous visitor, Asplin seized my arm and whispered feverishly: 'You take the car. I've got to get downstairs to the cipher room. Things are happening. Tell you later.'

He raced away, leaving me with an unsettled feeling that a few too many things were happening, some of which were contradictory, but each of which was supposedly underpinned by certainty. To me, certainty and strong opinions seemed unnatural, contrary to the usual flow. Like Gerald Wray, I was of the view that ambiguity and allowance for chance seemed closer to the natural order. A feeling for contingency kept people alert, ready for adjustments. It was with these thoughts in mind that I told Brusa to take me to the Panhellenion Café in Omonia Square, confident that at this hour I would find Mavros at his table by the entrance.

This prediction proved mistaken. I found the table but occupied only by Guido Viscarra, sipping coffee and staring at the street morosely. Mavros was not far away, he informed me, at the Grande Bretagne Hotel where he had arranged to meet his wife and daughter for a special dinner. Viscarra added, as an afterthought, fixing me with his brooding, dance-instructor's gaze, that I was not the only one in search of his friend. Detective Diakis had come by not so long ago and wouldn't be put off by the news that Mavros was committed to a family occasion.

'So you must use your discretion,' Viscarra concluded. 'Personally, if I were you, I would leave what you wish to say to another occasion. Our friend doesn't take kindly to being interrupted in the course of an outing.' He smiled mischievously. 'And, as *you* know full well, his wife is easily vexed.'

'I have to see him.'

Viscarra shrugged, examined his fingernails for a moment, and reached for his coffee cup. 'It is up to you. I have said my piece.'

Undeterred, I hurried back to the car and told Brusa to drive onwards to the Grande Bretagne. I had to see Mavros before I spoke to Asplin. That was clear. I was not yet entirely convinced that Mavros was committed solely to the Allied cause.

The sense of urgency possessing me was heightened by the bustle of the city at this hour, the comings and goings of the waiters in the cafes, the flow of their customers, the ever-present tumult of carts and cars and pedestrians. A smart four-wheeled Phaeton trotted alongside us for a moment drawn by a horse with dark, shining, well-groomed flanks, before it swung away at the next corner and was lost in the current. The marble buildings along the boulevard glimmered in the waning light. The trees adjoining King Constantine's palace, where Lord Kitchener had presented himself to the monarch at midday, were etched in black against the sunset's afterglow, a lilac heaven pricked with early stars.

The secret that had been imparted to me was like a silhouette too: the shape, the essence of it, was imprinted upon my consciousness, becoming ever-sharper in its outline, but with the details left indistinct. And what was I to make of the suggestion that Mavros had been so affected by Michael Carter's death that he had offered his services to the Allied cause? The businessman's parents were British admittedly, and he himself had been schooled in the home counties, but when one turned to the course of his adult life, the diversity of his experience, England could hardly be described as the country that had claimed his sole allegiance. Or was he doing this for his daughter's sake, from a sense of having let her down, of guilt?

The magnificent foyer of the Grande Bretagne was busy with its usual quota of wealthy businessmen with pointed beards and their richly-attired wives, swishing by in silk dresses, all pearls and rice-powder. Here and there could be seen members of the diplomatic corps and their advisers, immersed in the low murmur of polite conversation, including the eminent jurist, Hans Van Riebeck, from the Grotius Institute in Den Haag, equipped with a sombre briefcase. He was said to be advising the King about territorial disputes on the borders of the crumbling Ottoman Empire. The new French Minister, M.Guillemin, standing by the entrance in a frock coat, glanced at me suspiciously before turning back to his aide, castigating the poor fellow with Gallic fury, listing the faults of the social function they had just attended.

It didn't take me long to spot Diakis, for apart from the hotel staff, he was one of the few figures in uniform to be found within the foyer. He and Peter Mavros were seated by the swing doors leading to the main dining room. They were conversing with the intense look of a pair of race-goers at Ascot reviewing the entries for a forthcoming event. I joined them.

Diakis greeted me warily as I pulled a chair into place.

Mavros managed a faint smile. 'First the City Police. Now the British School. I'm glad I scooped up a few spoonfuls of soup before I left the table. It won't be getting any warmer.'

The inconvenient visitations he had just mentioned should have left him in a sour mood, but the gleam in his handsome brown eyes was to the contrary. He quickly disclosed the cause of his good humour.

'The Cy Lapides thing,' he informed me. 'I've just been told the investigation is over. They've got their man.'

'The perpetrator?'

'Exactly.'

'Not so,' Diakis remonstrated. 'You are jumping too far ahead. We know the one. That is for sure. But the man himself has disappeared.'

'Carl Bessen!' Mavros sat back in his chair with the air of a tipster who has picked a winner. 'Our friend Diakis has been liaising with the head of the Palace Police – Christos Veveris. A few days ago they traced the knife to a purchase made by Bessen in the Plaka. And they have a witness who saw him leaving the end room upstairs.' He smiled. 'Or should I say "your room".'

'Why not? Everyone else seems to be saying it.'

'A strong and reliable witness. He saw Bessen leaving the room before Furnell arrived. A German with a guilty look. The one with a scar on his arm. He had blood on his clothes.'

'And we have a waiter,' Diakis added. 'who saw Bessen threaten Lapides the day before the murder.' The detective drew a finger across his throat. 'Like that. In the street outside the Panhellenion Café.'

'It's all over,' Mavros assured me. 'The file's closed.'

'But no,' Diakis interjected, correcting him. 'It is not quite. We have gone to his import agency where he pretends to work, but he has been tipped off and left for Bulgaria. Someone has got to him first to say the police are on their way. Or paid him to leave. Which is why I am having to speak to you so urgently. In case you have some information about his whereabouts. Or the route he has taken.'

'I scarcely know the man,' Mavros told the policeman. 'My good friend Guido Viscarra saw him some nights ago, I believe. In a fight at Piraeus. A taverna on the waterfront.' The speaker must have felt my gaze upon him, for he managed to suppress the mischievous imp that was always dancing about inside him. 'It was a brief encounter I am led to believe. Which left little time for talking.'

'I can't assist,' I advised Diakis. 'I know Carl Bessen by sight, but nothing about his movements.'

'Ditto for me,' Mavros chipped in. His tone was so good-humoured that I was beginning to wonder whether political influence lay behind the closure of the file, and whether the sudden involvement of Christos Veveris from the Palace Police, and the finding of a vital witness, was connected to the Kitchener visit and the rekindling of the King's affection for the British, but this wasn't the time to explore all the ins and outs of the affair. If it suited the powers-that-be to hold a German operative responsible for the man from Smyrna's death in the end room, then it suited me too, as the man whose name was on the rental slip.'

'If we find Bessen,' Diakis assured me. 'We have our evidence. More than enough. So these can be yours as they are not wanted on the file. The objects found in your room.' He handed me the Cyzicus coin, the square of tissue paper, and the halves of the menu card.'

I accepted the bits and pieces, nodding impassively, surmising that the real purpose behind his gesture was to avert the possibility of these inconvenient objects being found upon the file at some later date. 'I will keep them at the British School in case they are needed.'

Diakis rose to leave. 'If you hear anything at all?'

'If we hear anything at all about the movements of Carl Bessen or anyone who knows him,' Mavros declared, as if on oath, 'we shall certainly tell you. You have my word on that.'

I placed the bits and pieces on the table as we watched the detective depart. Mavros patted his substantial midriff in a contented way, as if to say: 'that's that.' He glanced at the swing doors leading to the dining room. 'I should be getting back to my soup. A special night out! My wife and daughter will be furious.'

I couldn't let him escape without attending to some unfinished business. I pointed to the objects on the table as a card-player does after displaying his hand and singling out its merits. 'Do you want them?'

My companion's good-humoured mood evaporated. He studied me suspiciously. 'What makes you say that?'

'They are yours, I believe.'

'You're losing me.'

'I don't think so. I've just come back from Gallipoli and I may be going again. Now that I know what's going on.'

I proceeded to lay out what I suspected and what I had just been told by Furnell, including reference to my conclusion that as Mavros and Viscarra had engaged the man from Smyrna the objects found upon him probably came from them.

Mavros let me say my piece until close to the end when he felt obliged to interrupt. 'Very clever, and everything you say is very close to being right. Yes, for several months I've been working closely with Furnell to facilitate the evacuation which now seems inevitable, to me a least, and largely because of Michael Carter's death. I owe him that. I handled things badly at Ephesus and I regret it. But that's why the story you've put together isn't quite straight.'

He leaned closer and lowered his voice. 'If I were a spy by profession or a dedicated patriot, I would have been more efficient, especially at a time like this, and in a matter of such importance. I would have found a better man than Cy Lapides to spread the misinformation required by Furnell's cover story. But the fact is that I'm not a spy and not much of a patriot, having been stateless for most of my life. I employed Lapides at the outset for what was essentially a private purpose.'

Mavros picked up the coin and showed it to me. 'This is the keepsake coin that Michael found at Ephesus and gave to Anita. I found out from my South American friends aboard the *Aragon* that Michael's battalion had been sent to Lemnos for rest and recuperation after the August offensive, so I sent Lapides to seek him out, with the keepsake coin to identify himself, so that Michael could be sure that the letters Lapides brought with him from my daughter and myself were genuine. We were planning to meet Michael, until I found out what had happened to him and the circumstances of his death. That grieved us, here in Athens, and it angered me to dwell upon the futility of this and so many other deaths. So I went to Alexandria with Lapides and found my way to Furnell. He and his colleagues knew what they had to do but they needed help to do it. In the absence of formal orders approving their analysis they had to go outside the usual avenues, while waiting for approval. I fitted the bill. Lapides and others like him were provided with cards and notes hinting at a new offensive to give the German and Turkish informers something to think about.'

He put the coin back on the table with the profile of King Cyzicus upwards. 'Cyzicus was on the coin so why not fabricate a new offensive centred on the Sea of Marmara? We needed a cover story of some kind, so why not that? The coin got caught up in Furnell's process of spreading misinformation but it wasn't really part of it. The coin came first. The coin belongs to Anita. When Lapides approached me at the Panhellenion, the day before his death, it enraged me to find him wanting money for it to pay his gambling debts. Then trying to blackmail me. I can't say that I was particularly sorry when the news reached me on the following day that he had been disposed of. The irony is that in the end he came close to completing the job we gave him – we now know that he was successful in leading the Germans to believe that a new Allied offensive is on its way. If Carl Bessen and his cronies had waited a little longer, and offered Lapides a higher price, he probably would have told them the real plan.'

Mavros shrugged. 'Who knows? He was probably destined to finish up as he did. He was just a man from Smyrna. When the small private journey he was asked to make initially turned into a mission fit for a hero, he couldn't rise to the occasion.'

The speaker chuckled wryly. 'I've spent many hours trudging around sites with Gerald Wray and his colleagues and most of what they say passes right over me. But some things stick. They strike a personal chord. If there's one thing we know from Homer, so I'm told, a man only becomes a hero by finding a way of acting in the world that lifts him out of himself and exceeds the grasp of others. It was true at Troy and it's still true, on the battlefield or in the belly of a wooden horse.'

Mavros pocketed the coin and gathered up the fragments of the card. He held up the piece of tissue paper. 'The line between truth and fiction is as thin as that, but now you know the truth. I had a soft spot for that boy, as my daughter did, and many years ago his father lent a hand when I needed help. Espionage! It isn't usually my thing, but if the aim is to winkle out the actual facts of a matter and to stop the enemy learning secrets of importance to us, then you can rely on me in coming weeks to keep my mouth shut and do what has to be done. It's too late to save the young fellow I cared about, but it's a way of saving other lives.'

My confidant paused, as if reminded of something else he felt compelled to say. 'Wray told me about *The Odyssey* on one occasion. There is a chapter in it when Odysseus, on his journey home, came to the deep stream of Oceanos at the world's edge and visited the kingdom of the dead. Within that realm he encountered a good many of the friends and heroes he had once known. He tried to console them by mentioning the exploits for which they had won renown and for which they would always be remembered. The answer he received from the great Achilles was simply this: "Spare me your praise of death, Lord Odysseus. Put me back on earth."'

Mavros had spoken with an intensity that had nothing to do with archaeology or learning. It came from within, and possessed him again as he gripped my sleeve. 'Stay alive! Thanks to Gerald Wray, that's the one piece of wisdom from the classics I've never forgotten. Keep going! And look to where you are!' His grip tightened. 'Michael's friends. We have to save them. We have to bring them back. We have to see the situation for what it is – get out, or go under. We have to do what has to be done, which is what I've been doing all my life. I put it no higher than that.'

There was nothing more to be said. I shook his hand and walked away. The diplomats and the businessmen with their pointed beards were still coming and going in the foyer. The jurist was still there with his heavy briefcase, stuffed with maps depicting hazy borders and emerging realms. On the front steps of the establishment I found the French minister still dressing down his hapless aide, comparing him to a toothpick.

It was typical of Peter Mavros, I thought as I strode down the steps, so typical of the man to present himself in a heroic light, even at the very moment when the consequences of the proposed line of action were not yet known, and the future was little more than a faint horizon shimmering with mirages. In coming to the truth of a situation in a time of war the words we seize upon to explain or justify our actions were so often wide of the mark. But in this case there was a wild force, a kind of certainty, in what he had just put to me. It rang true. For better or for worse, I believed him. I was willing to trust him. I felt sure that he would act as he had promised.

* * *

On the morning after the Minister's reception I managed to catch up with Asplin on his way out of the British School. I blocked his path for long enough to let him know the outcome of the police investigation, but I couldn't detain him for a longer talk, a chance to lay out the full story behind Lapides' death. Not now! Too much was happening, Asplin exclaimed, as he pushed away.

A cable had come in from C In Whitehall. Admiral Wemyss and other senior figures were pushing for a renewed naval assault upon the Straits. If the French agreed, troops from Salonica could be sent to Gallipoli to support the attack. Asplin had to get back to the Legation right away. He was waiting on fresh instructions.

I cornered him eventually, much later in the day, by waiting on the porch of his little cottage. When the Sunbeam drew up beside the gatehouse and Brusa released his boss, I hailed Asplin from afar. He strode towards me briskly.

'You'll have to make it quick,' Asplin rapped out as he waved me into his parlour. 'Whitehall's in a flap and its hard to get any sense out of them. Things seem to be changing hour by hour. I've got to hurry back to the Legation for a meeting with Sir Francis and the French minister. With Bulgaria providing free passage for the Central Powers, there are ugly rumours afoot. The Turks will soon be upping their firepower with a battery of Austrian heavy siege howitzers.'

I had heard the rumour, I confirmed, and others like it. I managed to stop him pacing by dragging up a chair and insisting that he use it. 'The Legation can wait a bit. We have to talk.'

I came straight to the point, revealing what I had discovered about the proposed evacuation. I went on to say that Furnell and a small group close to him, including Mavros and Lapides, had been spreading misinformation about a new offensive in order to dupe the enemy.

Disconcerted, then appalled, Asplin made his feelings known before I could wind up the story. 'So much for "coordination"! What's it add up to? Going behind our backs! *Intelligence!* What's it mean in this case? Don't make me laugh! A stunt to leave us dashing all over the place on a fool's errand. And facing a murder charge!'

Within these agitated mutterings, I detected a degree of personal anguish, a realisation that he had been deliberately left out of the picture, but I could sense also, as his agitation subsided, that the enormity of what lay ahead, the risks involved, was beginning to take possession of him. I didn't attempt to answer his critique. I let him ponder, while he sat there silently with a tortured expression, the fingers of one hand drumming the arm-rest of his chair, raised to his moustache absent-mindedly from time to time as if for reassurance that he hadn't been deprived of this feature of his personality by an unexpected trick.

I expected a further outburst, but the silence ran on. I had seen this happen with others, and in the twelve months since my enlistment I had faced such moments myself – a dire disclosure, the reversal of one's understanding, the need for adjustment, breathing space. But this might not be new to a former barrister, I reflected, a man whose livelihood had once depended upon being able to cross-examine a surprise witness at short notice, or deal immediately with some devastating question from the bench. As the silence continued, I felt that Asplin was drawing upon such experiences in order to work out a way to handle this unexpected challenge.

He drew a deep breath. 'Point taken. If that's the way things are, we shall have to make do.' He laughed bitterly. 'Self to blame, of course. I should have guessed. Rumours. Innuendos. Fabrications. They're our stock-in-trade, these days. I was sent to Mytilene before the August offensive to run a similar operation. Deceiving even our own man on the spot. The British Consul! Poor fellow! He thought I was completely mad, utterly reckless, with all the supposed secrets I let slip in the presence of the Chief of Police and the local burghers. But the ploy worked. I have reason to believe that the German submarines sat tight in the Straits when they could have been hard at work off Suvla Bay.'

He slapped the arm-rest of his chair and leapt up. 'Yes. I should have guessed. The leg spin and the googly. A catch close to the wicket. But no matter. The next best thing is to make it work. We'll draw a line beneath Cy Lapides and do what we can to assist this Damaso chap, if he's standing in for the man from Smyrna. Although, from what you say, he doesn't sound much better than Lapides.'

'That could be so,' I agreed. 'But he's cheerful. And doesn't gamble. And seems quite decent. And besides, in wartime, I recall you saying, one has to make do with whatever is to hand – from manpower to weapons.'

Asplin had obviously forgotten the appraisal made when I joined his unit. 'That doesn't sound like me. I simply shape what I have to the purpose. We'll make the best of it until we hear from Whitehall or Furnell as to whether the evacuation is going ahead.'

'That's about it, then. That's what I had to say.'

'So be it.' Asplin had been restored to his usual energetic self, but he paused to ask another question before rushing off to his meeting. 'And what about you? Will you be going back to Gallipoli?'

'Probably.'

'Keep me posted. There's so much happening at the moment. So much to take in. Peter Mavros, you say. And that friend of his. That little worm Viscarra. I wonder whether they can be trusted?'

'We'll soon find out.'

* * *

I wasn't entirely surprised when Guido Viscarra turned up at the British School with a note from Anita. I had been half expecting it. Our earlier meeting had been inconclusive and I had little doubt that, upon returning to the dining room at the Grande Bretagne, her father must have said something about my visit to Gallipoli, and his retrieval of the Cyzicus coin. Viscarra waited in the School's front hall as I slipped into an empty office to find out what Anita had written.

It struck me as I tore open the envelope that her father's story had made it very difficult to construe incoming messages of any kind. Furnell had been keeping me informed and I knew by now that upon Kitchener's return to Lemnos the Secretary of War's principal advisers had tabled the draft of an evacuation plan which was then sent on to London for approval, although the stratagems and ruses required to pull it off were still being worked out by Birdwood's Australian Chief of Staff, Colonel Brudenell White. After a period of further vacillation, I was led to believe, the War Committee had arrived at their decision: evacuation. As soon as possible.

According to Furnell, everything depended upon certain critical factors, including the weather. A strong southerly blow on either of the two nights in late December selected for the final embarkation would wreck the whole adventure. And secrecy was a critical factor. The troops singled out for the first phase of the withdrawal – those at Suvla Bay and Anzac – were still in the dark, but steps had been taken to seal off the neighbouring islands from Greek caiques trading with the mainland and to place cordons around certain villages on the pretext that an outbreak of smallpox was suspected. I knew also that I was to play a part in the final phase.

I took all of this into account as I crumpled up the envelope and scanned Anita's note. When it became clear that she wished to see me right away, I knew I had to go. Furnell was in Salonica at present but the call to join him on a return trip to Lemnos could come at any time, in which case I might not see her again. She spoke of her need to discuss an important matter, but it was hard to tell what exactly she had in mind.

Letter in hand, I went back to Viscarra and within a few minutes we were on our way to the Mavros residence. Hands on the wheel of the family car, staring straight ahead, the Chilean said little to me in the course of the journey. When the car pulled up at the front door, he paused to make it plain that Anita Mavros knew nothing about the Lapides investigation or the evacuation plan. I was to keep away from these matters. I was to take care not to be drawn into any conversation about Detective Diakis or Carl Bessen. She was aware that I had been to Lemnos and Gallipoli in recent weeks to act as an interpreter but, even so, I was to make sure that I didn't, as he put it, 'let the pussy cat out of the bag'.

He unlocked the front door and took me upstairs to the studio adjoining the outdoor terrace. I could see Anita standing at the far end of the enclosure, by the parapet, gazing at the square below. I was pleased when Viscarra, without having to be asked, quietly withdrew, leaving me to find my own way outside.

Anita was less agitated than when I had last seen her. To my surprise, she seemed quite composed, almost peaceful, as she thanked me for coming and invited me to join her in admiring the view.

Composed? Or was there a sense of resignation in her manner, sadness perhaps? It was hard to tell, but it certainly didn't seem unusual for us to stand beside each other in silence for a little while as we surveyed the shopfronts and the square. A number of the businesses below, as I had noticed previously in her father's presence, were closing up at this hour and the women at their sewing machines on the pavement were standing about as if waiting for confirmation that it was time to go home.

'The photographers,' Anita murmured.

There was no need to say more. I could see them too, these denizens of the marble square, gathering up their stools and tripods, about to depart.

'They've had enough for one day,' I ventured, aware that, unlike our previous encounter, we were already beginning to communicate without anything of consequence being said. She was very beautiful, standing beside me in the dusk, but I felt somehow that our coming together had more to do with bringing to an end what had happened in the past than with renewal, or with any desire on her part to look for counsel. She had something to tell me and that would be it. The section of the past I represented was about to be shut down.

She slipped away to pick up a large manilla envelope from the table nearby and returned a moment later. Without a word, she lifted the flap of the envelope and extracted a photograph, glancing at it, before handing it over.

'Your gift,' she said. 'The walk you gave us that afternoon in Smyrna.' And now, at last, she smiled. 'It wasn't just a walk. It gave us a chance to have our picture taken. A place in the hereafter.'

Wandering about on the waterfront, in the hour or so before the ferry for Athens departed, they must have found their way to a photographer's studio. As I studied the sepia print I was surprised to see them standing side by side in costumes, with a painted vista of doric columns and mountains in the background, like the ruins at Delphi. They were clad in what was probably the photographer's standard outfits for gods and goddesses: a long white robe and a javelin for her; he in a toga and with a laurel wreath on his brow. They seemed pleased with themselves, their unnatural grins inevitably held for too long before the flash went off, making them look like performers smiling brightly on the billboard of a music-hall.

The photographer had obviously got them to stand up straight, and very still. But they looked so young, and there was something about the way that Michael had placed one sandalled foot on top of hers – a subterfuge unnoticed by the photographer, but an artful, god-like bit of knavery nonetheless – that illustrated the playfulness of the occasion, as if they were indeed performers, adding a touch of mischief to the scene.

For a moment, reminded by this vignette of Michael's youth, his happy-go-lucky nature, I could picture him at Ephesus in that carefree summer, sparring with his friends in the encampment, or pumping the primus stove on bended knees, or at the villa with a flirtatious grin, flicking water from a bucket.

Anita upended the envelope and cupped a hand to receive the coin that slid out of it – the Cyzicus coin. She handed that to me also, but without her earlier fleeting look of gaiety. 'I want you to have these,' she said. 'If you go back to Gallipoli, and I believe you will, I want you to leave them somewhere close to where he died. That will bring it to an end.'

I glanced at the photograph again, and at the coin. 'Things like this,' I suggested, unsure of myself, but feeling that I had to say something about that peculiar moment in time, the afternoon at Smyrna that had brought us together, then driven us apart. 'They never quite go away. Perhaps it might be best to keep the photograph. Or any letters.'

She shook her head. 'No. He has gone back to where he came from. He will be there in everything we did or that ever comes to me. But this will bring it to an end.' The memory of that sunlit moment on the quay, infused with love, had made her eloquent, but the passage of time, it seemed, or the whimsy of the photograph, had forced her to see things in a different light. 'I have to leave it well behind me,' she added. 'So that what was there stays with me in a different form. Besides, the coin has proved unlucky.'

'You know about Lapides?'

'Of course. They tried to keep it from me, but it came out when my father gave me the coin at dinner the other night. I've thought a lot since then. My father doesn't want any more deaths, and nor do I.'

'None of us do.'

'Then this is the best way.'

I took the envelope from her and returned her keepsakes to it. First the coin. Then the photograph. 'If I get back to Anzac,' I promised. 'I'll do what you ask.'

212

'I feel certain of one thing. This is the way he would have wanted it. No shadows left behind to worry about'.

'When I think of Smyrna,' I assured her, remembering my walk along the quay with Michael by my side. 'I think not of shadows, but of sunlight on the water.'

'As I do. So find a place that fits. That will make it more real for me than a coin with a jinx upon it and the two of us in fancy dress. Can I trust you?'

'I'll do my best.'

She placed her hands upon the parapet, looking over the city streets below and the Parthenon in the distance: as if everything had become clear at last, the unlucky coin disposed of, their sepia images bound for immortality, 'Spoken like a man from Smyrna,' she murmured, as a last reminder of the fleeting moment we had shared but which had proved illusory. 'I hope you come back safely. And with more than a scrap of paper and a coin like that upon you.'

* * *

THE NEXT ROOM

T HIS PARTICULAR DUG-OUT, Captain Emery told me, was safe enough on the whole from bullets and shrapnel, being reasonably close to the protected end of North Beach. He stamped his foot on the earthen floor to show me the ground was damp but not muddy. His boot print was visible but faint. He used the toe of his battered boot to erase the mark he had just made and invited me to look around.

The earth in the dug-out had been hollowed out to a depth of about three feet. The walls were made of grain-bags filled with sand and the roof from spars collected from the wreckage of a picket boat, covered over with a tarpaulin and weighted down with an overlay of earth and rubble. He used his boot again to kick the nearest sandbag. Rock solid after all this time. No way through a lump like that. Safer here than at the front, he reckoned. As the previous occupant had found out.

The tiny room was furnished with a camp-chair and two bully-beef boxes lashed together, serving as a table. The bed consisted of two planks bearing a layer of dirty hay and hessian flanked by a couple of biscuit boxes. He pointed out the candle stumps on the top box. The boxes could be used as shelves, he said, a place to put a few things, although I probably wouldn't be here long enough for that.

The south side of the cramped enclosure lay above the ground line and had been left open to provide a view of Ari Burnu Point with a glimpse of Imbros island on the far horizon, a small black node in the sunset's panorama, as if it were an opal risen from the sea. There were a number of other dug-outs immediately opposite the entrance to my quarters, positioned at different angles to suit the vagaries of the hillside. Further on, sheltered to some extent by a rocky overhang, lay a little burial ground walled off from the track running by it, embellished with wooden crosses. That was where the previous occupant of my dug-out had finished up, I was told in a matter-of-fact tone. Out there.

I dumped my kit-bag on the bed as my companion showed me how the room's open side was fitted with a curtain made of ration bags that could be let down to keep out the afternoon sun, or the drift of snow if it came to that. The blizzard a few weeks ago, he told me with a wry expression, had been hard going. The best way to get through it was with a tot of rum.

He re-attached the primitive curtain to its hook. 'But you probably won't be needing luxuries like that.' He paused for a moment to stare at the burial ground and the burnished seascape before turning back to me. 'One way or another, for better or for worse, we'll soon be gone.'

This was said in the uneasy tone I had heard used in several places since coming ashore less than an hour ago, something close to a tone of resignation, but usually followed by an attempt to lighten it with humour. *Luxuries like that. Here today; gone tomorrow. If you go, you can't come back.* Laconic sayings like these were used to lift morale. The men had been told they had to leave, the time had come, but it was hard to abandon what they had fought for, to leave their friends behind.

The man beside me was bound to have experienced these feelings, more so than others perhaps. Captain Emery's superior, Colonel Brudenell White, had devised and attended to every facet of the departure plan. Emery was bound to be familiar with the underlying appraisal and the insistence upon a systematic destruction of facilities that had to be carried out before the last boat left – precious supplies, ammunition dumps, hard won positions, tunnels that had been fiercely contested.

Thoughts of this kind must have been running through my companion's mind. He completed the handing over of my newly-acquired burrow by saying brusquely, as if I had been pressing for more than my bare entitlements: 'So there it is. It'll have to do.' He put a finger to his temple. 'Which reminds me. There's something else I have to show you. Back in a minute.'

I watched him leave, stumbling down the gully in his gross, mud-caked boots and tattered army greatcoat, shouldering past a line of mules on their way to the beach. These emaciated creatures, attended by a small contingent of Maltese and Cretan muleteers, were simply part of the larger pattern, I reminded myself, the process of thinning out, removing stores and equipment while continuing to hold the upper trenches, keeping the front line intact, or at least the appearance of it.

I had spent half and hour or so with Colonel White and his staff officers but it had been left to Emery to finish off the briefing. Even at this late stage, close to the final night, how much did Emery or other Australians in the Anzac sector know about the toing and froing that had taken place in recent weeks, the shifts of opinion in high places as the pros and cons of the evacuation were debated?

I understood from Furnell, and from what Asplin had managed to pick up in the cipher room at the British Legation, that when Kitchener's recommendation for withdrawal went to the next level the War Cabinet was divided and couldn't reach a decision. Upon his return to London, Kitchener found that Admiral Wemyss was still pressing for a renewed naval assault upon the Straits with the result that Kitchener himself began to have second thoughts and canvassed the possibility of sending more troops to Gallipoli. This was unacceptable to the French, so finally a joint decision was made at Calais by the Entente Powers to withdraw from Suvla and Anzac simultaneously, from Cape Helles later.

The preliminary arrangements put in place by Colonel White and his team pending approval – the periods of silence, the gradual removal of troops to Lemnos and other islands supposedly for recuperation – had given rise to rumours that a withdrawal might be imminent, but it was now less than a fortnight ago that news of the evacuation had become generally known to those on the front line. The plan depended upon providing enough small boats to remove the remaining troops under cover of darkness while holding the existing front line with a skeleton force until the last possible moment on the final night – the night of 18/19 December when a full moon was expected. The plan depended essentially upon deception.

I glanced at the dug-outs and darkening ground outside my shelter, listening to the jingle of the mule harnesses and the muffled accents of the handlers guiding them. As I dwelt upon the complexity of what was taking place, and the possibility of things going wrong, I felt again the flutter of apprehension that had been with me since I landed. The hillside before me and the fractured slopes beyond it were speckled with tiny glimmers of flame as men sat by their fires and incinerators while night fell, a scene reminiscent of a sprawling city anywhere, although, in this case, gossip around the fires would inevitably be accompanied by the crackle of sporadic gunfire, and the whine of shells.

The walled enclosure 'out there' with its array of tiny crosses was almost invisible now, disappearing in the dark. It was there, I decided, that I would leave the envelope Anita had entrusted to me as a gesture to commemorate Michael Carter's life. So I left the entrance to my dug-out and began rifling through my kit-bag in search of it.

By the time I had found what I wanted, and lit one of the candle-stumps, Emery was back, half-crouching as he stood in the open doorway, breathing heavily. He was carrying a rifle to which two tin cans were attached by lengths of string. I pocketed my envelope in order to take a closer look at his peculiar weapon.

'It's a drip rifle,' he explained, placing it on the makeshift table beside the candle. 'Simple but ingenious. A means of tricking the Turks into a belief that our lines are still manned. In the final hours of the evacuation.'

'It may be ingenious, but I can't see how it works.'

'String and two empty bully beef tins. The upper tin is filled with water and either perforated or so placed as to allow the water to trickle slowly into the lower tin. That's attached by a string to the rifle trigger. The lower tin is so placed that when it fills it falls with a jerk and fires the shot. Or a candle, like that one, can be used to burn through the string so a weight attached to the trigger falls with a jerk. On the final night these and rifles fired by a small group of 'die hards' left in the upper trenches, moving from one loophole to another, will lead the enemy to believe that we're still in position. As will the bombs with delayed fuses. Until the last boats leave the beach.'

He straightened up and came back to a point he had put to me a number of times on our way to the dug-out. 'All sorts of stratagems and devices are being put together in preparation for the final withdrawal. But everything has to be done as though we're simply carrying on as normal, getting ready for winter. But we don't know to what extent the Turks have been deceived.'

Frowning, his face half in shadow, Emery scratched his unshaven chin, as if not entirely sure about the next step in the process. 'This is where you come in. If any Turkish prisoners are captured between now and the final night we're depending on you to help me question them. Find out what they know. Whether the Turks in the front line positions have any inkling as to what is going on – the gradual reduction of our numbers, preparations for departure. If they are suspicious, we'll have to work out what to do about it. The evacuation on the final night is going to be every bit as dangerous as the initial landings. If the Turks get wind of what's going on it'll be a disaster.'

'Colonel White said much the same.'

'I bet he did.'

Emery found a place for himself on the makeshift table and invited me to use the camp-chair. Without further ado, he began running through those features of the operation planned by Colonel White which were of critical importance. It was hoped that by now the Turks had become accustomed to periods without gunfire and had concluded that the Allied forces at Suvla, Anzac and Cape Helles were bunkering down for winter. There was a reasonable prospect that the Turks attributed the sounds of increased water traffic at night – as the numbers ashore were reduced – to the bringing in of supplies and the rotation of troops before winter arrived. So long as the piers at North Beach were concealed from the view of the Turks' forward positions they couldn't tell whether troops were embarking or disembarking. The fact was that each evening after dark small boats had been coming in to pick up troops and animals and guns. Most of the wounded had been removed.

He spread his hands. 'A storm or a strong blow on the final night could wreck the whole adventure. But that's in the lap of the gods. There are some things we can't control. It's a full moon on the final night. On the one hand, that adds to the risk of movements in the trenches being observed, but on the other – it will make it easier for the ships and boats moving about offshore. The one thing we can control is the way the front line is thinned out without any sound or sign of it as men move down to the beaches.'

The more details my companion laid out for my benefit the more animated he became, face thrust forward, keen blue eyes upon me. He raised one foot and tapped his heavy boot. Troops in positions closest to the Turks would be instructed to wear socks or place empty bags on their feet, he said, to muffle the sound as they left the line. Steps and crevices on the routes to the beaches were being whitewashed so that they would show up clearly in the dark, and in some places sacks of salt and flour would be on hand to mark the way. At Lone Pine, where the opposing trenches were separated by only a few yards the trench floors were being broken up into soft soil and where that wasn't possible, because the ground was too hard, blankets would be laid. The piers were being carpeted with sacks.

In the course of questioning prisoners, Emery emphasised, we should be on the lookout for any mention of such matters, or anything else that was thought to be unusual. He took me through some more examples. Over the last few days working parties had been assembled to bury ammunition and stores in the latrines and to get rid of anything that might assist the enemy when they eventually took possession of our sector. The water pumping station, the electric light plant, the condenser – these were all being dismantled and shipped off the peninsula.

Whatever was being done in the daylight hours was being accompanied by the movement of men and carts and mule teams in the usual way to foster an appearance of normality. Cooking fires would keep on being lit and trenches repaired so that the

Turks could see what was going on. Soldiers in the front lines were being instructed to keep on raising their periscopes and tapping picks in the tunnels, as though they were still digging.

He moved on to the arrangements for the final night. By then the garrison would have been reduced to about 10,000 men. These would be removed from the jetties by boats and cutters and towed out to sea by launches. The A party would leave the firing lines at dusk, the B party before midnight and the C party, consisting of a carefully selected group of 'die hards', would be responsible for holding the entire Anzac line from that time onwards. They would have to move from one firing mound to another along the line, firing at irregular intervals to maintain the illusion of normal, sporadic gunfire, until the time came to set the drip rifles and delayed fuses, and slip away.

In those areas where spurs and gullies were difficult to negotiate in the dark wire gates had been erected so that if the C party were attacked the gates would be closed to obstruct the enemy and protect the embarkation on the beaches. The die hards would be left to fight where they stood, assisted by shelling from British ships offshore. If they weren't attacked, and were able to slip away quietly as the parties before them had done, the last men would leave Anzac before dawn.

Emery reached into his greatcoat and produced a typed sheet. 'This order will be issued shortly. I was told to give you a copy so that you will know exactly what is going on. I understand that, in addition to questioning incoming prisoners, you may also be needed at the casualty dressing station. If, on the final night, the number of wounded are so great that they can't all be evacuated with the rest of the troops before daylight, Red Cross flags will be set up and the Commander of the station will have to apply to the enemy commander for clemency. I understand that you will be working with our medical team in coming days to prepare letters in French and other languages asking the Turkish Commander-in-Chief to allow medical personnel and the wounded to be taken off by British hospital ships.'

'That is so,' I confirmed. 'I went through all of that with Colonel White and the Army Corps Commander a short time ago.'

'Well then,' Emery replied.' You had better have a look at the Order.' He passed the sheet of paper to me and held up the candle.

The Army Corps Commander wishes all ranks of the Division to be informed of the operations that are about to take place the success of which will largely depend on individual efforts. If every man makes up his mind that he will leave the trenches quietly when his turn comes, and that up till that time he will carry on as usual, there will be no difficulty of any kind, and the Commander relies on the good sense and trustworthiness of every man of the corps to ensure that this is done.

In case, by any chance, we are attacked the Commander is confident that the men who have to their credit such deeds as the original landing at Anzac, the repulse of the big Turkish attack on 18ᵗʰ May, the capture of Lone Pine, the Apex and Hill 60, will hold their ground with the same valour and steadfastness as heretofore, however small in numbers they may be. He wishes all men to understand that it is impossible for the Turks to know or tell what our numbers are, even up to the last portion of C party on the last night, as long as we stand our ground.

* * *

The pale morning light above the seascape brought me to the open door of my dug-out and gave me heart. The guns were firing, as they always were, but there was something about the promontory before me, its thick brown paw in the ocean, that was enough to get me moving, entice me into the world outside. I knew immediately that this was the moment to find a niche for the photograph and keepsake coin that Anita had entrusted to me. So I borrowed a pick from a bloke in the dug-out next to mine and scrambled across to the walled enclosure nearby containing its array of wooden crosses.

I threw a leg over the little stone wall separating the burial ground from the track beside it but, even as I did so, a burst of gunfire somewhere on the slope above sent me toppling inwards, ducking for cover. I raised my head a moment later to find that I was not alone. An army chaplain was on his knees in the dirt accompanied by a young soldier in a torn jacket, his neck swathed in bandages. We all looked up at about the same time and glanced at each other. The chaplain was clutching a canvas pouch, protectively, so I asked him what he was doing.

He smiled, a broad-faced fellow with a tiny crucifix on his chest. 'It looks odd, I agree.' He held out the palm of his free hand for my inspection. This prompted his bandaged companion, a gap-toothed digger, with a grimy, slightly-crazed expression, to show me what he was holding – a tin can with a wad of paper in it.

'Seeds,' the chaplain said. 'We'll be leaving soon so we're sowing wattle and manuka. We have to give things a final touch. Don't we, Colin?'

The youngster nodded vigorously, head bobbing up and down. 'Show them. That's what I say. Show them we're not just buzzing off.' He was talking as if to himself. Then suddenly began scratching at the ground, trying to straighten the cross nearest to him, as if he had suddenly noticed something wrong about the angle of it. 'Yes, we have to show them.' He was fumbling with the stones holding up the cross now, trying to adjust it, and it struck me that he was not so much talking to himself in a manic way as talking to the ground. 'No. We're not just buzzing off. We're not.'

The chaplain, not much older than his jittery companion, smiled again and distributed the seeds he was holding, scattering them here and there in a furrow he had created, saying, as if to include me in the venture: 'Work to be done.' He had a look at what his companion was trying to do and managed, by adding another stone, to straighten the tilted cross with a single movement. 'Is that right, Colin?' he asked, gently. 'Work to be done.'

'Work to be done,' the youngster echoed. 'Yes. Yes. Work to be done.'

The chaplain put one hand on the ground and was about to lurch to his feet when another burst of gunfire not far away drove us all into the dirt again. While we waited for the firing to subside the chaplain told me, in a matter-of-fact tone, that in the few days that had passed since it became known that there was to be an evacuation, men who had lost their mates had spent a lot of time tidying up existing graves or erecting new crosses. 'They've been living with their dead alongside them for months', he explained, as we lay there in the dirt, the gap-toothed youngster somewhere nearby. 'Which makes it hard to leave. There's been a constant demand for prayers. And for paint to touch up names and numbers ruined by the weather.'

He was whispering to me now and I gathered that what he had to say was meant more for me than for his companion. 'Some can't bear to think of leaving. Although most know it has to be done. And those they leave behind would want it that way, I feel sure. If we could ask them about it.'

The chaplain had noticed my pick and must have presumed that I had come to straighten a cross or improve the resting-place of a friend, for as the sounds of gunfire died away, he asked me politely if I felt in need of any assistance, or spiritual support. This made me uncomfortable at first. I had imagined that I would fulfil my undertaking while alone. But he was so straightforward in his manner, and so easy to talk to, that I felt comforted by his presence. I showed him the coin and photo and went on to tell him a little about myself, and why I had come to this enclosure.

I went on to confess to a sense of awkwardness about what I had in mind to do. My friend, Michael Carter, was probably buried somewhere else, near Hill 60 perhaps, and these were only mementos, but I had promised to leave them at Anzac. Was it fitting that they be left here, close to where others had been buried according to Christian rites?

The chaplain answered by showing me his pouch of seeds and explained that Colin and he would be going on to other places shortly, some without crosses. 'We are all enriching the earth,' he assured me. 'You must keep your promise. You must find a good quiet place, and that will be the right place for what you have to do. We will say a prayer for your friend. And I will add to that what I have said to many others in recent days. Your friend has simply slipped away into the next room. Whatever you were to each other, that you still are. Let his name be ever the household word that it was – spoken without effort, and without the trace of a shadow in it.'

I nodded, feeling comforted by this. By the quiet that had come to us after the last burst of gunfire. The stillness.

A few minutes later, having scraped out a niche in a quiet corner of the enclosure I buried what I had brought and knelt nearby, staring at the covering of soil, as the Chaplain said a prayer and repeated the words of consolation he had mentioned, words echoed by his bandaged companion who seemed to know them by heart, and was weeping softly to hear them again.

The chaplain shook my hand and put an arm around his companion's shoulder. 'Come along, Colin,' he said. 'There's work to be done.'

The youngster pushed away and gripped my elbow as he staggered to his feet, using his other hand to farewell me with a clumsy handshake. In an awkward, gap-toothed way he was trying to get some words out, but I couldn't quite hear what he said. When I asked him to repeat it, he turned me towards the beach below where the half-sunken ship *Milo* lay water-logged in the shallows at the far end of the main pier – a breakwater to assist the forthcoming evacuation. What he said sounded like. 'By their blessing.' And still trying to round off in his own way the little ceremony the three of us had just enacted, obviously believing, as one kindred spirit to another, that he had to say something to make me feel better, he released my hand and pointed to our patch of ground. 'I've heard them,' he said. 'Speaking to us. From the next room.'

His grimy, bewildered face was right up close to mine. 'I've heard them,' he repeated. 'They say go. You've done your bit. Get going.'

The chaplain patted his companion on the back as if to sympathise. He waited patiently, canvas pouch in hand, while the youngster gathered up his tin can. 'Work to be done, Colin.' the chaplain urged.

I saw them off and watched them working their way across the derelict landscape, the young man limping, shovel on his muddy shoulder, until they reached the next rise and disappeared from view.

* * *

A tent adjoining the casualty dressing station had been set aside for storing medical supplies and foodstuffs, but as most of these had been removed by now it had been taken over by Emery and was being used to interview prisoners brought in from the front line, before they were shuffled down to the pier. So far there had been only a few of them, and with little of importance to say. They were still astonished for the most part by the circumstances of their capture – caught most often in what they thought were their own trenches when tunnels being dug by one side or the other intersected unexpectedly. Upon being questioned, they all seemed to think that the Allied forces at Suvla and Anzac were digging in for winter. Answers of this kind were pleasing to Captain Emery.

Toby Asplin, assisted by Damaso Montiele, was with the British forces at Suvla. Arnold Furnell had gone to Cape Helles. I had little doubt that if in their sectors they were getting the answers that we had received, they would be pleased too. The process of deception that had been set in motion so many weeks ago seemed to be working well. An appearance of 'normality' was being kept up on all fronts.

From time to time, we slipped into the casualty dressing station itself to talk to wounded men brought in from the upper trenches to get a sense of what was happening on the front line in our sector. A complaint frequently voiced was that as a consequence of Colonel White's determination to 'school the Turks to silence' by withholding fire, there were now occasions when Turks in the opposing trenches seemed to be simply strolling about, much to the chagrin of our men, or exposing their heads and shoulders as if they owned the place. This was hard to take and certain of the wounded felt that they had finished up on stretchers because they were prompted by these acts of effrontery to 'dish it out to Abdul' when they were given permission to start firing again.

News of my presence – the interpreter bloke – must have spread, for at odd moments during the day an officer or a representative of one of the positions nearby would raise the tent flap and ask me to help them with a note, a message for the Turks to find when they reached our empty trenches. So I set about turning these handwritten effusions into French. My visitors must have assumed that Emery and his superiors would probably disapprove of such communications because the visitations mostly took place when Emery was conveniently absent.

Some notes were simple. '*Goodbye, Johnny Turk, we will see you later. You are a good fighter, but we don't like the company you keep.*'

Another note was so elaborate that I was only half way through it when Emery returned. I shoved it in my pocket and came back to it later. '*The Brigadier presents his compliments to our worthy opponents and offers those who first honour his quarters with their presence such poor hospitality as is in his power to give, regretting that he is unable personally to welcome them. For a little while we have been with you, yet a little while and you will see us not. We have left the trenches clean and in good order, and we shall be grateful if they may be so maintained until our return, particular care being taken in regard to matters of sanitation, so vital to the health and well-being of an army.*'

The jaunty tone reflected in these epistles wasn't echoed in all of the notes. What I remember principally about these hurried attendances at my tent, furtive, laconic or forlorn as the mood might be, was a pervasive sense of apprehension, for themselves, and for what might happen to the burial grounds. Surprisingly, it was Captain Emery himself who asked me to translate the draft of a formal communication that was to be left behind for the Turkish Commander, calling upon him to observe the usual, civilised conventions in a time of war. *I am confident that the graveyards of our soldiers buried in Turkish soil will be respected by your troops. They have fallen far from home, fighting gallantly in their country's cause and deserve that a gallant foe such as we have found the Turkish soldiers to be, should take special care of their existing resting places.*

* * *

The Commander of the casualty dressing station called for silence. A doctor with gaunt cheeks and a perpetually harassed look, a habit of sweeping aside the lock of dark unruly hair that always seemed to be bothering him, he waited until the group gathered around him had closed in: stretcher-bearers, men in ragged uniforms, two or three on crutches. His role on this occasion was to read aloud General Birdwood's final order, a reading that was taking place in much the same way in other places, no doubt, at Suvla and elsewhere in the Anzac sector.

The Commander glanced at his script. 'This special army order is from the General commanding the Dardanelles Army.' The speaker waited for the chattering to subside. 'Please listen carefully.'

I followed what was being said from my own copy of the order as the medical officer began reading in a good strong voice.

'*In carrying out our present operations, we are undertaking what no soldier ever likes – a withdrawal from the front of the enemy. In the present case, however, I know that none of you will feel in the least disheartened, because we all know we have never been beaten. By the tenacious hold we have kept on the Gallipoli peninsula, we have retained the best fighting troops of the Turkish army in front of us and prevented the Germans carrying out their plans of using them as they wished elsewhere.*'

The reader turned the page and continued:

'*We must remember, then, that in withdrawing from our present position we are simply carrying out the orders of the government, who after full consideration have decided that we can be better employed in fighting elsewhere. Remember in the final retirement silence is essential. Up to the end we shall always have sufficient men to withdraw according to our own arrangements. This will be done steadily, and without any undue haste or scurry. To withdraw in good order, and with hearts full of courage and confidence for the future, provides a test of which any soldiers in the world may be justly proud, and that the 9th and Anzac Corps will prove themselves second to none as soldiers of the Empire, I have not the slightest doubt.*'

The medical officer swept back his lock of hair and lowered the script. He surveyed the faces before him. 'So there you have it,' he said, briskly. 'Official confirmation of what you've heard from others. There's nothing more to be said, but "do your duty".'

Desultory gunfire could be heard on the ridges above us as the group began to disperse. The pale evening sky above the Sphinx was suddenly darkened by a swirl of migratory birds.

* * *

On this, the final day, staff officers appointed for the purpose were moving about the dug-outs and encampments to ensure that the usual number of cooking fires were being lit, although the population of the Anzac garrison had by now been considerably reduced. A party of men were recruited to smoke and lounge about on a rocky outcrop where they could be seen from the Turkish position at Gaba Tepe. But it wasn't long before the performers were forced off their little stage by a round of shells from the Turkish battery known as Beachy Bill.

Other parties of men moved up and down saps and gullies nearby to create an impression that fresh troops were arriving. In the trenches men were assigned to raise periscopes and present fire to the enemy as if it were just another day. General Birdwood came ashore in the afternoon and toured the lines for the last time.

As the day wore on I could see in all directions officers and men going silently about their preparations for departure. Most of the wounded at the dressing station had been evacuated. The Commander of the station and others in his team were hard at work feeding reports and documents into an incinerator, anything that might be of use or interest to the enemy. As there were no more Turkish prisoners to be interviewed I helped stoke the flames while Emery went off to confer with the Rearguard Commander and the small group of senior officers remaining. The command would be passed down through several hands as the operation proceeded until, in the early hours of the morning, it came to rest with the last senior officer left ashore.

Emery came back towards the end of the afternoon to say that the weather report was still in our favour. Beachy Bill and other batteries had kept firing throughout the day but the command group had no reason to believe that the enemy suspected anything. The men designated to move at dusk were being lined up in the trenches, ready to set off at specified intervals on their trek to the beaches. Orderlies had been placed at intersections to act as guides and specially appointed Embarkation Officers were standing by to control the flow on the piers as boats pulled alongside. The transports further out would move to their allotted positions offshore under cover of darkness.

'This time tomorrow,' Emery told me as he completed his report. 'We'll all be gone.' He skipped sideways for a moment to step on a half-burnt sheet that had suddenly flapped out of the incinerator. 'We'll be on our way.'

'If we get through the night,' an Embarkation Officer cautioned.

'Of course.' Emery glanced at the expiring sun and at the ravaged slopes above us. 'And if the weather holds.'

* * *

They were coming in now, moving inwards with muffled feet and moonlight on their shoulders, along the silent trenches, edging through the shadows in the gullies and at the intersections, these rivulets of weary men in single file or in twos and threes, filtering downwards to the piles of abandoned crates and boxes on the darkened shore, to the makeshift piers and jetties with their clusters of boats and rafts, and at last to the merciful calm of the ocean.

For hour after hour they kept coming in, they kept pushing onwards, downwards, conversing in whispers, pausing occasionally to check the breeze with moistened fingers, cocking their heads now and again at the sound of sporadic gunfire in the hills and ridges, but knowing, as they waited their turn to move forward again, that the sound of firing was there to make it easier for them, to suggest that this was just another normal night at Anzac. And as the men moved along the jetties to the small boats and lighters awaiting them they threw what remained of their grenades and ammunition into the water. That was it.

In the upper trenches the front line was gradually contracting. It was thinning out. Men had come in from the extremities of the line to begin with and they were now moving progressively downwards from positions closer to the centre, while a handful of men in the C party kept bustling about in the front line, trying to keep up the normal rate of firing and bomb throwing by shifting between different mounds and loopholes. Large parts of the line would soon be left open to the Turks if they chose to press forward and look.

Howitzers, machine gun, trench mortars, grenade catapults – these were steadily being dismantled and removed as the defences dwindled. From midnight onwards the skeleton force would have no chance of repelling an attack. Everything depended on the process of deception, and it would have to last.

The casualty dressing station had been closed and most of the medical team had left. I said farewell to Emery who was under orders to remain on shore until the Rearguard Command had finished up in the hands of Colonel Paton, designated as the last man to leave the beach, whose departure would establish that the evacuation had been completed.

I joined the Commander of the casualty dressing station in a group of ten men waiting in line at the main pier on North Beach. A fellow in our group whispered to me that he had been the last man to leave his post. He did so with a machine gun tripod on his shoulder, a full pack, a rifle, and ammunition, but the load had proved too heavy, so the pack was the first to go, then the tripod. He could scarcely go on. He was shaking so much by the time he reached the beach that an Embarkation Officer had promptly taken possession of everything else including a compass and a diary in his pocket. 'I've got nothing left,' he said, sadly, pulling out his pockets and showing me his empty hands. 'I'm down to nothing.' When I saw him next, in the barge carrying our group, he was weeping, but whether from what had happened before he left, or in thankfulness for having got away, I couldn't quite tell. Everyone was still trying to stay silent but the mood around me was strange. It felt as though we were on our way to another planet, and the only sensible thing was to savour the receding shoreline of the world we knew, flawed as it was, and to hold one's breath.

A section of the beach was suddenly engulfed by giant flames, probably the explosion of an ordnance dump, converting the sky to an orange inferno for a moment. The ropes holding down the kerosene-drenched tents on the foreshore must have burnt through for sheets of canvas like fireballs were flung upwards here and there, drifting away towards the dark mass of Ari Burnu Point. Several men around me feared that this explosion might be the first phase of a Turkish onslaught that would overrun the C party. They were momentarily desperate to see whether our die hards would detonate the mines left in the tunnels under The Nek as a diversion. But the bursts of shelling and gunfire on land simply ran on in the usual intermittent way. By the time we reached the waiting ship the inferno had subsided. What remained of the glow served only to accentuate the vast, impregnable shape of the landscape we had left.

I scaled the rope ladder and scrambled aboard the vessel, twisting my ankle as I did so. I straightened up to find that a mist was forming over the moon. The view across the water was becoming hazy, indistinct. Walker's Ridge, Chatham's Post, Courtney's, Quinn's – the names once known so well along the Anzac line would soon be left behind. By now the last few men would be leaving Lone Pine, drawing cages of barbed wire entanglements behind them as they closed the gate on everything it represented, and made their way to the beach. There, if all went well, and so far there were no indications that things would not go well, the remainder of the medical team and most of the Embarkation Officers would start pulling out.

When the last of the men emerged from the paths and gullies, Colonel Paton and his cohorts would ensure that the remaining dumps were ignited and they too would depart, leaving only a fiery glow on the vacant shoreline and the sound of occasional gunshots in the hills, aimed at nothing in particular as the drip rifles did what they had been primed to do, mimicking the habits of an army that had vanished, allowing the Turks in due course to clamber out of their saps and trenches and other diggings, and after a while, upon pressing forward to reach the lower slopes and silent beaches, to stumble upon certain unexpected truths and experience the awe that always accompanies the discovery of a ruined city or a labyrinth of abandoned rooms.

* * *

The years recede, leaving the horizon to itself, the reefs to capture traces of our mishaps, the shore to receive vestiges of how we dealt with the anguish of our time. Flotsam, fragments, relics: bits and pieces washed up, drifting into the mind at random, without forewarning. And so it is, within the drift, that a picture comes to me of the landscape we had just vacated, while the first faint streaks of dawn were still appearing, and of those beside me on the deck of a small naval steamboat as we edged along the silent coastline, looking out for stragglers, anyone left ashore.

The mood aboard our boat was subdued but cautiously triumphant. A wireless message had been received that the withdrawal from Suvla and Anzac had been completed without mishap and the indications were that of the many thousands of men involved there would be less than five casualties.

'We've done it,' Captain Emery informed the group at the rail of our vessel, showing us the radio operator's message. 'And I hope we won't have to use this.' He raised the copper megaphone he was holding. 'It makes me feel like the cox of a rowing crew! But you never know. Anything can happen in the dark. So let's get back to work and keep your eyes skinned for any movement.'

Like Emery and the others around me I had a pair of binoculars to magnify sections of the landscape, the fissures, the gullies, the ridges, but after we had completed the first leg of our journey without spotting any stragglers, and began working our way back along the coast, I left it to my companions to study the scene in detail. The roughly-hewn landscape was out there, vacant, featureless, for even landmarks such as The Sphinx seemed to have lost their aura, now that they would cease to be of any importance to the men who had named them.

I limped along the rail, feeling a need to separate myself from the others for a while, distancing myself from the mood of satisfaction.

Alone, a speck on the restless sea, what could one say about a scene like this? After months of conflict the Allied troops had looked at where they were and perceived that the time had come to withdraw. A plain appraisal of this kind might be sufficient for a member of the High Command, but was it enough for those who would never leave this tragic shore?

Fit young soldiers had been sent to this place from the fringes of an empire that would, in time, as empires always do, begin to crumble and fade away. Some, like Michael Carter, good-humoured, energetic, had barely got started before they were struck down – their lives brief; their jobs well done but few. The glimpses of love afforded to them, like shadows on a sunlit quay, would never be played out as a fully realised experience, or reimagined through the eyes of their descendants. The youngsters who came after them would have to take their place, be their offspring, heirs of a country strengthened by the heartache of the survivors and the example of the fallen.

Put me back on earth. Spare me. Peter Mavros had absorbed the lessons of this sombre landscape, reviewed the carnage perpetrated here, and as a man who prided himself on getting to grips with reality had said to himself: 'Enough!' He had combined with others to ensure that the departure was effected neatly.

For all his faults, there was a kind of wisdom also in what the self-professed adventurer had said when I challenged him about the outcome of my trip to Smyrna with his daughter. Betrayal? It was a will-o'-the-wisp, a spectre casting off its ties before the break. Deep down, Mavros had suggested, men and women of the world accept that the bonds attached to a promise can fray. But the shock of betrayal brings with it transformation, a sign that something new, perhaps predestined, is happening, or is about to happen.

The story of the landings at Gallipoli and of the mishaps and deaths that followed was bound to be unfolded in graphic detail, replete with descriptions of strategic errors and heroic exploits, statistics and recriminations. There was talk already of a betrayal of the dead, the abandonment of the ground they had fought for. Talk of that kind was bound to spread, but was it apt? There were two sides to the coin. The transformation that had just been effected – a complete withdrawal with scant loss of life – was a bold new step and probably inevitable. There was much in favour of such a finding.

I raised my binoculars and scanned the battered landscape again, pausing at the Sphinx. It would take a century or more for stories of an entirely different kind to emerge from the scene before me: the inscrutable rock formations and the blue Aegean. Legends would take shape perhaps, or an enduring myth. Looked at in that light, as it was at Troy, the past with its power to illuminate the present, to linger in a man's mind with the memories of his own life and of all those he had met along the way, might eventually become as real as the events portrayed.

I had been seconded to 'intelligence', a noisy wartime world of orders, despatches and coded cables. It occurred to me as I lowered my field-glasses, still pondering the events I had lived through, that one had to be schooled to silence before a word like intelligence could be truly understood or put to use. The meaning behind the word was probably inexpressible. It embraced ambiguity. It was large enough to include the clear thinking and determination that underpinned the evacuation plan. It almost certainly underlay the creation in ancient times of so many convoluted but absorbing myths, for some truths could only be told from behind a mask.

It was too early to think of describing what had happened here in such a way. Too early indeed. I found little difficulty in coming to such a conclusion. It was a task for others in another age. I dug into my trouser pocket and found the sheet upon which Gerald Wray had copied out a passage from the text book on his shelves in seamless copperplate, a passage which, at one stage, had seemed so important to us.

The words before me were both familiar and elusive. They had always been open to various interpretations, admittedly, but now, at the end of our operation, it came to me, as a kind of echo from the coast we had put behind us, that the true meaning of these words stood apart from everything we had brought to light and lay somewhere in the past or in the future – secreted in excavations or undiscovered rooms beyond us.

It only remained for me to read the concluding sentences once more before I let the page flutter into the ocean.

Until, at last, Rhea, the dead king's heavenly attendant appeared and sent the Argonauts a fair wind for their departure, but without their brave companion Hercules who had left them to go his own way. And so it was, after such a great ordeal, they departed. And from the waves around them as they pulled away, the sea-god Glaucus rose to say how Hercules, left ashore, was not destined to share the gaining of the golden fleece. He had served them well but now had work to do in other realms. Thus, with quiet minds, holding a new course along the coast, they went on, feeling sure their companion sanctioned their departure, for he would always be well-remembered and have honour enough awaiting him in times to come.

Lightning Source UK Ltd.
Milton Keynes UK
UKHW010029170820
368169UK00013B/114